T0129243

SEASON OF VALOR

BATTLES OF DESTINY

SEASON OF VALOR

AL LACY

MULTNOMAH
BOOKS

SEASON OF VALOR

© 1996 by Lew A. Lacy

published by Multnomah Books
a part of the Questar publishing family

Edited by Rodney L. Morris
Cover design by David Uttley
Cover illustration by Sergio Martínez

International Standard Book Number: 9781590528556

For information:
Questar Publishers, Inc.
Post Office Box 1720
Sisters, Oregon 97759

Library of Congress Cataloging-in-Publication Data
Lacy, Al.
    Season of Valor/Al Lacy.
        p.cm.--(Battle of destiny)
    ISBN 0-88070-865-4
    1. United States--History--Civil War, 1861-1865--Fiction. 2. Man-woman relationships--Maine--Brunswick--Fiction. 3. Brunswick (Me.)--History--Fiction. I. Title. II. Series: Lacy, Al. Battles of destiny series.
    PS3562.A256S43   1996
    813'.54--dc20   95-52595
                                                                       CIP

146651086

To my little sister, Patty Perkins, who will always have a
special place in her big brother's heart.
I love you more than you will ever know.

A special word of appreciation to my good friend and Christian brother, Bruce Droullard of Readfield, Maine, who was so kind to supply me with vital information concerning Joshua L. Chamberlain and Bowdoin College, which I used in this book. Thank you, Bruce!

PROLOGUE

General Robert E. Lee's Army of Northern Virginia had shown itself to be a superb fighting machine at Fredericksburg, Virginia, in December 1862 and at Chancellorsville, Virginia, in May 1863 by decidedly defeating the Union Army of the Potomac in both bloody battles.

Lee was fully aware that there was trouble within the Federal army. President Abraham Lincoln was having a hard time finding the right man to command his Union forces.

Although Major General George B. McClellan had turned back the Confederates in the Antietam battle in September of 1862, Lincoln was unhappy with McClellan's reluctance to move against the enemy with haste when needed.

After the bloody Antietam confrontation, Lincoln decided to relieve McClellan of his command. He replaced him with Major General Ambrose E. Burnside on November 5, 1862. Burnside immediately made plans for moving his army toward the Confederate capital at Richmond.

Lee was in Burnside's path at Fredericksburg. Burnside made a series of tactical blunders in the Fredericksburg battle, and although his forces outnumbered Lee's by fifty-two thousand men, the Confederates whipped the Federals soundly. The morale of the

Army of the Potomac sank to the lowest point since the war began.

When Burnside and his haggard men returned to their camps near Washington, D.C., in late January 1863, the general's career as commander of the Army of the Potomac came to an inglorious end. Lincoln chose Major General Joseph "Fighting Joe" Hooker as his new leader. But Hooker's defeat at Chancellorsville in May immediately put him on Lincoln's "doubtful" list. Lincoln made no move to replace him, but watched him closely.

General Lee, still basking in the glory of his victory at Chancellorsville, well knew that the victory had little more than postponed the day when Lincoln's army would again make a move on the Confederate capital. To seize and occupy Richmond was Lincoln's ultimate goal. Lee could either retire to Richmond and stand a siege or take the initiative and invade Union territory.

The considerations that had prompted Lee's invasion into Maryland in September of 1862—a drive that was blocked at Antietam—still remained valid. A successful invasion of the North might bring diplomatic recognition from England and France. There could very likely be foreign intervention on behalf of the Confederacy against the Union.

Such a victory, in Lee's mind, would also encourage the anti-war Democrats in their agitation of Lincoln's administration to force Lincoln to end the war under terms reasonably favorable to the Confederacy.

There was another reason Lee wanted to invade the North—the chronic shortage of supplies in the South. Lee's troops were operating in a war-ravaged region partly occupied by the enemy. It bothered him that he was unable to provide adequate food and clothing for his men and forage for the Confederate horses.

Pennsylvania was Lee's target. The rich farmland of that state would provide the food and forage, and while his army was laying hold on Pennsylvania's resources, the people in the South would have time to stockpile supplies.

On May 14, after Hooker's withdrawal from Chancellorsville,

Lee went to Richmond to discuss his plan with President Jefferson Davis and the Confederate cabinet. The Confederate leaders were uneasy about such a move, but Lee had a magisterial power about him, and the group finally approved his proposal.

On Monday morning, June 8, 1863, Lee arrived at Brandy Station, a whistle stop on the Orange & Alexandria Railroad a few miles north of Culpeper. Most of his Army of Northern Virginia was camped around the station. The Virginia sun shone down brilliantly from a clear blue sky.

Major General James Ewell Brown Stuart, Lee's chief of cavalry, had made preparations for a cavalry review for the supreme commander. In late afternoon, Stuart's cavalry mounted up. Lee looked on proudly as twenty-two cavalry regiments wheeled into a long column of fours in response to a bugle signal.

At that moment three Federal cavalry divisions, flanked by two infantry brigades, were only three or four miles away and moving toward the camp. The Union force had been sent by General Hooker, whose intelligence service had reported Stuart's recent move from Fredericksburg to the Culpeper area. Hooker's command was to "destroy the Rebel cavalry."

The Federal commander, General Alfred Pleasonton, decided to hide his troops in the woods and attack at dawn. When he began the assault the next morning, Pleasonton was surprised to find more than Stuart's cavalry in the camp. The hard-fought battle resulted in 866 Federal casualties and 523 casualties on the Confederate side. Pleasonton led his men in retreat, and General Hooker was in trouble with President Lincoln for ordering the ill-advised assault.

Things grew worse between Lincoln and Hooker, and on June 28, Hooker was relieved of his command and replaced by Major General George Gordon Meade.

The Brandy Station battle turned out to be the opening clash of a campaign that would come to a bloody climax just outside the small Pennsylvania town of Gettysburg. To that quiet farming community, the giant armies of blue and gray would be moved like pawns on a chessboard as if by some mysterious, inexorable hand of destiny. *Gettysburg* ... destined to be the bloodiest battle in the War Between the States.

You and I are about to embark on a journey into the lives of the people of both North and South who were touched by the Battle of Gettysburg, which has had more books written about it than any other Civil War battle. Most of those books are historical and documentary. Only a few novelists have undertaken the task of combining history with fiction to tell the story of Gettysburg. To those few—and with a little fear and trembling—I add this work of history-linked-with-fiction.

SEASON OF VALOR

CHAPTER ONE

The lowering sun cast long shadows across the creek as Mike O'Hanlon strung his last sucker on the line, smiling to himself. A catch of five wasn't bad in less than an hour. The fish were biting pretty good today.

He picked up his fishing pole, laid it on his shoulder like a soldier would his rifle, and climbed the steep bank lined with towering elms. It was mid-April in Maine. The air still had a nip to it, and the leaves were just now coming out on the trees and bushes. Even the grassy fields about him still had a slight tawniness. New England had experienced a hard winter that year of 1853, especially the northeast corner. The temperature had plummeted to near-zero on several occasions, and stayed there sometimes for days on end.

Mike was glad spring had finally arrived. He was tired of winter. Fishing was no fun when you were freezing. And besides, spring always brought May, and on the thirtieth day of next month he would turn fifteen.

He topped the bank and stepped onto the country road. He looked briefly toward Brunswick, which lay some six miles to the south. His home was northwest of where he stood about a mile and a half. He was about to cross the road and angle through the fields toward home when he happened to glance up the road and saw

Shane Donovan chopping wood beside the Wimberly's woodshed. Mike was surprised to see Shane at the elderly couple's place. He usually headed for home right after school to do his regular chores.

Shane was so intent on his work that he didn't see Mike coming up the road. As Mike drew nearer, he noted the old man standing in the door of the woodshed, looking on. Mike was rather spindly, and he marveled at the strength of his best friend. Shane could split logs as well as most men. Of course, knowing how was also an asset. Shane's father, Garth Donovan, was a lumberjack, and had started his oldest son working with him regularly when he turned ten.

Calvin Wimberly saw Mike turn into the driveway and called to him from the door of the woodshed. Shane turned to look at his redheaded friend and glanced at the string of fish.

"How many you got there?" he asked with a smile.

"Five. They were biting good this afternoon." Mike glanced at Mr. Wimberly, then looked back at Shane. "It's sure nice of you to chop wood for Mr. and Mrs. Wimberly."

"I'm happy to do it," Shane said. "Mr. Wimberly's been having some arthritis trouble in his shoulders, so I came by on my way home from school to chop up enough to last them a while."

"And I sure do appreciate it, too," Mr. Wimberly said.

"Nice to have the weather finally warming up," Shane said, looking Mike square in the eye. "After all, it's the twelfth of April."

"Yeah," Mike said. "Sure is nice. I can get more fishing in."

Shane hoped his mention of the date would bring a "happy birthday" from his friend. Mike knew Shane's birthday was April 12, but hadn't even mentioned it at school.

"I imagine you can't wait till Sunday," Mike said. "Probably seems like a long time, huh?"

Shane gave him a blank look. "I'm not sure I know what you're talking about. I mean…I enjoy being in church and hearing the Bible taught, if that's what you mean."

"You know what I'm referring to."

"Sorry, but you're going way over my head like Mr. Olmstead sometimes does in Sunday school class."

"You miss Joshua Chamberlain too, eh?"

"Of course. It isn't that I dislike Mr. Olmstead. He's a fine man and a solid Christian…but he shoots in the clouds sometimes. Mr. Chamberlain just has a way of making the Bible real clear."

"Well, let me make myself clear. I was talking about Ashley Kilrain."

"Ashley Kilrain? What about her?"

"What about her? C'mon, Shane, you can't fool me. I saw how she was looking at you during church service. She may only be thirteen, but she's awfully pretty!"

Shane blushed, ran his fingers through his thick, wavy hair, and said, "Aw, she doesn't have eyes for me…and she wasn't looking at me on Sunday, either."

"Well, I'm not blind. Besides, I'm not the only one who noticed it. Moira was sitting right by her, and she mentioned it to me after church on Sunday night."

"So Shane's got a girlfriend, eh?" Calvin Wimberly said. "With a name like Kilrain, she's bound to be Irish too."

"Oh, she's Irish all right, Mr. Wimberly," Mike said. "She's got beautiful reddish-brown hair, eyes as blue as the Irish Sea, a slight droop to the corners of her Irish eyelids like meself…and that fresh-scrubbed look with the rosy cheeks like all the girls in good ol' Dublin!" Pausing, he cocked his head and asked, "But you know who she is, don't you?"

"Of course. I was just funning Shane. Who in these parts doesn't know the Kilrains? After all, I'm wearing Kilrain-O'Hanlon shoes this minute!"

✵ ✵ ✵ ✵ ✵

Ashley's father, Donald Kilrain, was co-owner of the Leprechaun Shoe and Boot Manufacturing Company in Brunswick, and Mike's father, Lewis O'Hanlon, was the other owner. Both men had come to America with their families in 1842 and established the company in Brunswick. Their fathers were co-owners of a company with the same name in Dublin. The fathers had provided financing for their sons to go to America and establish the new company. They had chosen Maine after reading about it in American magazines. They had made the right choice. The company was doing well, and the Kilrains and O'Hanlons were becoming wealthy.

Ashley and her sixteen-year-old sister, Moira, attended the Lewiston Finishing School for Girls in the town of Lewiston, some fifteen miles north of Brunswick. The sisters lived in a dormitory and came home on the weekends.

"Well, anyway," Mike said, "I sure wish it was me Ashley had eyes for instead of you, my friend!"

"Michael, Ashley Kilrain doesn't have eyes for me. But if she did, it'd be because she likes older men."

Mike gave him a bland look, then said casually, "Oh, yeah. It's your birthday, isn't it?"

"Yes, it is. A man's best friend shouldn't forget—"

"But that doesn't make you an older man. I'll turn fifteen on May thirtieth. You're only forty-eight days older than me!"

Shane laughed. "Yeah, *sonny*, and don't you forget it!"

Mike raised his fishing pole back to his shoulder and started toward the road. "See you at school tomorrow, grandpa!" he called.

Shane watched him go, then picked up the ax. Ten minutes later, he finished the chopping job. He carried the wood into the woodshed, hung the ax on nails provided for it on the wall, and said, "There you are, Mr. Wimberly. I'll be by to check on you in a few weeks. Have some more wood hauled in, and I'll chop it for you."

Calvin Wimberly pulled his wallet from his overall bib and

said, "I figure a job like you just did is worth at least three dollars, Shane, so I'll make it five for good measure."

"Oh, no, Mr. Wimberly. I did that job because I wanted to be a help to you. I don't want any pay."

"But…"

Shane walked away and called over his shoulder, "I'll be by in a few weeks. See you then!"

The sun had just set, leaving its golden glow on the western horizon. Shane knew his parents would be wondering where he was if he didn't get home soon. He hopped a fence and started running across a large field toward home. It was a four-mile jaunt through fields and woods of picturesque farmland.

Shane was about halfway home when he spotted black smoke roiling skyward from the farmhouse of a young widow named Elsa Brainerd. Shane sprinted toward the burning house and saw Elsa near the front porch, beating flames off her dress. Two of her three children were with her, screaming in terror.

Terror was in Elsa's eyes as she looked up and saw Shane. He dropped to his knees and finished beating out the flames with his hands. Tears streamed down the widow's cheeks as she cried, "Shane! My baby is in the house!"

Shane looked toward the house. The front door stood open, and the smoke that billowed out the door and flattened against the ceiling of the porch was tinged with red flame. The windows on the bottom floor were closed, but angry flames licked against the panes and thick smoke was turning them black.

"What room is Darlene in?" Shane asked.

"The upstairs bedroom in the far east corner! The fire must have started in the kitchen. The back doors and windows are worse than these. The only possible way I could see to get inside was the front door. But look at it! No one can get in there now!"

Shane scanned the yard, looking for something he could use as a shield to get him through the flame-filled door. His eyes fell on a heavy blanket on Elsa's clothesline. Not far from the clothesline was a small corral next to the barn where a horse and a cow stood looking on. Inside the corral, butted up against the split-rail fence, was the stocktank, full of water.

"Oh, my baby!" Elsa wailed. "My baby! I should never have left her!" A trembling hand went to Elsa's mouth as Johnny and Melissa clung to her, their little faces frozen in masks of terror.

Shane ran to the clothesline and grabbed the blanket. He hopped the fence, plunged the blanket into the water, then made a mad dash for the front porch. Elsa shouted something to him, but the roar of the fire drowned out her words. He wrapped the dripping blanket around him and plunged through the door.

The house had a vestibule with a door to the parlor off to the right, another that led to a hallway straight ahead. The kitchen was at the end of the hallway, which was a blazing inferno. To the left was the staircase. Shane's eyes smarted from the smoke, but he saw that the stairs were just beginning to catch fire. Lambent flames played lightly across the first few steps, but the staircase was not yet blocked.

The heat was unbearable. Shane had a fleeting thought that he was glad he was going to heaven when he died. He bounded up the stairs. Smoke was thick in the hall. As he hurried through the heavy cloud toward the bedroom, he suddenly realized that his pantlegs were on fire. Quickly he lowered the wet blanket around his ankles and calves to smother the flames.

He could hear baby Darlene crying and coughing in the bedroom at the end of the hall. He ran through the door and saw the tiny crib in the corner. He bent over the weeping infant and wrapped her in the wet blanket.

He picked her up and hurried out into the hall. The smoke was thicker yet. He pressed his face into the blanket, drew a deep breath, and ran toward the stairs. He was almost there when he saw that the flames had swept across the stairs to the wall and climbed higher.

The staircase was now blocked.

Outside, Elsa Brainerd held Johnny and Melissa close to her, weeping and praying. A sheet of flame now covered the front door.

Melissa's attention was drawn to the road. "Mama!" she shouted. "It's Mr. and Mrs. Cox!"

Elsa's closest neighbors were Wayne and Betty Cox, who were in their late fifties. Apparently Wayne had just arrived home in the family wagon. He had the team at a full gallop, and the wagon bounced furiously. Betty hung on for dear life.

Behind them Elsa saw George Frye on his horse, riding hard, and another wagon coming at top speed from the opposite direction. It was her neighbors to the south, Carl and Sadie Nelson. Their eighteen-year-old son, Jerry, was in the bed of the wagon, standing and bending over between his parents, gripping the seat. His hat flew off just as Elsa looked back at the burning house.

George Frye raced to the opening in the Brainerd fence that served as a driveway. Pounding hooves raised a cloud of dust as he rounded the corner and beelined for the house. He slid from the saddle before his horse even stopped.

"Elsa! Where's the baby?"

"Upstairs in my bedroom!"

Frye took one look at the flames filling the front door and windows and said, "I'll run around back! Maybe there's a way I can get in. Where's your bedroom located?"

"You can't get in the back either," she said, wiping tears. "Shane Donovan is in there already...but I'm afraid something's happened to him. There's no way out."

"You mean Garth's boy?"

"Yes! I tried to go in and get Darlene, but my dress caught fire. Shane came running up and beat the flames out, then grabbed a blanket and ran into the house to get Darlene."

Both wagons rolled to a halt as Frye looked back toward the inferno. "He'll never get out now," he said with a quaver in his voice.

The Nelsons and Coxes jumped from the wagons and hurried toward Elsa and George.

"Elsa!" Wayne Cox said. "Betty told me you left Darlene

home when you came over. Is she—is she—"

"Yes!" Elsa sobbed, clinging to her other two children. "Shane Donovan is in the house too! He went in to try to rescue her!"

The two women each put an arm around Elsa and one of the children. Sadie Nelson's hand went to her mouth.

"How long's he been in there?" Wayne asked.

Elsa's shaky fingertips touched her cheeks. "I'm not sure. Maybe seven or eight minutes."

"Dad, how about you letting me climb up on your shoulders?" Jerry asked. "If I could get up on the porch, maybe I could break a window and get inside. If Shane made it to the second floor, he might—"

The glass in an end window over the porch roof shattered. Every eye turned to see a foot kicking at the glass to clear the shards off the edge of the window. Then Shane crawled through the window, bearing the small bundle.

"Oh, thank the Lord!" Elsa said. "He's got my baby!"

Smoke lifted off Shane's clothing as he hurried to the edge of the porch and shouted, "Mr. Cox! Pull your wagon up close! I'll jump in the back!"

George Frye rushed up to the edge of the porch and said, "Just drop her down to me, Shane!"

"No, sir! It's too far down. No offense, sir, but I can't take the chance that between the two of us, we might let her fall. Please! Just give me a wagon to jump into!"

Wayne Cox was already to his wagon and climbing up to the seat. He grabbed the reins, gave them a snap, and guided the reluctant horses toward the blazing house. Both animals nickered in protest, but he snapped the reins again and shouted at them. They danced nervously as Wayne pulled the wagon directly under where Shane stood. The heat was intense and the roar deafening.

Shane hugged the baby close and jumped. When he landed in the bed of the wagon, he rolled onto his back and shouted, "Go!" The nervous horses were glad to trot away to cooler air. Everyone rushed to the wagon as Wayne pulled to a stop.

Elsa was first to reach the wagon, arms outstretched. Shane smiled as he leaned over and placed the baby into her mother's arms. With shaky hands, Elsa unwrapped the blanket, tears flowing, and looked at the infant, who was whimpering.

"Oh, Mommy's precious baby!" Elsa said, hugging her to her breast. "You're all right! You're all right!"

Johnny and Melissa jumped with joy. Shane swung down from the wagon bed, tiny tendrils of smoke still lifting from his clothing.

Elsa continued to weep as she stretched one arm toward him. "God bless you, Shane! God bless you! How can I ever thank you?" She hugged his neck tight, then released him.

"That was a wonderful thing you did, Shane," Betty Cox said. "You're a brave young man!"

"That's for sure!" Jerry Nelson said.

The others joined in, heaping praises on the fifteen-year-old boy. Shane scrubbed a palm across his sweaty, smudged face and said, "Any one of you fellows would've done it. I just happened to be here first."

"I'm not sure I would've had the courage to plunge through those flames," Jerry said, "even with a wet blanket. You did a wonderful thing, Shane. I'm sure little Darlene will cherish your name when she grows up…and for the rest of her life."

Again Elsa used one arm to embrace Shane around the neck. He felt her warm tears on his face as she said, "I'll always be so grateful to you, Shane."

The sun had gone down and twilight was slowly falling over the countryside. Standing in the brilliant light of the huge fire, the three men decided to soak the roofs of the barn and other buildings in case the sparks that were flying about should fall on them. Betty Cox invited Elsa and the children to stay with them until a new house could be built. She told her husband that she would go ahead and take Elsa and the children home.

Jerry offered to take the Nelson wagon and run Shane home. Weary from his ordeal, Shane took him up on it.

CHAPTER TWO

Poor Mrs. Brainerd," Jerry Nelson said as he guided the wagon along the road toward the Donovan place. "As if it wasn't bad enough losing her husband. How will she ever afford to build another house?"

"By herself, she never would," Shane said. "But she's not alone. The Lord knows that she and her children need a house to live in. He'll give it to her in His own way and in His own time. You'll see."

Jerry turned and looked at Shane in the gathering darkness. "I wish I had your kind of faith, my friend. There's not a trace of a doubt in your voice as you say that."

"David said, 'The Lord is my Shepherd. I shall not want.' The Shepherd takes care of His sheep, Jerry. He doesn't promise to give us everything we want, but He does promise to supply the needs we have. You're a young Christian yet. You've been saved how long now?"

"Since October. Six months."

"You'll learn as you grow older in the Lord. God keeps His promises. One way or another, Mrs. Brainerd will get her new house."

They were nearing the Donovan place and saw a wagon

pulling out of the driveway onto the road, heading their direction.

"Uh-oh," Shane said. "That'll be Pa. No doubt he's coming to look for me. When he comes home from the lumber mill, he expects me to have the chores done."

Jerry chuckled. "Well, I'm sure when he finds out what delayed you, he'll not be angry."

"I'd say you're right. Sure hope so, anyway."

The darkness made it hard to distinguish much more than silhouettes as the two wagons drew abreast.

"Mr. Donovan!" Jerry called out. "I've got Shane here. I was just bringing him home."

Garth Donovan pulled rein, stopping at the same time Jerry brought his wagon to a halt. Shane could make out his younger brothers in the back of the wagon. Patrick was eleven, and Ryan was nine.

"What's kept you, son?" Garth asked, a touch of anger in his voice. "You should've been home from school nearly three hours ago."

"Well, Pa, I stopped to chop wood for Mr. Wimberly. His arthritis is bothering him a lot, and he can't swing an ax without a lot of pain. I figured on doing my chores before supper, but I—"

"Maybe you shouldn't have tried to chop it all at once. I commend you for the deed, Shane, but you've had your mother and me worried. Why didn't you just cut up half the pile today and do the other half tomorrow?"

"Well, Pa — "

"It would've helped to have let your mother know you were planning to cut wood, Shane. I try to let you have some free rein with your time, but I don't want this kind of thing to happen again."

"Pa, I wasn't planning on it. I walk right by his house on the way home from school. He was out there trying to chop the wood as I came by and...well, when I stopped to say hello, I could see the pain in his face. I took the ax from him and told him I'd finish the pile. But you see, Pa — "

"Shane, I commend you for taking over the job for Mr. Wimberly. I want you to be that kind of boy. But shouldn't you have considered your parents? Didn't you realize we would be worried?"

"Pa, the job wasn't that big. I — "

"Come on and get into the wagon. We've got to get home. Thank you, Jerry, for picking him up."

"Sir…" Jerry said.

"Yes?"

"Sir, Shane is trying to tell you that something else came up that detained him."

"Something else? What, may I ask?"

"Go ahead, Shane. Tell him."

"Well, Pa, Mrs. Brainerd's house was on fire, and I had to stop and help her."

"Her house was on fire?"

"Yes, sir."

"So that's where those smoke clouds were coming from! I hope she and the children are all right."

"They're fine. Mr. and Mrs. Cox are taking them into their home till a new house can be built. They lost everything."

"We'll have to see what Elsa and the children need. I'm sure other neighbors will want to help, too."

"I'm sure they will," Shane said, jumping out of the Nelson wagon. "Thanks, Jerry. See you tomorrow at school."

There was a lengthy pause as Shane settled on the seat beside his father, then Jerry said, "Mr. Donovan…"

"Yes, Jerry?"

"There's…ah…there's something Shane hasn't told you. About the fire, I mean."

Garth looked at Shane, then back toward Jerry. "What's that?"

"Well, sir…your son is a hero. He rescued Mrs. Brainerd's baby girl. She would've died for sure if Shane hadn't gone into the house to get her."

There was a brief moment of silence, then Garth said, "Is that right, son? You went into a burning house and rescued the Brainerd baby?"

"That's exactly what he did, Mr. Donovan," Jerry said. "Your son risked his own life to save little Darlene Brainerd."

There was another moment of silence, this time a little longer. Then Garth turned on the wagon seat and wrapped his arms around his oldest son. "Shane, thank God you're alive! Are you all right, son? Did you get burned?"

"I think I might peel some skin, and my hair and eyebrows might be singed a bit. But I'm okay."

"Oh, thank You, Lord," Garth said. "Thank You for taking care of my boy! And thank You that little Darlene is all right!"

"Well, I guess I'd better head back," Jerry said. "Pa and Mr. Frye and Mr. Cox are soaking the roofs of the barn and sheds so they don't catch fire."

Garth again thanked Jerry for bringing Shane home, then turned the wagon around in the road.

"Shane, I want to tell you how proud I am. And I'm sorry, son, for not letting you get your story out."

"It's all right, Pa. You were just trying to tell me how I should've done things. You didn't know."

Garth swung the wagon into the yard and drove it to the barn.

"You boys go on in and wash up. I'm sure your mother's got supper about ready. I'll be right behind you."

Shane slid off the seat and his younger brothers hopped to the ground. As they walked toward the house together, Patrick said, "You really are a hero, big brother!"

"I just did what had to be done, that's all."

Shane headed for the rear of the house, intending to enter the kitchen from the back porch. As usual, lantern light could be seen flickering in all the windows on the lower floor. Suddenly there was movement on the back porch.

"Shane, are you all right?" Pearl Donovan called out.

"Yes, Ma. I'll explain why I'm late at the supper table."

"Boys, do me a favor and go through the front door, please."

Shane was puzzled by the unusual request, but said, "Sure, Ma," as he guided his little brothers toward the front of the house. Patrick and Ryan eased back to let Shane enter the house first.

Shane stepped into the large parlor and nearly jumped out of his skin when two dozen voices shouted, *"Surprise!"* then began a rousing rendition of "Happy Birthday." They all applauded when they finished.

Shane was pleased to see so many friends from church and school. When he saw Mike O'Hanlon's smiling face, he realized why his best friend hadn't said anything about it being his birthday. He let his gaze roam over the happy young faces, and his heart almost stopped when his eyes landed on Ashley Kilrain.

Shane had not told anyone how he felt about Ashley. He thought she was the prettiest girl he had ever seen. Not only that, but she was sweeter than any girl he had ever met, and she was a dedicated Christian. Ashley Kilrain, in Shane Donovan's estimation, was the epitome of Christian femininity and gracefulness. He loved her long, thick auburn hair, and her soft, rosy cheeks and deep-blue eyes were enough to take his breath.

And now she was looking straight at him, smiling warmly.

Pearl Donovan had positioned herself off to one side, standing with her husband and other two sons. It took her a moment to notice that Shane's shirt and pants were scorched, and that the hair at his forehead was singed. She leaned close to Garth and whispered, "What happened to Shane?"

"I'll tell you and everybody about it right now." Garth moved to the center of the parlor and said, "Listen, everybody. There's something you need to know."

When it got quiet, Garth looked at his oldest son and said, "Shane, as you can see, we planned a little surprise party and dinner for you. Your brothers and I had a scheme all worked out to get you off the place for about a half hour while your friends arrived and parked their wagons and buggies out behind the barn. You just unknowingly kept us from having to put our scheme into action."

Shane grinned, shook his head, and let his eyes brush over Ashley Kilrain's face. "Some schemers, all of you," he said.

"Now I want everyone here to know why our son was late and why his clothes are scorched," Garth said.

There was a low murmur among the group, then Garth told them of the fire at the Brainerd home and that Shane had risked his life to rescue the Brainerd baby. When the whole story had been told, everyone looked at Shane with admiring eyes. It seemed to Shane that Ashley Kilrain's eyes held the most admiration. There was a stillness in the house as the group realized how close their friend had come to death.

Pearl Donovan wept as she rushed to her oldest son and wrapped her arms around him. "Oh, Shane, I'm so proud of you! I'm so thankful to the Lord that you're still here to celebrate your fifteenth birthday! And I'm so glad that little Darlene Brainerd's life was spared!"

There were some amens among the group, and several spoke out, sometimes two or three at a time, showering the young hero with praise. Shane's features flushed with embarrassment.

"You're all very kind, but really…I'm no hero. I just happened to be the first one on the scene and did what had to be done. Any of you would've done the same thing."

"Takes a lot of courage to do a thing like that," Hector Donaldson said.

"That's right," agreed another. "A whole lot of courage!"

Pearl saw that her son was becoming increasingly embarrassed. "Well," she said, "we'd better eat or our supper will get cold!"

Shane was placed at the head of the main table, and his father sat at the other end. Three other tables were crowded into the parlor-dining room area.

Ashley was seated at the main table, next to Pearl, who sat

across the corner from her husband. From time to time during the meal, Shane let his eyes stray to Ashley, feeling a strange warmth whenever he looked at her.

When the meal was over, it was time for games. The favorite was "Musical Chairs," which was played enthusiastically while Pearl played the piano. Even Garth joined in. After nearly an hour of games, it was time for Shane to open his presents.

When all the gifts had been unwrapped, Pearl, Patrick, and Ryan came from the kitchen carrying cakes — Pearl a large chocolate cake with lighted candles, and the boys smaller cakes. Everyone sang "Happy Birthday" again, and Shane easily blew out the fifteen candles. There was laughter and applause, then they all ate cake while mingling and chatting.

Shane made his way amongst his guests, thanking them for coming and for their gifts. He purposely saved Ashley till last so he could spend more time with her. She was talking to Hector Donaldson and a girl named Patricia Reynolds as he drew near. Patricia said a few more words to Ashley, then she and Hector excused themselves and walked away, joining a small group close by.

Ashley gave Shane a coy smile and said with a hint of Irish brogue, "I sure am thankful to the Lord that He protected you in that burning house, Shane. I know you've heard it already tonight, but you *are* a very courageous young man."

"You're very kind, Ashley, but I really don't think *courageous* is the right word to describe me. Maybe *determined* is the word. I was very determined to save that little baby's life, but to tell you the truth, I was scared to death."

Ashley smiled and said, "That's why I used the word *courageous*. Courage doesn't mean without fear. It means doing what has to be done in spite of your fear."

"Really?"

"Yes, really. You're a very courageous young man, Shane, and I'm proud to know you."

"And I'm proud to know such a smart girl who's also the

prettiest girl I've ever seen in my life and I'm wondering why you're not in Lewiston at school since you only come home on weekends and this is only Tuesday."

While Shane was taking a breath, Ashley giggled and said, "Thank you for the kind words, Shane. The reason I'm here and not at school is because I wanted to come to the party. Daddy came and picked me up after school this afternoon. I didn't want the other kids in the youth group to be at your birthday party without me."

Shane wasn't sure Ashley meant that she wanted to be there for *him* or for the socializing. He hoped it was because she wanted to be there for him. He was trying to think of something else to say when he noticed Mike O'Hanlon looking at him from across the room. Or was he looking at Ashley?

Shane was about to ask how her Uncle Buster was when Ashley said, "I suppose you're going to the church picnic a week from next Saturday."

Shane struggled to free his tongue while the Irish lass held his gaze with her own. "Well, yes. I...I'm going to the picnic. Would...would you be my date?"

Ashley sucked in a tiny breath and said, "Why, I'd be delighted to go as your date, Shane. I'm honored that you would ask me. I mean that."

Shane's heart was pounding so hard he wondered if Ashley could see the front of his scorched shirt move.

"The honor will be all mine, Ashley. May I come by and pick you up in our family wagon? *With* my parents and little brothers, of course."

"You may," she said. "The picnic's at noon. What time should I expect you?"

"I'd say about a quarter till, if that's all right."

"I'm sure that will be fine."

"Then it's a date!" Shane said.

Moments later, the guests piled into the wagons and drove

away. Shane kept his eyes on Ashley until she was swallowed by the night. Only Mike O'Hanlon remained. He had made arrangements to spend the night with his best friend, and Shane was happy to have him. They had often stayed at each other's homes over the years. Shane's second-story bedroom was large and equipped with two three-quarter beds.

Shane had been dying to share his good news with Mike ever since the party was over. Finally alone with his friend, he lay in his bed with his arms behind his head, looking toward the dark ceiling.

"Mike…"

"Yeah?"

"I sure am glad Ashley likes older men."

"Oh? Why's that?"

"Because when I asked her to be my date at the church picnic, she accepted!"

There was a brief moment of silence. Then Mike said, "Hey, that's great, old man!"

There was a smile in Mike O'Hanlon's voice, but the darkness hid the grim form of his lips.

CHAPTER THREE

On Sunday morning, the bell in the tower of the First Parish Congregational Church in Brunswick was ringing as people came to the services in buggies, surreys, carriages, wagons, on horseback, and afoot.

The story of Shane Donovan's heroic deed had spread all over Brunswick and the surrounding farm area. When the Donovan family arrived in their wagon, people crowded around to commend the fifteen-year-old boy for his courageous act and to ask questions about it. Shane was not yet accustomed to his newfound fame and found all the attention embarrassing.

While he was answering questions, Shane saw the Kilrain carriage pull into the churchyard. Ashley was wearing a new hairstyle under her small plumed hat, and she was smiling at him. He hoped the new hairdo was for him.

In the Kilrain carriage, Donald and Mavor sat together on the front seat, along with Donald's brother, Vivian Kilrain. In the second seat, Moira sat beside her younger sister, while eleven-year-old William and nine-year-old Harvey rode in the third seat.

Vivian, at forty, was a year older than Donald, and a widower. He hated his first name and insisted that everyone call him Buster. He was short and muscular, and his carrot-red hair and ruddy complexion gave him the look of a man with a quick temper. Buster Kilrain had served as a soldier in the Army of Ireland before coming to the States to work in the Leprechaun Shoe and Boot Manufacturing Company. Everyone in the family adored Uncle Buster.

The Kilrains pulled up and parked beside the Donovans. Shane was still surrounded by curious people, but while he talked to them, he looked at Ashley. She gave him another smile. Shane was about to excuse himself to go help Ashley from the carriage, but Uncle Buster beat him to it.

The Donovan boys, being the same ages as the Kilrain boys, hurried off to their Sunday school classes together. The rest of the family members greeted one another. Shane finally was able to politely break away from the curious ones and hurried to talk with Ashley. Before he could get to her, Buster clapped him on the shoulder.

"Well, Shane me boy, sure and if ye didn't go and become a hero! I think what ye did was grand and quite unselfish. Me compliments to you."

Shane grinned shyly and said, "Thank you, Uncle Buster."

A surrey pulled up next to where they stood, loaded with the Calvin Stowe family.

"Hey, Shane," Calvin said, "we heard about the fire at Elsa Brainerd's and about what you did. God bless you for being such a brave young man!"

"Thank you, sir," Shane said.

Calvin Stowe was professor of rhetoric at nearby Bowdoin College, a Christian liberal arts school. Harriet, his wife, had already made a name for herself with her novel that had been published two years previously. *Uncle Tom's Cabin* was creating quite a stir both above and below the Mason-Dixon line.

As Shane was speaking with the famous author, Wayne and Betty Cox pulled up in their wagon with Elsa Brainerd and her children aboard. Little Darlene was wrapped in a blanket and held in her mother's arms.

The crowd moved toward the Cox wagon, wanting to talk to Elsa and get a look at the baby. Shane stood back, looking on. He was glad to let Elsa and her baby girl have the limelight. As the people spoke to Elsa, Shane heard her say, "Yes! Praise the Lord for His protective hand on my baby...and praise the Lord for Shane Donovan! He's the bravest young man I've ever known."

Later, the choir opened the morning worship service with a rousing song, then two congregational hymns followed. At the close of the second hymn, the pastor, Dr. George Adams, rose from his chair on the platform and went to the pulpit. Adams, a distant cousin of John Quincy Adams, was a tall, stately man. Though he was only in his early fifties, his hair was silver.

Dr. Adams gave his normal announcements, then said, "My brothers and sisters in Christ, I believe that by now all of us have heard about our dear sister, Elsa Brainerd, losing her house in a fire this past Tuesday."

Shane Donovan was sitting between Mike O'Hanlon and Ashley Kilrain. He tensed up, hoping the pastor would not say anything about him having rescued the Brainerd baby. He heaved an inward sigh of relief when Dr. Adams proceeded to ask the people to sacrifice in a special offering for Elsa and her children. He said that if everyone would go the extra mile for the widow, they could raise enough money to build her a new house. There were scattered amens in the crowd, and the offering plates were passed.

While the money was being counted, Dr. Adams introduced twenty-four-year-old Joshua Lawrence Chamberlain, an 1852 Phi Beta Kappa graduate of Bowdoin College who was now studying for the ministry at Bangor Theological Seminary. While a student at Bowdoin, Chamberlain had been music director at the church, and he was now engaged to Frances Adams, the pastor's adopted daughter. Frances — better known as Fannie — was the church organist.

In the pulpit, Dr. Adams spoke highly of Chamberlain and told the crowd how proud he and his wife, Sarah Ann, were that

Joshua would one day be their son-in-law.

Shane and Mike set admiring eyes on the handsome seminary student who during his college years had been their Sunday school teacher. His slim, muscular frame lacked an inch and a half of reaching six feet, but he had a way of carrying himself that gave the impression he was taller. His face was long and slender with prominent cheekbones and deep-set, gray-blue eyes under heavy brows. His hair was dark brown, and he was clean-shaven.

The congregation sang another hymn, and during the last stanza, one of the ushers hurried to the platform and handed the pastor a slip of paper. Dr. Adams read it and smiled.

When the hymn was finished, Adams stepped to the pulpit and said, "Friends, the Lord has worked in hearts here this morning in a marvelous way. I did not suggest any kind of a figure that it would take to build a house for Elsa Brainerd and her children, but I discussed it yesterday with Clyde Domire, who you all know is in the construction business. Brother Domire estimates that it will cost about four thousand dollars for the materials. He has already volunteered to build the house for no cost."

Elsa Brainerd, who sat between Melissa and Johnny with baby Darlene in her arms, began to weep. Betty Cox was seated next to Melissa. She reached over and patted Elsa's arm, saying, "The Lord takes care of His own, honey."

Elsa nodded, biting her lips and wiping tears.

"Mrs. Adams and I did some figuring the past couple of days," the pastor said. "We think the house can be furnished for about eight hundred dollars with another six hundred dollars needed for clothing and shoes."

Sarah Ann Adams was seated in the choir behind her husband. He heard her whisper, "George!"

He asked the audience to excuse him momentarily and went to his wife. She whispered something to him, and he nodded, then returned to the pulpit.

"My wife reminds me that there were toys burned up in the

fire, as well as furniture and clothing. We had figured them in our total, but I forgot to mention them just now. You men know how wives are — sticklers for details!"

Laughter swept through the crowd.

"Anyway, Sarah Ann and I figured the grand total needed to start Elsa and the children over again — the cupboards stocked with groceries, too — would be around fifty-five hundred dollars."

The congregation waited in eager silence as the pastor looked back at the slip of paper, smiled broadly, and said, "My brothers and sisters in Christ…in checks and cash, a total of six thousand one hundred dollars was in the offering, with a few notes promising an additional thirteen hundred and forty-four dollars to be given in the service tonight. How do you like that? A total of over seven thousand four hundred dollars!"

The crowd cheered and applauded, many shedding tears. Elsa wept for joy. The Coxes both took her into their arms, reminding her how much she and her children were loved.

When the crowd noise subsided, a man stood and said, "Pastor, I'm volunteering my labor to help build the house."

That was all it took to trigger the same response throughout the congregation. Elsa cried the more, overwhelmed with the generosity of the people and the goodness of the Lord.

At the organ, Fannie struck up a song of praise. The pianist blended in, and the music director stood and led them all in singing praises to the bountiful God of heaven.

Dr. Adams then returned to the pulpit and opened his Bible. Shane heaved another secret sigh of relief. He wouldn't have to endure any more embarrassment. The pastor hadn't said a word about Shane's act of courage in rescuing the baby.

"This morning," the pastor said, "I want to speak to you on the subject of courage."

Shane swallowed hard, blinking in disbelief. Mike elbowed him, and Ashley gave him a smile.

Dr. Adams began his sermon by explaining that courage was

not the lack of fear, but the wherewithal in a person to perform a necessary task in spite of fear. He then took his congregation into the Scriptures, giving biblical examples of courage. He showed that the supreme example was the Lord Himself, who set His face as a flint to go to the cross, knowing He would be forsaken by His Father while suffering the fire of God's wrath, the onslaught of the devil, and the fierceness of the jaws of death. Yet because He loved a lost world of condemned sinners, Jesus went to the cross with undaunted courage in spite of all He faced at Calvary.

After citing other examples of courage in the Bible, Adams took his audience to the three Hebrew children in the book of Daniel who went into Nebuchadnezzar's fiery furnace rather than bow before the golden image and deny their God. Shadrach, Meshach, and Abednego acknowledged that God might not deliver them, but showed their courage by going into the flames in spite of their fear.

Shane Donovan wanted to slide off the pew and hide on the floor when Dr. Adams used his act of courage as a closing illustration. Adams showed that in spite of his fear, Shane demonstrated courage by going into the blazing inferno after little Darlene Brainerd at the risk of his own life.

When the service was over, Shane was again surrounded by people who wished to congratulate him. His parents, Ashley, and Mike stood by looking on. They smiled at each other, seeing how embarrassed Shane was at being the center of attention.

The crowd around Shane had begun to diminish when he saw Joshua Chamberlain approaching him with Fannie Adams on his arm. Shane smiled broadly at Chamberlain, spoke first to Fannie, then extended his hand to Chamberlain.

"It's good to see you again, Mr. Chamberlain," Shane said.

"Thank you, Shane. I'm honored to be able to shake the hand of such a courageous young man."

"Well, thank you, sir. But I'll be glad when everyone can just forget about this whole incident. I don't much like being compared to Shadrach, Meshach, and Abednego. What I did wasn't anything like what they went through."

"Perhaps not, but commendable all the same."

"Mr. Chamberlain, Pastor Adams didn't mention a wedding date. When are you and Miss Fannie planning on getting married?"

"We haven't set a date yet, Shane. We both feel the Lord would have us finish our education first. Fannie is making plans to go to New York City to further her music studies, and I'm going to continue preparing myself for the ministry at Bangor."

Shane saw that his parents and younger brothers were heading toward their wagon. "Well, sir, I hope I get to see you again sometime soon."

"Who knows? I'm sure one of these weekends I'll be back...even if Fannie's in New York."

They shook hands again, and Shane joined his family at the wagon.

The following Saturday, Shane and Ashley had their date at the church picnic. They paired up for games and entered the three-legged race, the pie-in-the-face contest, and the egg-tossing competition. That day drew them closer together.

Over the next several months, they spent more time together, making sure they always sat side by side in Sunday school class and in the church services. Shane became more and more attached to the pretty Irish lass.

In late spring, Moira Kilrain graduated from the Lewiston Finishing School for Girls and married a young man from Portland, and they made their home in that city.

When summer rolled around, Shane worked ten hours a day, six days a week at the lumber mill with his father. In the evenings and on Sunday afternoons, he was allowed by his parents and Ashley's to visit her at the Kilrain home. He was often invited for meals by Mavor, and became well-liked by the family. Uncle Buster had a special liking for Shane, for they had become fishing partners, squeezing in fishing time after work hours and before supper.

Elsa Brainerd's house was finished by early July. The entire community gave her a housewarming, adding kitchenware she needed and some things for the bedrooms.

Mike O'Hanlon worked eight hours a day during the summer at the shoe factory, learning the business. His father and Donald Kilrain had promised to make him a partner after he graduated from college. Half of his work was doing manual labor in the shop, and the other half was spent in the office learning the management end of the business. Mike was bright and industrious and was catching on fast. He and his best friend saw each other very little during the summer.

They were both glad for school to start so they could be together more. Mike noticed, though, that Shane sorely missed Ashley on the weekdays when she was in Lewiston at school.

In late September, a lumberjack who worked under Garth Donovan was accidentally killed on the job. Garth had often talked to him about the gospel, but the tough, foul-mouthed lumberjack turned a deaf ear. The accident took him instantly. The man died in his unbelieving state.

Dr. George Adams preached the funeral, which was attended by a great crowd of area residents. His sermon was loaded with gospel, and many unbelievers were converted, including several teenagers. The tragedy also served to draw the teenagers of First Parish Congregational Church closer to the Lord and to each other. Ashley, Shane, Mike, and their friends in the church youth group took the newly saved teenagers under their wings to help them grow in the Lord.

On April 12, 1854, Pearl Donovan surprised her oldest son by springing another birthday party and dinner for him, with his friends from church as guests. All of the teenagers who had come to Christ after the lumberjack was killed were there.

Pearl placed Shane at the head of the table again, with Ashley on the corner to his left. Next to Ashley sat a pretty brunette. Shane leaned over and said to Ashley, "I assume this young lady is a friend of yours."

"Yes, she is. Shane Donovan, I would like you to meet Charolette Thompson."

Charolette smiled and offered her hand. As Shane took it, she said, "Ashley has told me so much about you, Shane. I feel like I already know you."

"Charolette and I have been friends for some time," Ashley said. "She's going to stay at my house this weekend and come to church with us."

"Wonderful," Shane said. "It will be nice to have you at church, Charolette. And thank you for coming to my party."

"I'm glad to be here."

"Has everyone else met her?" Shane asked Ashley.

"I introduced her around while we were waiting for your daddy and brothers to bring you home."

Garth Donovan stood at his end of the table and asked Mike O'Hanlon, who was seated across from Ashley, to lead them in prayer. After he had prayed and everyone began to eat, Mike asked Charolette where her home was and where she knew Ashley from.

"I was born in Ireland," Charolette said with a smile, "but Father brought our family to America when I was ten. He opened a general store in Lewiston. My parents put me in the Lewiston Finishing School for Girls the following year, and that's where I met Ashley. We've become close friends."

"I see," Mike said. "Well, I'm glad you could come to the party for the old man here."

Charolette laughed at Shane's feigned protest.

"Everyone here has been so nice to me. I guess you all go to the same church?"

"We're in the youth group together."

"Well, I'm looking forward to visiting there on Sunday."

On Sunday morning, to everyone's surprise, Dr. Adams had invited a guest speaker to fill his pulpit. He had been over to Bangor that week and had heard his future son-in-law preach in chapel. Adams was surprised at the eloquence and maturity Joshua Chamberlain had gained since his term as music director at First Parish, and he invited him to preach both Sunday morning and evening.

Ashley and Shane sat together, as usual, with Mike sitting on Shane's other side. Charolette Thompson sat next to Ashley. During the congregational singing, Ashley noticed that Charolette was unfamiliar with the songs. Her heart went out to her. Charolette was such a sweet girl, but had been raised in a home where neither God nor His Son were ever considered.

Ashley knew that Charolette's mother had died of consumption a little over a year ago, and that her father gave her little of his time. He was too busy running his store to pay attention to his daughter. The only thing he did was pay her bill at the school and tell her to stay there on the weekends...he didn't need her around the house. On more than one occasion Ashley had found Charolette weeping in her dormitory room, missing her mother and feeling all but abandoned by her father.

As a female soloist prepared to sing just before the sermon, Ashley leaned close to Shane and whispered, "Pray for Charolette. I think she's almost ready to come to Jesus." Shane reached down and squeezed her hand.

Dr. Adams introduced Joshua Chamberlain after the solo, and when he opened his Bible and began to preach, Mike and Shane looked at each other and smiled. They were amazed at how much his speaking had improved since he had taught them in Sunday school. He was a good speaker before; now he was excellent.

With his heart on fire for Jesus Christ, Chamberlain preached a powerful gospel sermon, warning sinners of the wrath to come and giving them the crucified, risen Christ as the only refuge. When it came time for the invitation, and the crowd was standing and singing, Ashley looked at Charolette from the corner of her eye and saw that she was weeping. She leaned close and said, "Charolette, would you like to respond to the invitation? I'll go with you."

Charolette nodded, wiped tears, and said, "Yes!"

Ashley took her friend by the hand and led her down the aisle. Others went forward also. There was great rejoicing throughout the congregation for those who were coming to Christ.

Ashley stayed with Charolette while the pastor's wife counseled her. When the service was over, the two girls embraced and wept. Charolette thanked Ashley for caring enough to talk to her so many times about salvation. Many of the teenagers in the youth group gathered around Charolette, rejoicing with her in her newfound faith.

During the following year, Charolette Thompson visited the Kilrain home on several occasions, staying over weekends and attending church. She became well-acquainted with the young people in the Sunday school class. She was growing in the Lord and becoming an avid student of the Bible. Though Shane's heart was fixed on Ashley, he found Charolette charming and a joy to be around. She had a vibrant sense of humor and a sweet spirit.

CHAPTER FOUR

S hane Donovan was now seventeen, but since Ashley Kilrain was only fifteen, her father would not allow her to declare herself Shane's steady girlfriend. Donald and Mavor Kilrain wholeheartedly approved of Shane, but they had decided that their daughter could not enter into that kind of relationship until she was seventeen. Though Shane and Ashley had not declared that they were steadies, everyone in the church knew it would be that way once Ashley was old enough.

In late April 1855, First Parish Congregational Church held another picnic on a Saturday afternoon. Shane rode to the picnic in the Kilrain carriage with Ashley, her parents, her brothers, and Uncle Buster.

It was a bright, sunlit day with only a few puffy white clouds drifting in the Maine sky. The picnic was held on the church property, which had open fields of grass fringed and dotted with trees.

Some four hundred people came. Elderly folks sat on chairs in the shade. Young mothers tended to crying babies and tried to keep up with their older children. Some men played horseshoes while others stood around and talked. Many of the women collected in groups to talk also. There were frequent bursts of laughter. Children ran about, laughing and having a good time. Boys with bugs in their hands chased girls, and the girls screamed.

Barry Flanders, a young man who had come into the church earlier in the year, brought Charolette Thompson to the picnic, and Mike O'Hanlon brought Minnie Weatherton.

The first organized competition was the teenagers' three-legged race. Shane took Ashley by the hand, looked around at their friends, and said, "C'mon everyone, let's race!"

"I can't, Shane," Barry said. "I twisted my knee yesterday, and it's still giving me a lot of pain."

"Did you have a doctor look at it?"

"No. Ma says I'll have to if it doesn't get better by Monday."

"I hate to see you miss out on the fun, Charolette," Shane said.

She smiled. "It's all right. I'll enjoy sitting here with Barry and watching the rest of you."

A good-sized crowd, including the pastor and his wife, gathered to watch. Nine teenage couples entered the race, which consisted of four heats. The race was a distance of fifty yards, so there would be a ten-minute rest period between heats.

Mike and Minnie lined up next to Shane and Ashley. Mike grinned at Shane, then looked at Minnie and said, "We'll put these two in our dust."

Minnie giggled, got a firm grip on Mike's arm, and said, "I'm ready!"

The start signal was given, and the race began. Mike and Minnie stayed abreast of Shane and Ashley until forty feet from the finish line when Shane and Ashley pulled ahead, along with two other couples.

Just as they crossed the line, Ashley stumbled and went down, taking Shane with her. From the ground, they turned to see who had stayed in the competition with them. Mike and Minnie were among the couples who qualified for the next heat.

As Shane started to get up, Ashley howled, gritted her teeth, and said, "I think I turned my ankle."

"Really? Does it hurt bad?"

"Enough to take me out of the race. I'm sorry, Shane."

Shane grinned. "Silly. There's nothing to be sorry about."

"But now you'll be out of the race."

"It's all right, Ashley." Shane began to untie the rope that held their ankles together. "It's not that important."

When the rope was loose, Shane helped Ashley to her feet. "Here, lean on me. We'll go over to the bench where Barry and Charolette are and watch the rest of the race with them."

Mike and Minnie saw them and asked what had happened. After Shane told them, Mike kidded Ashley, saying she knew that he and Minnie would eventually beat them, so she turned her ankle on purpose. They all had a good laugh as they moved off the field to rest.

Donald and Mavor Kilrain, along with Uncle Buster, were waiting at the benches for them, having seen Ashley fall. She assured them it was only a slight twist. Satisfied that she was all right, the parents rejoined the other couples they had been talking with.

The three men who were officiating came up and asked about Ashley, wanting to make sure she had not been hurt seriously. When they learned that the injury was minor but enough to take her out of the competition, one of them said, "You were doing real good, Shane. You've still got about six minutes. Maybe you can find another partner."

Ashley turned to Charolette and said, "Do you suppose Barry would mind if you entered the race as Shane's partner? I hate to see him eliminated because of me."

"Of course I wouldn't mind," Barry said. "How about it, Charolette?"

Charolette looked at Barry, smiled, and glanced at Shane. "Would that be all right with you?"

"Sure, as long as Barry doesn't mind," Shane said. "I've got a feeling you'd be a good partner."

Charlotte looked at Ashley. "Honey, are you sure you don't

mind the love of your life being tied to me?"

Ashley smiled. "You're my best friend in all the world, Charolette. I'm not worried about that."

"You're a dear," Charolette said, patting her arm. "I really am happy to get into the race, but I'm sorry it has to be because of your ankle."

"It'll be all right in a day or two," Ashley said. "Better hurry. The second heat is about to begin."

Shane gave Ashley a tender look and said, "Thanks. Charolette and I will do our best to win."

There was cheering on the sidelines as the second heat got under way. Shane and Charolette seemed perfectly synchronized as they ran, and came in first. Mike and Minnie came in on their heels.

By the time the third heat was finished, the two couples left for the final heat were Shane and Charolette, and Mike and Minnie. During the rest period, Mike chided his best friend, saying he and Charolette didn't have a chance.

"Oh? And just what makes you think so?" Shane said.

"Cause you're the old man here, my friend. You just won't be able to hold up. Too bad Charolette had to get stuck with a nine-teenth-century Methuselah!"

They had a good laugh together, and soon lined up to the sounds of a shouting crowd, ready to run the final heat. The start signal was given, and the race was on.

The race was neck-and-neck for nearly thirty yards, then Shane and Charolette began to edge ahead. When they were within ten yards of the finish line, Mike and Minnie were three strides behind.

"What's the matter young whippersnapper?" Shane called over his shoulder. "You gonna let this old man and his partner beat you?"

Mike shouted back a retort, but because of the noise from the crowd, Shane couldn't tell what he was saying. Shane and Charolette crossed the finish line first, and both couples fell on the grass, laughing. While the ankle ropes were being untied, Shane asked, "Now, what was it you shouted back at me, ol' pal?"

"I said you were ahead because that youthful girl was carrying you!"

The four of them laughed again, and the boys helped the girls to their feet. The grand prize was a huge watermelon. The crowd cheered the winners again, then the officials began preparing for a footrace between teenage boys.

"I don't suppose I could interest you in entering the next race, Shane, seeing as how you're so old and tired," Mike said.

"We'll see who's old and tired."

Shane called to his father to come and take the watermelon off his hands. Garth was there in seconds, offering his congratulations to Shane and Charolette and his condolences to Mike and Minnie. He hurried back to Pearl, carrying the prize.

Shane smiled at Charolette and said, "Thank you, young lady, for helping this old man win the race."

"Oh, you're welcome, Shane. The pleasure was mine."

Minnie and Charolette headed for the benches and found that Ashley was alone. Barry had gone to get them some lemonade. Minnie offered to get some for Charolette and herself, saying it should be her task since she lost the race. Charolette laughed and told her to hurry back as she sat down beside Ashley.

"How's the ankle feeling?" Charolette asked.

"It's not hurting quite as much, but it does seem to be swelling a little."

"Honey, I envy you."

"What do you mean?"

"To have such a fine, handsome, Christian boy like Shane interested in you — you're truly fortunate."

Ashley sighed. "You're right. He's a wonderful young man. I hope as we grow older that the love between us grows and deepens so we can marry. I can't think of anything more wonderful than being married to Shane Donovan."

When the picnic was over, Charolette watched Shane and

Ashley ride away together in the Kilrain carriage. Lord, if You have another boy in this part of the world like Shane Donovan, would You bring him into my life?

A caravan of buggies, surreys, and wagons from Brunswick made the fifteen-mile trip to Lewiston for graduation day at the finishing school in late May 1855. Ashley Kilrain and Charolette Thompson graduated, both being sixteen, which was the average age for girls to graduate from the school. Fifty-seven other girls graduated at the same time.

It was hard for Charolette to observe families of the other graduates congratulating them. She was the only one whose mother was missing. Her father, Alfred Thompson, had come to the graduation and stood beside his daughter as friends offered their congratulations. Charolette introduced them to him, but he was cool and showed little interest in them.

Alfred excused himself for a few minutes and walked away, and Charolette began to cry. Ashley saw it, went to her, and wrapped her arms around her. Mavor saw the two of them together and came to see what was wrong. Charolette wiped tears from her cheeks and drew a shuddering breath. She was about to reply when Pearl Donovan walked up and asked if there was a problem. Ashley released her hold on her best friend, and Charolette explained with quivering lips and shaky voice how desperately she missed her mother and wished she could have lived to see her graduate.

The two mothers embraced her at the same time, speaking words of comfort. As they were doing so, Alfred Thompson returned.

"What's the matter?" he asked. "What happened, Charolette?"

"I...I miss Mama, Papa. I wish so much she could have been here to see me graduate."

"Well, she's gone, Charolette, and there's nothin' we can do about it. You ready to head for home?"

"I guess so."

"Then let's go."

"What plans do you have now that you've graduated, honey?" Mavor asked.

"I'm going to find a job, Mrs. Kilrain," she said, sniffing and dabbing at her tears with a hanky Pearl had just placed in her hand. "I'm going to look in Portland first, since it's the largest town around."

Mavor looked at Alfred and said to Charolette, "Your father has a thriving business, I understand. Doesn't he have a spot for you in his store? That way you could stay at home."

"C'mon, Charolette," Alfred said. "Let's get goin'."

Charolette's brow furrowed as she looked at the women and Ashley with fear in her eyes. She thanked them for being so kind to her, told Ashley she would see her as soon as possible, and hurried after her father, who was already heading toward the graveled lot where the vehicles were parked.

She was about to catch up to him when she saw Shane Donovan running toward her across the school lawn. She stopped and forced a smile as he drew up. From the corner of her eye, she could see her father untying the reins of the horse that pulled his carriage.

"Charolette," Shane said, "I saw that you and your father were leaving, and I wanted to ask if you'll still be coming to church on Sundays."

"I'll come whenever I can arrange a ride. I'll be looking for a job in Portland, and if I find one, I won't be able to come to Brunswick very often. I'll just have to see how the Lord works things out."

"Well, I'll be praying that He'll fix it so you can still come to church. I figured your dad would give you a job in the store."

Charolette glanced at her father, who was climbing into his carriage.

"Papa says it's better if I live and work elsewhere," she said, a trace of a tremor in her voice.

"Oh. Well, you'll be keeping in touch with Ashley, I'm sure."

"Of course."

"Good. Then we'll know how things are going for you."

She glanced again at her father, who was now settled on the seat, glaring at her. She hurried toward the carriage and looked back at Shane. "See you Sunday if I can."

Alfred Thompson scowled at his daughter as she climbed into the carriage. He said something Shane could not distinguish, but whatever it was hurt her, for her shoulders slumped and her head dropped forward. She didn't look back at Shane as the carriage rolled away.

Shane hurried to the others and said to Ashley as he drew up, "Poor Charolette. Her father really treats her bad."

"I know. He's downright mean to her."

"He needs some man to take him out behind the barn and give him a good whipping."

"Now, Shane," Pearl said, "you shouldn't talk that way. No matter how he treats Charolette, he's still her father."

"I know, Ma, but that doesn't give him the right to mistreat her. She's a sweet girl. Did you know she's going to be looking for a job in Portland?"

"Yes, she told us," his mother said.

"Well, if she finds one, she won't be coming to church much, if at all. I asked her if her father couldn't give her a job in his store. She told me he said it's better if she lives and works somewhere else."

"I asked Charolette the same thing in front of him, Shane," Mavor said. "He didn't even respond. Poor girl. Somebody needs to take her in and give her a home and some love."

❋ ❋ ❋ ❋ ❋

The next Sunday, Shane Donovan and Ashley Kilrain were standing in front of the church building before Sunday school, chatting with other young people. Elsa Brainerd pulled her wagon up close to where they stood, smiled and said, "Hello, Ashley...Shane."

They greeted her, and Shane stepped up to help her out of the wagon while Johnny and Melissa hopped out of the back. Shane then reached onto the seat and picked up two-year-old Darlene, who smiled at him and said, "Unca Shane!"

"That's my girl!" he laughed, kissing her cheek and holding her close.

"She loves you a lot now, Shane," Elsa said, "but when she finds out what you did for her, she'll love you even more. I'll probably tell her about the time she turns five, so I can be sure she'll understand."

Shane kissed Darlene's cheek again and handed her to her mother. "I don't mind you telling her. Just don't make me sound more important than I am."

Elsa smiled at him, then hurried inside the church with her children.

Just then Ashley pointed to the street and said, "Shane, look!"

It was Charolette Thompson. She was driving her father's carriage, alone. Charolette raised a hand of greeting and pulled rein. When the carriage stopped, Shane stepped up, offered his hand, and helped her down. Charolette felt a tingle all over when she placed her hand in Shane's.

No, Charolette, she said to herself. Ashley is your best friend, and Shane belongs to her.

Ashley rushed to Charolette and embraced her. "Your father actually give you permission to drive here?"

"Well, not exactly. He got married last night, and he and my new stepmother are taking a two-day cruise down the coast. He didn't say I couldn't take the horse and carriage, so here I am."

"New stepmother!" Ashley said. "You haven't told me your father was seeing someone."

"It all happened real fast," Charolette said as they started toward the church together.

"Do you like her, Charolette?" Shane asked.

"I don't really know her. She…"

"She what?" Ashley said.

"Well…I…I guess I'd better not talk about her."

Ashley stopped and looked her best friend in the eye. "You're upset, aren't you? This new stepmother of yours…what's her name?"

"Ethel."

"Well, this Ethel…she doesn't like you, does she?"

Charolette cleared her throat nervously. "Well…I — "

"You don't have to say any more," Ashley said. "I knew it just by the look in your eyes."

"We'd better get inside, girls," Shane said, "or we're going to be late."

Charolette sat in Sunday school and barely heard the lesson. She was upset over her father's marriage, but even more, she was overcome with guilt because of her feelings toward Shane Donovan. While Chester Olmstead taught, she prayed inwardly, O Lord, forgive me. I shouldn't be having these feelings for Shane. You know I've been struggling with this attraction for him for several weeks. And You know I love Ashley and would never try to come between them. Please help me to smother these feelings. Please, Lord!

Charolette Thompson was unable to find employment in Portland, so her father reluctantly let her help in the store. She and her new stepmother did not get along well. Ethel seemed to resent Charolette's presence in the home and at the store. Alfred allowed Charolette to use the horse and carriage on the weekends so she would be out of the house. He knew she was spending them with

Ashley Kilrain and going to church on Sundays.

Donald and Mavor were glad to have Charolette in their home and came to love her more as the weeks passed. Charolette said little about her new stepmother, but Ashley and her parents suspected that the reason Alfred allowed his daughter to spend the weekends with them was because neither he nor Ethel wanted her around.

Charolette continued to struggle with her feelings toward Shane Donovan. Whenever she was near him, she prayed that the Lord would send the man he had chosen for her life's mate into her life. The love between Shane and Ashley was deepening before Charolette's very eyes, and though she rejoiced for Ashley, it was painful to watch. Until the Lord helped her to get over him, Shane had Charolette's heart. She vowed she would never let it show. If only there was another Shane Donovan!

One Monday morning in late July, Buster Kilrain happened to be at his brother's house. Buster knew of the unhappiness Charolette was experiencing at home. When she drove toward home after breakfast, Buster said to Donald, Mavor, and Ashley, "Poor Charolette. The likes of her misery is tearin' me heart out. She deserves some happiness. She ain't gonna find it as long as she has to live in that home and work in that store. How can her own father treat her like that?"

"I don't know," Donald said, "but something's got to be done for her."

"Well, I'd let her come and live at my house, 'ceptin' it wouldn't be proper for me and her to be livin' under the same roof. Besides, then she wouldn't have a job at all."

Donald spoke again. "Tell you what, family. I've been thinking there's no reason Charolette couldn't live with us. She's got her own room on the weekends. Why not just let it be her room all the time?"

"Oh, Daddy!" Ashley said. "That would be wonderful!"

"You know I'd love to have her," Mavor said. "But she still wouldn't have a job."

"Well, I think I've got that figured out too," Donald said. "Matilda Owens is leaving the factory to get married and moving to Bangor with her new husband. We're going to need someone to replace her. With her sweet personality and bright countenance, Charolette would be perfect for the receptionist's job."

"So what's our next move, dear?" Mavor asked.

"Well, we'll ask Charolette if she wants what I've just proposed…and if she does, the next thing will be for us to go and ask her father if he'll let us have her."

"I don't think we'll have a problem on either count, Daddy," Ashley said.

"I'll talk to Lewis about offering her the job. I'm sure he'll be agreeable to it. But since he's half-owner of the company, we always discuss this kind of thing. Then we'll talk to Charolette this weekend. If she likes our proposal, we'll go talk to her father."

Tears welled up in Ashley's eyes, and she wrapped her arms around her father. "O Daddy, this is the answer to my prayers! I've been praying so hard that the Lord would get Charolette out of that miserable situation. I know it's going to work out. I just know it!"

CHAPTER FIVE

U pon arriving at the factory that morning, Donald Kilrain entered Lewis O'Hanlon's office and explained Charolette Thompson's unhappy situation and his desire to hire her as the new receptionist. Lewis's heart went out to the girl, and he agreed that they should offer her the job.

The following Saturday evening, Charolette was again at the Kilrain home for supper. Donald offered thanks for the food, and everyone began to eat. After a few minutes, Donald looked at Charolette and said, "We're sure glad you can spend your weekends with us."

"Why, thank you, Mr. Kilrain. You've all made me feel so welcome here."

"As far as we're concerned, you're family," Ashley said, her heart pounding with excitement.

Charolette's eyes filmed with tears. She laid her fork down, looked around at the family, and said, "It's so kind of all of you to let me be a part of your family on weekends. I can't tell you what it means to me."

"Charolette," Donald said, "how would you like to be part of the family every day, not just on weekends?"

"I…I'm not sure what you mean, sir."

"I mean that I've talked it over with everyone at this table, and we're offering to let you come and live with us on a permanent basis if you so desire."

"Well, I — "

"Let me explain something before you speak. We know that you tried to find a job in Portland because your father and stepmother want you out from underfoot, so to speak. But you weren't able to find a job, so you're living at home and working in your father's store."

"Yes, sir," she said.

"We have a receptionist's job opening at the factory in a few days. I've talked it over with my partner, and he's in full agreement that we offer the job to you. We have no doubt in our minds that you can handle it with a little training. If you'd like to come and live with us and take the job, all you have to do is say so. The next move will be for Mavor and me to talk to your father about it. From what I know about the situation, I believe he'll let us have you. So…tell us what you think."

Charolette used a napkin to dab at her eyes, then said with a quavering voice, "I…I'm so overwhelmed, I can hardly speak. Yes! I would love to come and live here. And yes! I would love to have the receptionist's job. Papa will gladly let you take me off his hands, I can assure you."

Ashley broke into joyful tears, dropped her fork, and wrapped her arms around her best friend. "Oh, Charolette, I'm so happy! I've got a sister again!"

The family rejoiced together for several minutes, then made plans for Donald, Mavor, and Charolette to drive to Lewiston after church Sunday night to talk to Alfred Thompson. If all went as expected, they would load her belongings in the Kilrain carriage and move them into their home.

✳ ✳ ✳ ✳ ✳

Alfred Thompson sat in his living room with Ethel beside him and said without emotion, "Sure, you can take her, Mr. Kilrain. She and my wife here don't get along too good. Besides, since Charolette got into that church stuff over there at Brunswick, she gives me the willies with all that holy talk." He paused, pointed a stiff finger at Donald, and said, "And don't you start in on this Jesus stuff. I don't want to hear it, and neither does Ethel."

Donald and Mavor were sitting together on a small couch. Charolette was on a hardback chair next to them.

Charolette rose to her feet and spoke softly. "I'll get my clothes and things, Papa, and we'll be on our way."

"Fine," said Thompson, also standing.

Moments later, Charolette's belongings were in the Kilrain carriage. Alfred and Ethel stood at the door in the soft rays of the porch lantern and looked on. Charolette stood beside the carriage and looked back at them. The Kilrains stood beside her as she said in a quiet voice, "Good-bye, Papa."

Thompson had his arm around his wife. He nodded stiffly, but said nothing.

"Don't bother to drift back this way, girl," Ethel said. "We won't be here. I've been tryin' to get your pa to sell the store and move to Chicago. With you gone, it'll be easier to get him to do it."

Mavor bit her tongue. She wanted to tell Alfred and his wife what she thought of them, but didn't. She put her arm around Charolette's shoulders and said, "Come on, honey. Let's take you home."

When the carriage pulled away into the night, Charolette was sitting between her new parents, weeping. She did not look back. Mavor wrapped her arms around the girl, held her close, and said, "I'm sorry, sweetheart. I don't know how a father could treat his daughter like that, but we'll make it up to you."

Charolette laid her head on Mavor's shoulder. "May I call you

Mama, Mrs. Kilrain?" she asked, sniffling.

"You sure may."

"And you can call me Papa," Donald said.

It was almost ten-thirty when the Kilrain carriage swung into the driveway of the stately home. The Kilrains were surprised to see the O'Hanlon carriage parked in front of the house.

"What do you suppose this means?" Mavor asked.

"I don't know," Donald said, "but we're soon going to find out."

Donald halted the carriage next to the O'Hanlon vehicle, and with Charolette between them, the Kilrains hurried onto the porch. The door came open before they reached it, and Ashley stepped out into the soft orange glow of the porch lantern. They could see the O'Hanlon's standing just inside the door, somber looks on their faces.

Ashley looked at Charolette, then at her parents, and asked, "How did it go?"

"She's ours, honey," Mavor said. "We have her clothes and things in the carriage. But...what's wrong?"

"Come on inside," Ashley said, putting an arm around Charolette. "Lewis and Maureen have some bad news."

"What do you mean, bad news?" Donald said.

"Lewis will tell you, Daddy."

They moved inside the house and saw that Uncle Buster and Mike O'Hanlon were also there.

Mavor ran her gaze over their somber faces and asked, "Well...what is it?"

Lewis suggested that they sit down. When all but himself were seated, he explained that they had just received a letter from the post office. It was marked *emergency*, and had arrived on the ship from Ireland that morning. The postmaster had delivered it himself about an hour ago.

Donald's father, Marcus Kilrain, and Lewis's father, Jacob O'Hanlon, had gone hunting together nearly a week ago. Somehow Jacob had stumbled, and his gun went off. The bullet hit Marcus in the head and killed him. Alice Kilrain had sent the letter to ask for help. Jacob O'Hanlon was in a bad mental state and wanted Donald to move his family back to Dublin to take his father's place. Jacob would not be able to handle the factory alone. Alice was also pleading with Donald to return and take over the factory. She desperately needed him and his family with her.

A cold dread settled over Ashley. How could she bear to climb aboard a ship and leave for Ireland, knowing she would not be coming back? It was hard enough knowing she had lost her grandfather, but if the family returned to Ireland, she would lose Shane, too.

Mavor took her husband by the hand and said in a tight voice, "Darling, I don't think we have a choice. Your mother needs us...and the factory needs you. Jacob is going to need your help."

Donald looked at Lewis. "Maybe it should be you who returns to Ireland. You could be a great help to your father."

"I'm sure I could, but it's better that there not be two O'Hanlons running the business. Best to keep it one O'Hanlon and one Kilrain. Besides, it's your mother who's been widowed. She needs you and your family, Donald."

"Lewis, I'll do all I can to help you here," Uncle Buster said. "I've been around long enough that I can handle some of the management details and problems that come up."

Lewis smiled. "I'm sure you'll be a great help, Buster. I'll be glad to have you in that position."

"I'd like to help you in the management end, Pa," Mike said, "but I'm still too young and inexperienced."

Lewis laid a hand on his shoulder. "You'll be a real asset someday, son. But you're right. You need to get your college education and a few more years on you first."

Lewis's attention went to Charolette, who was holding onto Ashley, her features pale and her eyes shadowed with fear. "Charolette..."

The girl's gaze found his eyes. "Yes, sir?"

"Did your father give his consent to let you come live with the Kilrains?"

"Yes, sir, he did. All my things are outside in the carriage."

Lewis cleared his throat. "I want to tell you, dear, that the job is still yours. Maureen and I discussed the fact that if your father did give permission for you to live with the Kilrains — and they decided to move back to Ireland — you would either have to go back to your father, or you'd need another home."

"Yes, sir."

Lewis looked at Maureen. She walked across the room, laid a hand on Charolette's shoulder, and said, "Honey, we want you to know that you're welcome to come live with us. We have a large house. You'll have your own room, even as you do here."

Ashley turned to her and said, "Charolette, I'm sure my parents would take you with us to Ireland."

"Of course," Mavor said.

"We will if you want to go with us," Donald said.

Charolette tried to smile. "Thank you. I appreciate that. But with my father here in America, I — well, I just want to be where he can find me if he ever needs me. I so desperately want him to be saved, and if the Lord brought something into his life that would break down his stubborn will, I would want to be here for him."

"We understand," Mavor said. "And more than anything, we'd all love to see him come to the Lord."

Ashley hugged her best friend and said, "Oh, Charolette, I hate to go away and leave you!"

Mavor wrapped her arms around both girls. "You can write to each other. And who knows? Maybe Charolette can come to Ireland some time and see you."

Ashley nodded, but her throat ached and she couldn't speak.

Mavor squeezed Charolette and said, "You can stay here until we leave for Ireland, or I'm sure the O'Hanlons will let you move in with them right away."

"Yes," Maureen said. "Whatever you prefer, Charolette."

Charolette turned to Maureen, glanced at Lewis, then said,

"Thank you both so much for opening your home to me. I appreciate it more than I could ever tell you...but I'd like to stay with Ashley as long as I can."

"We understand," Maureen said.

Charolette thanked Donald and Lewis for giving her the job, then the men went outside to carry in her belongings.

Ashley held onto Charolette's hand, but her mind went to Shane. A sick dread settled in her stomach. Her mother had invited Shane for dinner tomorrow night. Ashley would have to tell him that she and her family were moving back to Ireland. Not only did she dread telling Shane, but she wondered how she could face life without her dream of one day becoming Mrs. Shane Donovan. With an ocean between them, their lives could never be molded together. Ashley wished she was old enough to stay in America...but wishing couldn't add one day to her age, much less two or three years.

The next day, Shane left work at the lumber mill early enough to bathe, change clothes, and make it to downtown Brunswick before the stores closed.

Jeweler and clockmaker Hans Dinkler looked up from his worktable when the bell over the door signaled that a customer had entered the store.

"Ah, Shane Donovan!" said Dinkler looking over the thick spectacles on the end of his nose. "Goot afternoon. Vat can I do for you?"

"Hello, Mr. Dinkler. I...ah...I want to buy a necklace for someone very special."

The wrinkled old man smiled, raised his bushy eyebrows, and asked, "Vould her initials be A. K.?"

Shane grinned sheepishly and nodded. "Yes, sir."

"You going to marry that girl someday, eh?"

"Well, Mr. Dinkler, we...ah...haven't discussed that possibility.

Her parents won't let us even be steadies yet, which I understand. But once we are, I'll bring the subject up with Ashley."

"Ah, that's a good boy," said Dinkler, tilting his head down to look at Shane over his spectacles. "I think these young peoples get married too soon these days. It is vise to vait until they are older."

"Yes, sir."

"Is it Ashley's birthday, Shane?"

"No, sir. I just want to show her how I feel about her, so I thought I'd give her a necklace."

"That is very thoughtful of you, my boy." Dinkler moved to a glass case at the end of the counter. "Look at vat I have here."

The case was laden with jewelry of all sorts — pocket watches, rings, necklaces, brooches, cameos, earrings, bracelets, and ladies' timepieces.

"Many to choose from, Shane. Vat price is your limit?"

"None, sir. I've saved for this. I want Ashley to have something real nice."

"Mmm." Dinkler nodded and reached under the glass for a necklace on a delicate gold chain. A heart-shaped locket adorned the chain. Engraved on the locket was a male hand and a female hand in a tender grasp of love.

Shane's eyes lit up. "Yes!" he exclaimed. "That's it exactly!"

"Now, son, this is rather high-priced. If you vant, I could let you pay me half now and half at a later time."

"How much is it, sir?"

"Vell, it is fifty dollars, my boy. Is too much?"

"Oh, no, sir. I'll take it."

Moments later, Shane left the store, carrying the necklace in a black velvet box with a white satin lining. His heart raced with excitement. This would convey to Ashley what he felt for her until the day he could put an engagement ring on her finger.

Shane would not consider proposing marriage until he and Ashley were older and he was making a good living. He would graduate from high school next spring at eighteen, then enroll at Bowdoin College. His dream was to be a professor in a Christian college and teach such subjects as history, English, and Bible. He would like to teach right there at Bowdoin someday, and go home every night to his beautiful wife.

At the Kilrain home, Ashley and Charolette were busy in the kitchen helping Mavor get supper ready. The dining room table was set, and savory aromas from the kitchen filled the house. Donald was in the parlor with his sons discussing their upcoming move to Ireland.

"It's Shane, Papa," William said as he looked out the front window.

Donald stood and said, "Now remember…don't say anything to Shane about our moving back to Ireland. Your sister wants to be the one to tell him."

Donald waited until Shane mounted the front porch, then opened the door before he could knock. "Good evening, Shane. Step inside and get a whiff of what's coming from the kitchen."

Shane drew a deep breath and said, "Mmm-mm! Smells good enough to eat!"

"That's what the boys and I have been thinking. Right, boys?"

William and Harvey both nodded.

Donald gestured toward the kitchen. "Well, gentlemen. I think the ladies are about ready for us. Let's not disappoint them!"

They entered the kitchen, and the women welcomed Shane. He was surprised to see Charolette, though he greeted her warmly. Ashley quickly explained that Charolette had come to live with them, and Shane said he was pleased to hear it.

During the meal, Shane could tell something was awry, though every member of the Kilrain family did their best to hide it. When he noticed that Ashley was absently picking at her food, he turned to her and asked, "Are you all right?"

"Of course," she said, forcing a smile. "Why do you ask?"

"You're not eating, and you seem preoccupied."

"Oh," she said, stabbing a bite of beefsteak with her fork. "I've just got a lot of things on my mind." She placed the meat in her mouth, forced another smile, and chewed.

"Is one of those things on your mind unpleasant?" he asked.

Ashley looked at her mother.

"Shane," Mavor said, "we've had a bit of bad news from Ireland."

"Oh?"

"Yes," Donald said. "My father was killed in a hunting accident."

"Oh, I'm very sorry, sir."

"We would have told you upon your arrival, but Ashley was going to tell you after the meal. She plans to have a talk with you."

Shane glanced at Ashley. "I'm very sorry about your grandfather. Please forgive me for — "

"There's nothing to forgive. How could you have known?"

"Well, I knew something was wrong, but I didn't have to stick my big nose in and start asking questions."

"It's all right," Ashley said. "You were just showing concern."

"How did it happen, sir?" Shane asked, looking again at Donald.

"Hunting accident. He was shot accidentally by Jacob O'Hanlon, Lewis's father."

"Oh, how terrible. This must be awfully hard on the O'Hanlon's too."

"You can imagine how they must feel, especially Jacob and his wife. They've been friends of my parents for as long as I can remember."

"Will you be going back to Ireland for a while to be with your mother?"

"Ashley," Mavor said, "maybe you and Shane should go on out to the front porch for your talk. Charolette and I will do up the dishes."

"I can wait if Ashley wants to help, ma'am," Shane said.

"No, that's all right. Charolette and I discussed it this afternoon. You two go on now."

Ashley took Shane's hand and said, "Come on. Let's go out on the porch."

Charolette prayed silently that the Lord would help Ashley as she broke the news and that He would ease the pain in Shane's heart when he heard it.

Donald had lighted the two porch lanterns just after supper, and they gave off a soft yellow glow across the front of the large house. When Shane and Ashley stepped outside, she led him to the porch swing. The summer evening was warm. The aroma of honeysuckle was in the air, and the crickets were giving their nightly concert.

Shane felt the small bulge in his coat pocket as they sat down on the swing together. He wondered whether to give Ashley the necklace before she brought up whatever it was she wanted to talk to him about or wait until after. On impulse, he decided to give the necklace to her first. It would make the rest of the evening sweeter, no matter what subject was in the offing.

Ashley's mind was racing. How would she begin? She was hoping that Shane would ask what she wanted to talk about. Instead, she saw him reach into his coat pocket and pull out a small black box. Her gaze went from the box to his sky-blue eyes.

"Before we have our talk, there's something I want to give you," Shane said.

Ashley looked at the box again. "O Shane, you shouldn't be buying me gifts."

"This is more than a gift," he said, casting a glance toward the door to make sure they were alone. "This is my way of telling you...that I love you, Ashley."

Ashley's heart skipped a beat as he placed the velvet box in her hands. Her eyes found his as she said in a half-whisper, "I love you too, Shane."

She looked back at the box and slowly felt along its edges.

"Well, go ahead," he said. "Open it."

She drew back the lid, and the lantern light shone on the exquisite locket and delicate chain. Tears filled Ashley's eyes and spilled down her cheeks.

"O Shane, it's beautiful! I...I don't know what to say!"

"You see the clasp of those two hands? Just say that we'll never let go of each other. That we'll always be together. Ashley and Shane...forever."

CHAPTER SIX

shley Kilrain's throat tightened. The pulse throbbed in her temples. Tears flowed like miniature rivers down her face as she tried to find her voice.

She took the necklace from the box and held it close to her heart, her head down. For a long moment she wept quietly. The only sound was when she drew a shaky breath.

Shane put an open hand under her chin, tilted her head up, and asked, "You like it, don't you?"

She looked up at him through a wall of tears and nodded. Suddenly it all gave way and she blurted, "Shane, I love it, but we can't ever have each other! My family is moving back to Ireland, and I have to go with them!"

Shane felt as though he had been punched in the stomach. He stared at Ashley, paralyzed in a swell of disbelief and horror. "But you can't leave me! I'll...I'll talk to your parents. We'll work out a place for you to live here. Ashley, I can't let you go! I — "

"There's no choice, as Ashley said, Shane," Donald Kilrain said from the door.

The couple looked up to see Donald and Mavor move together onto the porch.

"I'm sorry to interrupt," Donald said, "but there's no reason to let your conversation follow the path it's taking."

Shane rose to his feet. "Mr. Kilrain, I love your daughter. I can't just let her sail out of my life!"

Donald and Mavor moved closer as their daughter wiped away tears and left the swing.

"Son, Ashley is still shy of sixteen. We cannot, and we will not, return to Ireland without her. You're only seventeen yourself. You both have plenty of time to fall in and out of love a dozen times before you find your life's mate."

"Neither of you are old enough to be in the kind of love that you build a marriage on," Mavor said. "There's a lot of maturing needed before that day comes."

"Mr. and Mrs. Kilrain," Shane said, "I love and respect you both. I would never do anything to cause a problem in your home. It's just that…this has hit me like a runaway coach. I do love your daughter very much — at least as much as a seventeen-year-old can. And the thought of her sailing across the Atlantic thousands of miles is more than I can bear. I — we will never see each other again. I hope you can understand how we feel."

Donald placed an arm around Shane's shoulder as Mavor folded a trembling Ashley in her arms.

"Shane," Donald said, "you're a fine young man, and a fine Christian. Mavor and I have allowed this relationship between you and Ashley to go on because we both love and admire you. You're certainly the kind of young man we want our daughter to marry. But I'll say again, you're both too young to be marriage-serious about each other. The Lord has seen fit to allow my father to be killed. He knew we'd have to return to Ireland when that bullet took my father's life. He has a plan for your life, Shane, and for Ashley's. As painful as it is right now, the two of you must allow Him to work it out. Does that make sense?"

"Yes, sir. But no matter what happens, sir, I'll always love her."

"I understand that's how you feel right now, son. And I wouldn't expect you to feel any other way. But God will make everything just right for both you and Ashley. And if He wants you two together, He can span the thousands of miles of ocean and bring you together again. He's able to perform His will, miles of ocean or not."

"Yes, sir," Shane said, his voice quavering.

"Daddy?" came a weak voice.

"Yes, honey?"

Ashley opened her hand and held the chain and locket so both parents could see it. "May I keep this? Shane just gave it to me."

"I gave it to her before I knew about the move," Shane said. "I wanted her to know how I feel about her. I wanted her to know that I never wanted us to let go of each other."

Tears welled up in Mavor's eyes, and her lower lip trembled.

"May I keep it, Daddy? Please?" Ashley said.

"Honey, I think not," Donald said. "Shane needs to save it for the young woman God has for him."

"Sir," Shane said, "even if the Lord has someone else for me...I couldn't give it to her, now that I've given it to Ashley."

"He's right, dear," Mavor said. "I think Ashley should be allowed to keep the locket. It will always be a token of her friendship with Shane."

Donald was silent for a moment, rubbing his chin in thought. "Well, okay."

"Thank you, Daddy," Ashley said, letting go of her mother to hug her father's neck.

"I think I'd better be going," Shane said.

Mavor hugged him. "Just stay close to the Lord, Shane. He'll work His perfect will in your life."

"Yes, ma'am, I'll stay close to Him. Right now, I don't understand why this has happened, but I'll stay close to Him."

Ashley was wiping tears again. Shane looked at her, then at her father.

"Mr. Kilrain, I've never held Ashley close before...but in your presence, sir, I'd like to embrace her."

"You have my permission," Donald said.

Shane looked deep into Ashley's eyes for a brief moment, then folded her in his arms. "I love you," he said. "I always will."

"I will always love you too, Shane."

Biting his lower lip, Shane released Ashley. He told her he would come by to see her the next evening, then he bid her parents goodnight and left quietly.

Donald Kilrain put an arm around his daughter, and they followed Mavor inside where William, Harvey, and Charolette stood together, their faces reflecting their concern for Ashley.

Donald gave Ashley a hug and said, "Everything will be all right, honey. You'll see."

Mavor spent a few minutes consoling her, then Ashley said she wanted to go to her room. Charolette asked if she could go with her, and Ashley consented. When they moved into Ashley's bedroom and the door was closed, Charolette took her into her arms and held her while Ashley wept.

"I couldn't help but overhear about the locket," Charolette said. "May I see it?"

Ashley opened her fist, took hold of the chain with her other hand, and let the heart-shaped locket dangle in front of Charolette's eyes.

Charolette held the locket between her fingers and said, "Oh, it's beautiful. How thoughtful of Shane!"

"Before I told him we were moving back to Ireland, he said the clasped hands meant we would never let go of each other. And now — "

Ashley burst into heavy, heart-rending sobs. Charolette held her tight and spoke in low tones, trying to comfort her. Even so, Charolette envied Ashley. She had the love of the young man Charolette could not get out of her heart.

✵✵✵✵✵

Shane Donovan and Ashley Kilrain spent as much time together as possible during the next two weeks, their hearts aching. The Kilrain house sold quickly, which was a relief to Uncle Buster. He would have had to oversee the sale and handle all the paperwork if it had not sold before his brother and family sailed for Ireland.

On Saturday, August 18, 1855, the church had a going away picnic for the Kilrains. They were to embark from Portland Harbor on Monday.

When the dreaded day arrived, many friends from First Parish Congregational Church gathered on the dock to bid the Kilrains good-bye. Buster Kilrain was there, along with the O'Hanlons, the Donovans, and Charolette Thompson. The Kilrains' daughter, Moira, was expecting her first child any day, but was having some complications and had been in bed for a week. Her husband would not leave her side. Donald, Mavor, and their children stopped in Portland to see them before heading for the harbor.

The huge ship loomed over them, and people filtered past the group to mount the gangplank and go aboard.

Shane and Ashley stood apart from the others, while good-byes were being said. Ashley was wearing the locket Shane had given her.

Mike O'Hanlon walked up and said, "Please forgive my butting in, but I want to tell Ashley good-bye." Mike hurt for Shane, but he felt his own pain, knowing he would probably never see Ashley again. "I...I'll miss you, Ashley."

"I'll miss you, too, Mike," she said, giving him a sisterly embrace. "Thank you for being such a good friend to me."

"You're welcome. I hope you have a real happy life." Mike blinked against the tears that flooded his eyes as he stepped away.

Ashley looked up to see Charolette standing next to Shane. She opened her arms to her, and the girls wept as they held each other tight. When they let go of each other, Charolette turned to Shane with tears streaming down her face.

"Shane, I'm sorry this terrible thing had to happen. I've been praying for you and Ashley, that the Lord's will be done in your lives."

"Ashley and I have talked a lot these past two weeks, Charolette. We've committed ourselves to His will. As much as it hurts right now, we must let Him have His way in our lives."

"That's a beautiful way to put it, Shane," Charolette said, smiling through her tears.

It was almost time for the Kilrains to board the ship. Mike and Charolette moved away to give the young couple their last few moments together.

Ashley held the locket between her fingers and said with tremulous voice, "Shane, even if the Lord doesn't have us for each other, you will always be a very special person in my life. I will love you in a special way, and I'll keep this locket forever."

"And you will always be a very special person in my life, Ashley. I will always love you in a special way, no matter what."

Ashley's parents walked up and Donald said, "Honey, we have to board now."

Ashley nodded, excused herself to Shane, and ran to Uncle Buster, embracing him. She loved her uncle very much, and told him so. She then hurried to each friend who stood on the dock, gave them a quick hug and a few parting words.

Donald and Mavor told Shane how much they thought of him, and expressed their gratitude for the mature way he was accepting their leaving.

When Ashley returned, she drew close to Shane and said, "Well, I guess it's time to say good-bye."

Shane looked at Donald and Mavor and said, "Mr. and Mrs. Kilrain, may I have your permission to kiss your daughter good-bye?"

"Certainly, Shane," Donald said.

The lips of the young pair touched briefly and discreetly, then Shane stood aside and watched Ashley walk up the gangplank with her parents and younger brothers. He felt as if his heart would burst.

The Kilrains were the last to step aboard, and the ship's shrill whistle blew as one of the crew closed the railing gate and the massive vessel began pulling away. The passengers stood along the railing, waving to those they were leaving behind. People on the dock wept, shouted, and waved back.

Mike and Charolette stood close to Shane, who thumbed tears as he watched the ship move out of the harbor toward the Atlantic Ocean. Almost unaware of their presence, he watched until the ship became a dot on the horizon, then vanished from sight. Mike drew up on one side of him and Charolette on the other, each putting an arm around him.

Day after day, Ashley stood on the deck of the ship with the ocean breeze brushing her face and fluttering her long auburn hair. She held the locket between her fingers and prayed for Shane, asking the Lord to watch over him. Her heart seemed to break as she thought of the good times they had enjoyed together and remembered the dream she had of one day becoming Mrs. Shane Donovan.

The ship arrived in Ireland on September 6, having stopped in a few seaports along the way.

Donald Kilrain took command at the Dublin factory, and the family settled in, caring for Grandmother Kilrain. When they had been in Dublin a week, Ashley wrote to Shane. She told him she was still wearing the locket and would always have a special love for him in her heart.

Shane thought of Ashley continuously, praying for her…and long-ing for her presence.

Charolette had settled in with the O'Hanlons and loved living in their home. She also loved her job at the factory. And she looked forward to seeing Shane at church on Sundays and Wednesday nights. Each time Shane and Charolette talked, Shane found that his admiration for her was growing. Though he had no idea how she felt about him, he often called her his "sweet little friend."

In mid-September, Bowdoin College began its fall semester with a few new instructors. Among them was Joshua Lawrence Chamberlain, who had attained his master's degree and had joined the faculty to teach logic, theology, rhetoric, and Greek.

Fannie Adams had finished her schooling in New York and was back on the organ at First Parish Congregational Church. Sunday morning, September 16, was the first time Chamberlain had been in the church in several months. His future father-in-law had asked him to sing just prior to the sermon.

Shane and Mike were sitting together, with Charolette and some other girls from the youth group on the same pew. Shane was on the aisle, Mike was next to him, and Charolette was next to Mike, wishing she was next to Shane.

When Joshua Chamberlain stepped to the pulpit, ready to sing John Newton's "Amazing Grace," Shane whispered to his friend, "When I go to Bowdoin next year, I'm going to take every class he teaches!"

At the organ, Fannie began to play the introduction to "Amazing Grace." Joshua lifted his voice above the sound of the organ and said, "Friends…"

When Fannie realized he wanted to say something before he sang, she lowered the volume, but kept pumping and playing.

"Friends, many of you have wondered if Fanny and I are ever going to get married. Well, let me be the first to tell you that we have set a date for the wedding. We'll be married right here on Friday, December 7, this year."

There was an immediate chorus of amens and some applause from the congregation. Fanny then raised the volume, skillfully went into the introduction, and played while her fiancé sang. There were more amens as the song was finished and Chamberlain stepped away from the pulpit.

After the service, Joshua Chamberlain spoke with Shane and Mike. Charolette looked on as the two young men congratulated him on his coming marriage and talked of days gone by. While they chatted, Chamberlain's attention drifted to the pretty brunette who stood near. He finished something he was saying to the boys, then smiled at the girl, and said, "Hello, Charolette."

Charolette was surprised that Chamberlain remembered her name, and her face showed it. "Hello, Mr. Chamberlain. How nice of you to remember me. After all, it's been a year-and-a-half!"

"Has it really been that long? Well, anyway, I recall your name because you opened your heart to Jesus when I was preaching. That makes you special."

"Thank you, sir. I'll never forget that sermon."

Fannie came off the platform, greeted the young people, and whisked her fiancé away for Sunday dinner at her parents' home. When they were out of sight, Charolette turned to the boys and said, "My what a memory! He must have a brilliant mind."

"That he does," Shane said. "He received many honors at Bowdoin and at Bangor Seminary, and he's also mastered seven foreign languages."

"Seven! Really?"

"Really. He knows Latin, German, Old Testament Hebrew, New Testament Greek…ah, let's see…Latin, German, Hebrew, Greek…and Italian, Arabic, and Syrian. That's seven, isn't it?"

"I think so," Mike said. "Pretty impressive, huh?"

"I should say," Charolette said.

"Like I told Mike," Shane said, "I'm going to take every class

Mr. Chamberlain teaches when I go to Bowdoin. He's a great teacher and a great Christian."

"So you're going to Bowdoin?" Charolette said. "I didn't know that. What do you plan to study?"

"I'm going to major in education. Two of Mr. Chamberlain's courses will fit into my major, and I can take Greek and theology as electives. I've already checked. I want to teach in a Christian college someday. In fact, I'd like to teach at Bowdoin if the Lord will let me."

"I think that's a wonderful ambition, Shane. I hope it works out for you." Charolette then turned to Mike and asked, "How about you? What are your plans?"

"Oh, I'm going to Bowdoin, too. I'm going to major in economics to prepare for the partnership my dad and Mr. Kilrain are going to give me when I get out of college."

"So one day you'll be my boss!"

"That's right. And then, girl, you'd better watch your step!"

Shane received Ashley's letter the first week of November. He was thrilled to learn she was still wearing the locket. That night he answered her letter, telling her he still carried her in his heart and missed her very much. At church the next Sunday, Shane told Mike and Charolette about the letter. Charolette also had received a letter from Ashley. She said Ashley was missing Shane a lot and spoke of missing her other friends, too.

During the next four months, Shane and Ashley exchanged three more letters. Shane detected that Ashley was settling into life in her home country, and though in the letters she spoke of her special love for him, she said no more about the locket. He began to read between the lines. Ashley had resigned herself to the fact that they would never see each other again, a fact Shane was slowly resigning himself to as well.

✳ ✳ ✳ ✳ ✳

On Shane's eighteenth birthday, the youth group gathered at the Donovan home for a party. Shane noticed that Mike O'Hanlon had Betty Helms, the newest girl to join the youth group, with him.

After the meal, and during cake time, Shane saw Betty talking with some girls. He slipped up beside Mike and said, "You've sure got a knack for latching on to the pretty ones."

Mike grinned and said, "Don't get any ideas, pal! Besides, you're still tied to Ashley."

"Only in memory, my friend. I'll never forget her, but we both know we'll never be together again. We've resigned ourselves to it."

Mike was serious for a moment. "Well, I'm glad you're able to face the situation honestly, though I'm sure it must be hard to accept." Then a grin curved his lips. "But if you're thinking of shining up to Betty, forget it. She doesn't go for you old duffers!" Even as the words were coming from his mouth, Mike found his heart longing for Ashley.

Shane turned to see Charolette standing behind him.

"What are you smiling about?" he asked with a chuckle.

"You two," Charolette said.

"What do you mean?" Mike asked.

"You're forty-eight days apart in age, and you talk about one being old and the other being young."

"Well, we've gone on like this for ages, Charolette," Shane said.

"Doesn't change a thing," Mike said. "Betty still likes younger men!"

"Well, I like older men," Charolette said before Shane could give his usual retort.

The look in Charolette's eyes startled Shane. He found himself really noticing her for the first time. He had never seen what a beautiful person she was...inside and out.

"Thank you, Charolette," he managed to say. "I'm glad you

prefer older men." He paused, then smiled. "I like your hair. It's a new style for you, isn't it?"

"Why…yes."

"I mean, I always like the way you fix your hair, but this…well, it really looks terrific on you!"

CHAPTER SEVEN

As the weeks passed into months, Shane Donovan found a growing attraction for Charolette Thompson. But he had promised his love to Ashley, and he felt guilty over his feelings for Charolette.

Charolette was maturing into a beautiful young woman and into a strong Christian. Though she was warm toward Shane, she did not reveal the deep love she had for him. Her daily prayer was for God to have His perfect will in both of their lives.

Shane continued to work with his father in the lumber mill and steadily put on stature and muscle. He graduated from high school in the spring, and when fall came, he enrolled at Bowdoin College. Though taking a full load, he earned money for his schooling by working after classes and on Saturdays in the lumber mill.

He often thought of Ashley and heard now and then through Mike O'Hanlon of things taking place in the Kilrain family in Dublin. Grandpa O'Hanlon still had not gotten over the hunting accident, and Donald Kilrain was having to carry the load in running the factory.

On one occasion, Mike told Shane that Mavor Kilrain had mentioned in a letter to his mother that Ashley was now dating several young men. Shane felt a stab in his heart at that news, but he knew it was only right that Ashley date other young men.

Shane was superbly happy in college, especially getting to sit in Joshua Chamberlain's rhetoric, logic, theology, and Greek classes. The young instructor had been elected to professorship by the college board of directors just before the fall semester. He replaced Calvin Stowe, who had gone to teach in another college.

The friendship between professor and student blossomed. Chamberlain found young Donovan to be his best student and spent extra time with him. Chamberlain saw exceptional character in Garth and Pearl Donovan's oldest son, recalling Shane's heroic deed in risking his life to save the Brainerd baby when he was barely fifteen years old.

Charolette was thrilled that without fail, Shane found her and sat by her in the young adult Sunday school class and in all the church services.

On Sunday, October 12, 1856, Dr. George Adams announced proudly to the congregation that he and his wife were now grandparents. Fannie had given birth the night before to a beautiful baby girl, Grace Dupee Chamberlain. Joshua, who was in the choir, received applause, and the crowd had a good laugh when he stood and took a bow.

After the service, Charolette was at Shane's side as he approached Chamberlain and said, "Congratulations, Professor, on your new daughter."

"Thank you, Shane."

"Did you want a girl, Professor?" Charolette asked. "Or were you hoping for a boy?"

"Neither Fannie nor I cared which it was, just so the baby would be normal and healthy. And she is, praise the Lord."

"I can't wait to see her, sir," Shane said. "Does she look like Mrs. Chamberlain?"

"I'll say she does! Has Fannie's coloring through and through. I mean, skin, hair, and eyes."

"She has to be beautiful then," Charolette said. "Mrs.

Chamberlain is such a lovely lady."

"Why, thank you. My sentiments exactly." Chamberlain paused, then said, "And you're becoming a stunning young lady yourself, Charolette. Has Shane taken notice?"

While Charolette blushed, Shane said, "Yes, I have, sir. I sure have."

Professor Joshua Lawrence Chamberlain's class schedule had him teaching theology the last hour on Monday, Wednesday, and Friday. On the Monday after the announcement in church of little Grace's birth, the professor mentioned in theology class that Christians can know the perfect will of God for their lives if they stay close to God and wait patiently for Him to reveal it to them.

When class was dismissed, Shane approached the desk as the professor was placing papers into a valise. Chamberlain looked up, smiled, and said, "Something I can do for you, Shane?"

"I think so, sir."

Chamberlain laid the papers and valise down, giving young Donovan his full attention.

"Well, sir, you mentioned in class that a Christian can know the perfect will of God for his life if he stays close to Him and waits patiently for Him to reveal it."

"That's right."

"Could you expand on that for me?"

"All right." Chamberlain gestured toward a straight-backed wooden chair that sat next to a far wall. "Grab that chair and sit down."

Chamberlain eased onto his own chair and picked up his Bible. When Shane sat down across the desk from him, Chamberlain said, "Get your Bible out and turn to Romans 12."

Shane flipped pages quickly and soon had the Bible open to the designated passage.

"All right," the professor said, "read me verses one and two."

"'I beseech you therefore, brethren, by the mercies of God, that ye present your bodies a living sacrifice, holy, acceptable unto God, which is your reasonable service. And be not conformed to this world: but be ye transformed by the renewing of your mind, that ye may prove what is that good, and acceptable, and perfect, will of God.'"

Shane looked up at his professor, and Chamberlain said, "It does say we can prove what the perfect will of God is for our lives, doesn't it?"

"Yes, sir."

"Now, there are some prerequisites to finding God's will. To sum up what both of those verses say, we're to be wholly dedicated to the Lord. We're to be living sacrifices, serving the Lord with everything that's in us. And if we are, we won't be conformed to this ungodly world system that is anti-God, anti-Christ, and anti-Bible. And you know that's the attitude of this world because Satan is the god of this world, according to Second Corinthians chapter four."

"Yes, sir."

"All right, then. In order to know the perfect will of God, we must be devoted to Him, living all the way for Jesus, and walking according to the Word of God."

"I understand that, sir."

"All right. Now, there are some things about God's will for us that are stated flat and plain in Scripture. Let's turn to First Thessalonians 4."

When both had found the passage, Chamberlain said, "Look at verse three. 'For this is the will of God, even your sanctification, that ye should abstain from fornication.' You already know that sanctification is being set apart by God for service. And down in verse seven, Paul wrote, 'For God hath not called us unto uncleanness, but unto holiness.' So God tells us that His will is that we live clean and serve Him."

"Yes, sir."

"There's another plain statement here in First Thessalonians. Look at chapter five, verse eighteen."

Shane flipped the page and found the verse. "'In every thing give thanks: for this is the will of God in Christ Jesus concerning you.'"

"That verse plainly tells us that God's will for every Christian is that we give thanks to Him for whatever comes along in our lives...the good and the bad, the pleasant and the unpleasant."

Shane grinned. "That's not always easy to do, is it?"

"No, it's not. But it is God's will that we do. Now, as for particular circumstances in our lives, God will reveal His will. He said He would. However, He seldom gets in a hurry to reveal it to us. He wants us to learn some patience along the way, and He wants us to keep coming back to Him...so He usually delays revealing His will. Go to the twenty-seventh Psalm."

Shane flipped pages again. "Got it."

"All right. Read me verse fourteen."

"'Wait on the LORD: be of good courage, and he shall strengthen thine heart: wait, I say, on the LORD.'"

"Let the word *wait* sink in."

"It already has."

Chamberlain chuckled. "Now, turn over to Psalm 37 and read me the first part of verse seven."

"'Rest in the LORD, and wait patiently for him.' So I not only need to wait, but I need to wait patiently."

"You're catching on. Now let's look at one more verse — Psalm 62, verse five."

"'My soul, wait thou only upon God; for my expectation is from him.'"

"So when we wait patiently for the Lord to do anything in our lives, we can expect Him to come through for us. Right?"

"That's what it says, sir."

"Now, there's another prerequisite — prayer. The Lord wants us to come to Him in prayer and ask for His guidance. Turn to John 14."

When Shane had located the chapter, Chamberlain said, "Read me verses thirteen and fourteen, and note that it is Jesus speaking."

"'And whatsoever ye shall ask in my name, that will I do, that the Father may be glorified in the Son. If ye shall ask anything in my name, I will do it.'"

"Okay, now look across the page at 15:7 and read me that."

"'If ye abide in me, and my words abide in you, ye shall ask what ye will, and it shall be done unto you.'"

"There's plenty more," Chamberlain said, "but that's probably enough for now. Let's sum it up. We are to be living sacrifices, serving God and living holy lives while following His Word and seeking Him in prayer. And when we ask Him to reveal His will to us, and wait patiently for the answer, He will show us."

"Sounds reasonable," Shane said.

"Now…one more thing. *How* does the Lord show us His will? This is the key to the whole thing."

Shane grinned again. "I'm listening."

"Okay. Philippians 4, verses six and seven. Read it to me."

Shane eagerly turned pages, found the passage, and read: "'Be careful for nothing; but in everything by prayer and supplication with thanksgiving let your requests be made known unto God. And the peace of God, which passeth all understanding, shall keep your hearts and minds through Christ Jesus.'"

"Note especially the 'everything by prayer,' the thanksgiving, and the making of your requests known to God. And note too that with this comes the peace of God. When your heart and mind are at peace, there is no disturbance, right?"

"Yes, sir."

"All right. One more passage — Colossians 3:15. Go ahead and read it to me."

"'And let the peace of God rule in your hearts, to the which also ye are called in one body; and be ye thankful.'"

"Notice that Paul says to let the peace of God *rule* in your heart."

"Yes, sir."

"As we seek to know the will of God for our lives, and follow the things we've already seen from Scripture, then as we aim ourselves toward what we believe might be God's will for us, there will be a disturbance in our hearts if we are aiming the wrong way. It takes a close walk with the Lord to be able to recognize this, but the peace of God will rule in our hearts if we let it. Notice Paul said, '*Let* the peace of God rule in your hearts.' We have a choice whether to let it rule or to refuse to let it rule. So if we aim only in the direction that gives us peace, we'll know we're following God's will for our lives."

"That's beautiful, sir," Shane said. "So when we know we're walking right before the Lord, and we pray and wait patiently, the Lord will give us peace in our hearts when we aim correctly or disturb our hearts if we aim wrong. If we're aiming wrong but keep heading in various directions until we get peace, we'll know when we've discovered His perfect will in our lives. The peace of God will rule and give the proper direction."

"Sounds to me like you've got the picture, my friend. Do you mind me using myself as an example?"

"No, of course not."

"Well, right now I'm seeking God's will for my life…and that of Fannie and the baby, of course. As you know, First Parish licensed me to preach better than a year ago, and I've preached in several churches in Maine, filling pulpits when the pastors have been away or been too ill to preach. What you don't know is that four different churches have issued me calls to be their pastor. Each one seemed quite inviting, but I just couldn't get peace about accepting any of them."

"Well, I'm glad of that, sir. I love sitting under your teaching."

"Thank you, Shane. Anyway, in spite of those tempting calls to pastor, I have absolute peace in what I'm doing here at Bowdoin. Maybe one day the Lord will put me in a pastorate, but right now I know He wants me right here teaching."

"I hope He leaves you here at least until I graduate, sir." Shane rose from his chair. "Thank you for your help."

Chamberlain stood up behind his desk. "You're very welcome."

Shane turned to leave, and Chamberlain said, "Shane..."

"Yes, sir?"

"Shane, you and I are friends."

"Yes, sir."

Chamberlain rubbed the back of his neck. "This, ah…this session we've had about knowing the will of God…I don't mean to be nosy, but does it have anything to do with your relationships with Ashley Kilrain and Charolette Thompson?"

"Well, sir, to be honest, it's the very reason I was asking about knowing God's will."

"I thought so. Look, Shane, I've been observing you and Charolette together since I moved back to Brunswick. Are you letting Ashley stand between you and Charolette?"

"Well, sir, I…I might be…a little."

"But you think enough of Charolette that you're wondering what God's will is concerning her in your life…and concerning Ashley."

"Yes, sir. You might put it that way."

"May I tell you my own thoughts about it?"

"Yes, please do."

"Shane, Ashley is out of your life now…for good. From what Mike has told me, the Kilrains expect to remain in Ireland permanently."

"That's right. But…there's a problem, sir."

"Do you want to tell me about it?"

"Well, it's just that even though it appears that Ashley will never be coming back to America, I…I made her a promise."

"Yes?"

"I promised that I would always love her, and I don't want to go back on that promise."

Chamberlain grinned a crooked grin and laid a hand on his student's shoulder. "My friend, you can always have a special place in your heart for Ashley. She was your first real girlfriend, right?"

"Yes, sir."

"That makes her special. But Shane, life must go on. Since the Lord took Ashley out of your life, He must have someone else for you. Shane Donovan needs to have his eyes and heart open for the woman God has for his life's mate. Since we've gone this far, and you know I care about you, Shane, I want you to open up and tell me how you really feel about Charolette."

Shane blinked and scrubbed a palm across his brow. "Well, sir, until recently I hadn't really noticed her as anything but a friend. But now I see her as a warm, beautiful, sweet Christian woman. I mean…she's really a wonderful person."

Joshua Chamberlain still had his hand on Shane's shoulder, and now he grinned from ear to ear. "Remember yesterday morning at church when we talked about the baby? Well, while you were saying something to me, I noticed Charolette looking at you."

"You did?"

"Yes. And I saw that certain look in her eyes, Shane. The girl loves you."

Shane blinked again. "Really? You think so?"

"I know love in a woman's eyes when I see it. Now, let me give you some sound advice, and I'll let you go. From this moment on, you should notice more about Charolette's being — how did you put it? — a warm, beautiful, sweet Christian woman. And I believe you added the word wonderful, too."

"Yes, sir. She's all of that, and more."

"Then accept my advice, Mr. Donovan, and take more notice!"

"I will, sir. I promise. I surely will!"

Shane Donovan and Mike O'Hanlon did not get to see each other often after they entered Bowdoin College. Mike's economics major placed him in different classes than his best friend's education major, and their jobs kept them busy and apart most of the time. Mike worked every hour he could at the shoe factory, and Shane's off-hours kept him busy at the lumber mill. What little spare time Shane could squeeze free, he spent with Charolette.

Shane showed more interest in her than he ever had before. Charolette soaked it all in, longing for the day Shane would say he loved her. When it came, she would tell him how long she had been in love with him.

Shane and Mike chanced to meet one evening in mid-November at a college social function. Mike had a girl with him Shane had not yet met. Her name was Marie Welton. She was from Augusta and in her first year at Bowdoin.

Charolette was with Shane. During the evening, Charolette and Marie became friends, and when they went to powder their noses, Mike asked if Shane was falling for Charolette. Shane told him about his counseling session with Professor Chamberlain some three weeks previously. Though he would always have a special love for Ashley, he admitted he had a growing attraction toward Charolette.

Mike casually said that Mavor Kilrain had written his mother again, and the letter had carried no news about Ashley's social life. Shane drew in a deep breath and said that Ashley had probably found her a steady young man by now. This time, it was Mike who felt a sharp pang in his heart.

Shane found Charolette on his mind continuously, whether he was in class, on the job, or doing homework in his bedroom. He was even having dreams about her. He began to use a pet name for her in the privacy of his mind. The only other person who knew about the name was the Lord Himself, for when Shane prayed for Charolette, he called her Charly.

In the last week of November, the Brunswick town council sponsored a concert at the town hall. Many of Bowdoin College's faculty and students attended. Shane and Charolette sat with Joshua and Fannie Chamberlain, and both couples fully enjoyed the evening.

When the concert was over and they were putting on their hats and coats, Joshua said, "I know you two walked to the concert, but Fannie and I will be glad to drive Charolette to the O'Hanlons and you to your home, Shane. It's a bit nippy out there."

Shane smiled and said, "We really appreciate the offer, Professor, but we came dressed warm enough to walk. It gives us a little more time together."

Chamberlain put an arm around his wife, winked at Shane, and said, "You know what, Fannie? I think Shane has finally noticed what a lovely young lady Charolette is."

"I've been noticing that for some time, sir. It's just that I've been noticing it a whole lot more lately!"

Fannie laughed. "Well, keep your eyes open!"

"Don't worry about that, ma'am. Charolette is so pretty, when I'm with her, I don't even blink!"

Charolette blushed, but inside she was reveling in Shane's words. The Chamberlains excused themselves, saying they had some people to see, and the young couple left the town hall and moved down the street arm-in-arm.

As they walked, Charolette looked up at Shane by the soft glow of the street lamps and said, "That was a nice thing for you to say."

"What was?"

"About not even blinking when you're with me."

"Well, it's the truth. Almost, anyway."

They came to a side street that led to the O'Hanlon home. Charolette noticed something in the shadows in front of one of the houses in the middle of the block.

"Shane...?"

"Yes?"

"I saw something up there."

"Where?"

"Right up there." She pointed with her free hand. "It's like someone is skulking, or something."

"Don't worry, you're safe with me. Probably just someone out for a walk, like us."

A street lantern on the corner at the far end of the block gave off enough light to throw a glow part way toward the middle of the block. The lantern at the corner behind them did the same. Charolette clung tightly to Shane as they drew near the dark void in the middle.

Suddenly, four figures appeared from behind a large oak tree and headed toward them.

"Shane," Charolette said with fear in her voice.

"It's all right, honey. Just keep walking."

The word *honey* did not escape Charolette's notice in spite of her fear.

There was enough light that Shane could see they were about to face four young toughs. The air was cold enough that their breath showed in small gray-white clouds.

As they drew abreast, one of the toughs bumped Shane, knocking him against Charolette and almost causing her to fall.

"Watch where you're going!" Shane said. "You almost knocked the lady down!"

The one who had bumped Shane stepped up close, putting his nose only inches from Shane's. He released a string of profanity, then said, "What are you gonna do about it?" The other three made a circle around them.

The tough's language lit Shane's fuse. "You're going to apologize to the lady for filling her ears with your foul language!"

"Is that right? And who's gonna make me?"

"You're looking at him!" Shane said.

The others laughed, and the tough cocked his fist, saying, "Let's see how you like the looks of this, buster!"

CHAPTER EIGHT

S hane Donovan ducked the flashing fist.

The young punk had no idea who he was dealing with. Shane was now six feet tall and weighed a solid, muscular one hundred eighty pounds. Though he never looked for a fight, it was not in him to avoid one if it was forced on him. He was no novice at fisticuffs.

When the hissing fist passed harmlessly over his head, Shane stayed in his crouch and sent a hard right to the tough's jaw. It caught him flush, staggering him. Shane followed with the other fist to the soft flesh under the man's ear, and dropped him to the ground.

The other three leaped for Shane, swearing at him. Charolette felt totally helpless. There was nothing she could do but stand there and pray.

Shane caught the closest tough with a blow to the nose, but the other two struck him on the side of the head twice in succession, and he felt his knees buckle. He managed to stay on his feet, but another fist banged him on the temple, and lights flashed inside his head. He felt himself falling. He could hear Charolette crying out, screaming for the toughs to leave him alone.

Two of them were on him now, pounding him wherever they could find a spot. Shane was on his back, using his arms and legs to try to fend off his attackers, with little success. Then he caught a glimpse of Joshua Chamberlain's buggy parked in the street. Fannie was climbing out to join Charolette, and the professor was swinging a roundhouse punch at one of the toughs. Fist met jaw, and the tough went down. Another one lunged at Chamberlain and was dropped with a stiff punch. Two of the punks were on the ground, and the other two took off running.

Shane got to his knees, then slowly stood. He wiped a hand across his mouth and found it crimsoned with blood. The professor was standing over the two toughs who remained. Shane saw that one of them was the leader — the one who had started it all. His jaw appeared to be dislocated, and blood ran from both nostrils.

Shane stood over him and said, "Either apologize to the young lady for your language, or you're going to get a lot more of what you've been getting."

The beaten tough looked up in the dim light and said in a mumbling sort of way, "My jaw is broke. I...I can't make it work."

"You can say that much, you can tell her you're sorry."

The tough looked toward Charolette, who stood by the Chamberlain buggy with Fannie. "I'm sorry, miss. I apologize for swearing in your presence."

"You satisfied, Shane?" Chamberlain asked.

"Yes, I'm satisfied."

"Okay, then," Chamberlain said, "you two hightail it out of here!"

As the toughs hurried away, Charolette ran to Shane. "You're bleeding, darling! Here, let me see if this will help."

Charolette pressed her hanky to Shane's bleeding lip, the word *darling* reverberating in his ears.

Shane turned his head, causing Charolette to stop dabbing at his lip for a moment, and said, "Professor, I'm sure glad you showed up. I'd have been a bloody pulp by now if you hadn't."

"Oh, I didn't show up to help you, Shane," Chamberlain said.

"You didn't?"

"No. I didn't want to see those men get hurt bad, so I figured if I pitched in, they'd take off before you really put some damage on them!"

Shane laughed in spite of the pain all over his body.

"So I assume this started over that punk using foul language in front of Charolette," Chamberlain said.

"It actually started when they came along and bumped Shane on purpose," Charolette said. "They were looking for trouble. When Shane reprimanded the one who bumped him because it almost caused me to fall, he swore at Shane and asked him what he was going to do about it. Shane told him he owed me an apology for using that kind of language in my presence...and right about then, the punk swung at him."

Chamberlain smiled and said, "You're to be commended, Shane. It's a gentleman's duty to protect a lady's ears from foul language. I want to commend you for your courage."

"I didn't think about being courageous, Professor. I just did what a gentleman ought to do. The odds made no difference."

"Well, a lot of fellows would've backed off," Chamberlain said. "I'm proud of you. Come on, get in the buggy. Fannie and I will take you both home."

"If you'll just take us to O'Hanlons, sir, that'll be fine. I can walk home from there."

The Chamberlain buggy rolled through the dark streets of Brunswick, and soon pulled up in front of the O'Hanlon house. The porch lantern was giving off a yellow glow. Shane thanked the Chamberlains for the ride and helped Charolette from the buggy. They stood and waved at the professor and his wife, then stepped up on the porch.

"Now that we have better light," Charolette said, "I want to take a good look at that lip."

Shane looked into her eyes. She held his gaze for a second or two, then focused on the cut.

"Looks like the bleeding's completely stopped."

"You're a good nurse."

A smile curved her lips. "And you're a good protector. You've got some pretty bad bruises on your face, but there's no blood. Does the lip hurt?"

"A little. Charolette, I…"

"Yes?"

"Well…whenever I had a cut as a boy, Mom always kissed it, saying a kiss would make it better."

"If I kissed your cut lip, would that make it better?"

"Oh, I'm sure it would."

Charolette's soft lips touched his ever-so-carefully. When their lips parted, Shane held her close. Charolette laid her head on his chest and tried to calm her runaway heart.

"Charolette…"

She drew back and looked into his eyes. "Yes?"

"I can't hold it back any longer."

"Hold what back?"

"The fact that I have fallen head-over-heels, mind-heart-and-soul in love with you."

Charolette's eyes brightened with a sudden rush of tears. She drew in a quick breath and said, "Oh, Shane! Shane, I'm in love with you too!"

Shane folded Charolette in his arms and held her tight. She clung to him for a long moment before saying, "Shane…what about Ashley?"

"She'll always have a special place in my heart, Charolette. She's a dear friend, but I'm in love with you. The Lord meant us for each other. I love you, my sweet Ch — Charolette. And I always will."

Shane had almost revealed the pet name he had secretly given her, but decided to keep it a secret. He let her move back so he could look into her eyes, and said, "I realize marriage has to be a ways off yet, but I just as well get it all out. I want you to marry me when the time is right."

She raised up on her tiptoes, kissed him sweetly, and said, "Yes, darling. When the time is right, I will marry you. Just knowing that you love me and want me to be your mate for life is enough to keep me going. O Shane, I love you so much!"

And their lips met softly again.

Garth and Pearl Donovan were elated when their son announced that he and Charolette were officially courting. They loved the girl and had known for some time that she had eyes for Shane. The O'Hanlons rejoiced with their house guest when she told them of the courtship.

Mike said he was happy for them and that the Lord always did things just right. In private, Shane asked Mike if he had heard anything about Ashley lately, and Mike said he had not. He added, however, that a letter had come to his father, advising him that Grandpa O'Hanlon's mental depression over the hunting accident had improved and he was back at the factory, helping Donald Kilrain carry on the business.

As the days passed, the love Shane and Charolette had for each other grew deeper and stronger. Every time they were together, he found her more loving and more lovable, and thanked God for giving him such a wonderful young woman.

One cold night in the third week of December, they were leaving the college campus in the Donovan buggy after attending a Christmas program. They were bundled up under a heavy blanket, and Charolette was clinging to his arm. The sky was clear and a three-quarter moon cast its silvery spray on the snow-covered ground.

Charolette looked up at Shane and said in a half-whisper, "Oh, darling, I love you so much!"

Shane smiled at her. "And I love you, Charly."

Charolette sat up straight. "What did you call me? Charley?"

Shane cleared his throat nervously. "I guess I might as well confess. I've called you Charly to myself for quite a while."

"How do you spell that?"

"C-H-A-R-L-Y. Why?"

"Because my mother used to call me that, and she spelled it the same way."

"Well, if you rather I didn't think of you as Charly, I won't do it anymore."

"Oh, no! I think it's sweet of you. I want you to think of me that way, and from now on, I want you to call me Charly."

"Really? You don't think it sounds, well, too masculine?"

"Please. It will mean more to me than you'll ever know because you came up with it without knowing that's what Mom called me."

"Okay. If you want, I'll have Pastor Adams say, 'Do you, Charly, take this man to be your lawfully wedded husband?'"

"No, I just want you to call me that."

"All right. Charly it is."

The horses hooves were muffled by the blanket of snow that covered the ground as the buggy approached the O'Hanlon house.

"About your mother, Charly..."

"Yes?"

"How old was she when she died of consumption?"

"Thirty-three."

"Awfully young."

"Yes, but I have many fond memories of her."

"But not many of your father, I take it."

Charolette was quiet for a moment, then said, "Not many."

"But you still love him, don't you?"

"Of course. He's my father."

"Would you like to go to Lewiston and see him?"

"I'd love to. If he's still there. Ethel was trying to get him to sell the store and move to Chicago."

"But you don't know any more than that?"

"No. I haven't had any contact with him since the day he so gladly gave me over to the Kilrains."

"How about I take a little time off work and drive you over there on Saturday?"

"Would you really?"

"Of course. The Bible tells us to honor our father and mother. No matter how poorly he's treated you, he's still your father. Who knows? He might even be glad to see you."

"Maybe. But I can guarantee you Ethel won't be."

"We'll just ignore her," Shane said.

On the following Saturday afternoon, it was snowing lightly when Shane and Charolette emerged from the store her father had owned. The new proprietor explained that he had bought the store from Alfred Thompson the last week of November. He had no idea where they went. They had talked about Chicago, but three or four other places were often spoken of too — Minneapolis, St. Louis, and one or two he couldn't recall.

As the couple climbed into the buggy to head back for Brunswick, Shane saw the pain in Charolette's eyes. "I'm sorry, honey," he said. "I know you wanted to see him."

"Yes, but there's something worse than not getting to see him. I have no idea where they went for sure...and now I have no way of ever reaching him with the gospel. My mother died without being saved. I don't want the same thing to happen to him. I talked to him about Jesus many times, but he always turned a deaf ear."

"I guess all we can do now is pray for him. The Lord knows where he is, and He can send someone to witness to him."

"Thank you, darling, you're right. We'll pray just that way."

*****

Christmas fell on a Thursday in 1856, and the O'Hanlons invited Buster Kilrain and the Donovans to Christmas dinner late in the afternoon. Buster had been with the O'Hanlons that morning when the gifts were opened, and Shane and Charolette had been at both places for the opening of gifts. Shane had a special gift for Charolette, but kept it a secret until it was almost time for dinner.

Charolette was busy in the kitchen, helping Maureen and Pearl. The men and children were in other parts of the house. Charolette was cutting freshly baked bread at the cupboard when she saw Shane enter the kitchen. She smiled at him as his mother said, "We'll be ready to eat in about ten minutes, son."

"I know, Mom," Shane said, heading toward Charolette. "I want to see my girl alone just before we eat. Charly, can we talk in the sewing room for a couple minutes?"

"Of course. Just give me a minute to finish cutting this bread."

"Sure smells good," he said, drawing a breath through his nostrils.

When Charolette laid the knife down, Shane took her by the hand and led her to the sewing room at the end of the hall on the ground floor. Shane closed the door, slid his hand into his pocket, and said, "I have a special present for you."

Charolette cocked her head, frowned, and said, "What is this? All presents for this Christmas have already been opened."

"Not all," he said, holding a small ring box for her to see.

Everyone was gathering around the table when Shane and Charolette appeared in the dining room. Her dark eyes flashed with happiness as she held up her left hand and said, "Everybody please notice!"

Pearl spotted the ring first and gasped, "Oh, how beautiful!"

Then she threw her arms around the girl and began to weep.

Garth was second to embrace Charolette, telling her he was so happy that she would one day be his daughter-in-law. Uncle Buster was next, planting a kiss on her cheek and congratulating Shane on getting such a wonderful girl. The children followed Uncle Buster, then Lewis O'Hanlon hugged her and told her she had become like a daughter to him. Mike wrapped his arms around his best friend, congratulating him, then kissed Charolette on the cheek.

Lastly, Maureen tearfully congratulated the couple, hugged Shane, then took Charolette into her arms. "I knew this was coming sooner or later. I'm already dreading the day you leave our home. I feel the same way Lewis does — you're just like a daughter to me. We're going to miss you terribly!"

Charolette thanked her, hugged her good, and then all sat down to eat.

That night at bedtime, Mike was alone with his mother in the kitchen. The rest of the family was upstairs, getting ready to retire for the night.

Maureen took her son in her arms and said, "Michael, I have to confess something."

"What's that, Mom?"

"Well, I had entertained hopes that you and Charolette would fall in love, and I could have her for my daughter-in-law. She's such a precious girl. I love her so much."

Mike patted his mother's cheek and said, "The Lord already has one picked out for me, Mom…one that you'll love even more than you love Charolette."

The following Sunday, Dr. George Adams announced the engagement in the morning service, and by Monday morning, word had spread to the college. Everyone was happy for Shane and Charolette. God's hand was on them, without a doubt.

CHAPTER NINE

The winter of 1857 was hard, and spring was late in coming. But by the first week in May, it finally was out in full bloom. Graduation took place at Bowdoin College two weeks later, and school let out for the summer.

Shane and Charolette were often asked if they had set a wedding date, but they had not. Because Shane's part-time income was low and he had tuition to pay, he and Charolette agreed they should wait until he had graduated from college and obtained employment. Then they would marry. He would work on his master's degree a little at a time after that.

Fall came, then winter.

One day in early January of 1858, Lewis O'Hanlon visited Garth Donovan at the lumber mill and asked to see him for a few minutes. When the two friends sat down behind a closed door in Garth's office, Lewis said, "I've heard a rumor, and I want to know if it's true."

"A rumor? About what?"

"About you having made a deal with your employer to buy him out."

Garth grinned. "Now where did you hear that?"

"Your wife. Actually, I didn't hear it from her own mouth, I heard it from Maureen. Pearl told her to keep it under her hat, so I'm the only one she's told. She also said that Shane doesn't even know it…that you're planning to surprise him with the news just after the sale takes place."

Garth smiled warmly and nodded. "That's it. I've got something in mind, but I didn't want to tell him until it becomes a reality."

"And that is?"

"Those sweet kids are so in love…and it's obvious that the Lord has them for each other. They want to marry, but just can't see their way clear to do so."

A pleasant grin worked its way across Lewis's face. "So when Daddy Donovan becomes his son's employer, the boy gets a raise in pay."

"You're pretty smart for an Irishman. I want that boy to finish college…even get his master's degree if he wants it. But I'd like to see those two go ahead and get married. They're both mature for their age, and I know they can handle it."

Lewis threw his head back and laughed.

"What's so funny?" Garth asked.

"I'm having a good time realizing that great minds run on the same track."

"How so?"

"Garth, my friend, I've had this same thing going through my mind…and when Maureen told me about you're deal to buy the mill, I figured to come and talk to you about giving Shane a substantial raise so those two can get married."

It was Garth's turn to laugh. "I have a feeling that isn't all you came to talk to me about. You're going to give Charolette a raise too, aren't you?"

"You know me too well, Garth. But yes — that girl is voluntarily handling more and more work, and she deserves a good raise. Before I decided what 'good' is, though, I wanted to see if we couldn't put our heads together. So when does this sale take place?"

"In five days — January 12."

The two men discussed what income they thought the young couple would need while Shane completed his education, and agreed on the raises they would give to meet that need.

Lewis made a note on a slip of paper drawn from his coat pocket, and said, "All right, my friend. When will you tell Shane you're the new owner of the lumber mill, and that he's getting a raise?"

"On the morning after I sign the papers."

"Okay. I'll tell Charolette about her raise the same morning, but I won't mention a thing about the raise you're giving Shane. We'll just let nature take its course. Okay?"

"It's a deal."

The two friends shook hands and parted with a warm glow deep inside them.

"You what?" Shane gasped at the breakfast table on Wednesday morning, January 13. "You bought the mill?"

Patrick and Ryan looked on with bulging eyes and gaping mouths. Pearl smiled to herself.

"But Pa," Shane said, "that means you're my employer! My boss!"

"That's right, son. And it means something else."

"What's that?"

"It means that as your employer, I'm giving you a raise in pay."

Shane glanced at his mother, then said to his father, "You are? May I ask how much of a raise?"

"Triple what you're making now."

"*Triple?*"

"That's right. Starting today."

"Hallelujah! Now I can put more money aside for when Charly and I get married!"

"That's good thinking, son." Garth looked across the table at his wife. "Don't you think so, Mother?"

"Yes, it sure is. It's wise to have a good financial foundation when entering marriage. Not everyone can, of course, but it makes that difficult first year so much easier."

It was midmorning the same day when Lewis O'Hanlon came from the rear of the factory and passed by Charolette's desk on his way to his office. Without breaking stride, he said, "Charolette, when you have a minute I need to see you."

"I can come in right now if you wish," she called after him.

"Fine," he said, turning and smiling at her.

Charolette picked up her notepad and pencil and hurried to meet her boss. He gestured for her to enter the office ahead of him, then closed the door as she took a seat in front of his desk. He rounded the desk and sat down.

"Busy morning?"

"Yes, sir. I've been going over those orders from New York and Boston as Uncle Buster asked me to do. We're picking up a lot of new business in both cities."

"Great. That's what we like to hear."

Charolette held pad and pencil ready to take down whatever instructions he had for her.

"Now," Lewis said, "I want to talk about you, my dear."

"Me, sir?" she asked, eyes wide.

"Yes. Charolette, I cannot tell you how pleased I am with your work. Everybody in the factory appreciates you, especially Uncle Buster and me."

"Why, thank you, Mr. O'Hanlon. I appreciate your saying so."

"In fact, I appreciate you and your fine work so much that I'm going to double your salary."

"You…you're going to *double* my salary?"

"You heard me right. From your first day on the job, you've gone beyond your own responsibilities and taken on work that you saw needed to be done. I like that. It shows me what you're made of. You certainly are going to make Shane a wonderful wife."

"Thank you," she said shyly. "But Mr. O'Hanlon, you're already paying me well…let alone the fact that I'm living in your home, getting free room and board. You really don't have to give me this raise."

"Charolette, Maureen and I are delighted to have you living in our home. We've both expressed it before, and I'll say it for both of us again — we're going to miss you terribly when you and Shane get married. By the way…any date set yet?"

"No, sir. We plan to wait until Shane is out of college and working full time."

"But that's still more than two years away for his bachelor's degree, let alone if he goes for his master's."

"I know, but our finances won't allow us to marry any sooner."

"This raise won't help that situation?"

"Oh, yes, it'll help. I'm just not sure how much. I'll see what Shane says when I tell him."

"We're not trying to get rid of you, you understand. I just hate to see you have to wait so long to get married."

Charolette was smiling from ear to ear. "Thank you, Mr. O'Hanlon. Your confidence in me means more than I can ever tell you. And this raise is appreciated very, very much. I can't wait to tell Shane!"

That evening, Shane knocked on the door of the O'Hanlon home, eager to tell Charolette about his father's purchase of the lumber mill and the tripling of his pay.

The young couple had previously set the evening for a date, and because the weather was so cold, the O'Hanlons told

Charolette that she and Shane could spend the evening together in the library, which had its own fireplace.

Mike opened the door, smiled and said, "Why, Shane, how nice of you to come and see me!"

Shane moved through the door and removed his hat. "I hate to break your heart, friend, but it isn't you I came to see."

Mike took Shane's hat, coat, and scarf. "I'll make it through this devastating disappointment somehow."

Shane cuffed him playfully on the chin. "She in the library?"

"I'm here," came Charolette's voice from the winding staircase that ended in the vestibule where the two young men were standing.

Charolette was wearing a black dress with white lace trim on the high neck and at the ends of the sleeves. Her raven-black hair was done in an upsweep, topping out in tiny ringlets that dangled onto her brow. Shane moved to the bottom of the stairs and gave her his hand as she reached the last step.

"You look splendid this evening, Miss Thompson."

"Why, thank you, Mr. Donovan."

"What's with all this formality?" Mike asked.

"Private stuff," Shane said, giving him a mock scowl.

"I guess I know where that puts me. See you two later."

"Thanks for the warning," Shane said.

Mike laughed and disappeared down the hall that led to the kitchen.

"I've got some real good news to tell you," Shane said.

"Oh? Well, it so happens I've got some real good news for you, too!"

Hand-in-hand, they moved down the hall and entered the library. The fireplace was crackling and giving off welcome warmth.

"Mike built the fire for us," Charolette said, leading Shane by the hand to the love seat that stood near the fireplace.

"Bless him," Shane said.

As they sat down, Charolette said, "Tell me your good news, darling. Then I'll tell you mine."

Shane took both of her hands in his, and with a lilt in his voice said, "My father just worked a deal with Mr. Throckmorton."

"The man who owns the lumber mill?"

"Yes. Mr. Throckmorton is retiring, and he's making it possible for Pa to buy the mill. They made it official yesterday."

"You mean your father is now owner of the mill?"

"Yes. And this morning at breakfast, he told me he's giving me a raise in pay starting today. And get this — it's triple what Mr. Throckmorton was paying me!"

Charolette's mouth dropped open. *"Triple!* Really?"

"Yes! Now we can set a date for our wedding! We can put a good amount of money away for a year or so, then we'll be in good financial shape when we get married."

Charolette placed her hand to her throat. "O Shane, this is wonderful! Praise the Lord!"

"Yes, praise Him! It is wonderful, isn't it. Now what's your good news?"

Charolette adjusted herself on the love seat, looked deep into Shane's eyes, and said, "I got a raise too!"

"You did?"

"This morning, Mr. O'Hanlon called me into his office and told me how pleased he is with my work. He's doubling my salary as of today!"

Shane hugged her. "Honey, that's wonderful!"

"Yes! Isn't the Lord good?"

"Yes, He is. He sure is."

Charolette eased back from his arms, put a hand to her chin, and looked at the floor.

"Something bothering you?" Shane asked.

"Oh, no." She raised her eyes to meet his. "It's just that — Shane, did your father mention our wedding when he told you of the raise?"

Shane thought a moment. "No. But when I said this would allow us to put more money aside, both he and Ma agreed it was a wise thing to do. Why do you ask?"

"Well, after he told me about the raise, Mr. O'Hanlon asked if it would make it possible for us to get married sooner. It's like — "

"Conniving?"

"I guess you could call it that."

"Seems so. I've got a feeling Pa and Mr. O'Hanlon got together and put these raises together so we could get married sooner."

"I think you're right. Mr. O'Hanlon sure seemed curious to know if it would affect our plans."

Shane was shaking his head in wonderment. "I just said that my raise would let us marry in a year or so, but now I'd say if we planned it right, we could get married in six months. What do you think?"

"Well, I would say we could get married even sooner with this much money coming in. But if we waited six months, we'd have a solid financial foundation under us. I agree. Let's drop it from a year to six months!"

Shane took Charolette in his arms and whispered, "I've got an idea. Let's get married on your birthday."

"My birthday?" she said, pulling back to look him in the eye. "You mean it?"

"Of course."

"O Shane, that'd be wonderful! I'll become your wife and turn nineteen on the same day."

The young couple went to the O'Hanlons and thanked them for conniving with Garth Donovan to give them both raises so they could get married sooner than they had planned. And Shane took Mike aside and told him that since the wedding date had now been set, he wanted to know if Mike would be his best man. Mike was elated and agreed.

It was announced at the church and at the college that the wedding was set for June 14. Friends expressed their joy to the happy couple.

*****

In March, news came from Ireland that Lewis O'Hanlon's father had died suddenly of heart failure. There were brothers and sisters there who could care for Lewis's mother, but Donald Kilrain was asking for help in managing the company. There was no one at the factory in Dublin who had enough knowledge of policies and procedures to step into Jacob's spot. Because Mike had been working some in the management end of the business in Brunswick, Donald requested that he come and fill his grandfather's shoes until a new man could be trained for the job. Donald explained in the letter that the experience would be invaluable to Mike, even though he would have to drop out of college for a while, probably no more than a year.

Mike was eager to go. The experience would be a great help to his career, but the main reason he wanted to go was to see Ashley Kilrain. He was sure if she had found a steady beau, it would have been mentioned in one of Mavor's letters.

Lewis prayed for several days about Donald's request and discussed it with Maureen and Mike and Buster Kilrain. Nine days after the letter had arrived, Mike was called to his father's office at the factory.

When Mike entered the office, he found Uncle Buster there, too. He closed the door behind him as Lewis said, "Come and sit down, son." Lewis waited for Mike to sit before proceeding. "Mike, all of us have been seeking the Lord's guidance concerning Donald's request. He needs to have an answer soon, and Buster and I have decided that if you really want to go, we should send you."

Mike's eyes lit up. "You can put it down and draw a line under it, Pa — yes, I want to go!"

"Well, you can thank Uncle Buster for the opportunity, son. I'm pretty dependent on you here, but he says he'll work extra hours to make up for your absence."

"Thanks, Uncle Buster," Mike said. "I know I'll learn a lot working in the Dublin factory."

Buster's Irish eyes twinkled. "Sure, and don't I know that, me boy! And somethin' else."

"Yes, sir?"

"It'll also put ye a whole lot closer to little Ashley too, eh?"

Mike's countenance crimsoned. His eyes flicked to his father.

Lewis grinned. "You aren't fooling anybody, son. It's been written all over you since you found out Shane and Charolette were sweethearts. Be sure to tell Ashley hello for Buster and me."

Lewis and Buster had a good laugh at Mike's expense, then serious planning began. Mike would sail for Ireland as soon as possible.

On the following Sunday, Shane and Charolette were walking toward the church from the parking lot when they saw the O'Hanlon carriage pull in. Mike waved, calling for them to wait. They stopped and greeted him as he drew up.

"Shane, I need to talk to you right after church," Mike said.

"You want this private, or is it all right if Charly hears it?"

"It's fine if she hears it. But it's important. We'll talk right after church, okay?"

"Sure. Right after church."

The cold March wind blew through the naked trees that surrounded the church grounds as Shane and Charolette stood near the O'Hanlon carriage, greeting people as they passed by. Mike hurried toward them, having stopped to talk to Pastor Adams at the door. Charolette pulled her coat collar up to fend off the biting wind.

"I'm sorry to hold you up," Mike said, "but I have to tell you, Shane, that I won't be able to be best man at the wedding. I'm really sorry about it, but it just won't be possible."

Though everyone at church knew of Jacob O'Hanlon's death, no one knew of Donald Kilrain's request for Mike to come and help him.

"I know there has to be a good reason, Mike," Shane said.

Mike then told them he would soon be leaving for Dublin, and why. "I hope you understand, Shane. You too, Charolette."

Both assured him they understood, but were sorry he wouldn't be there for their wedding.

"How soon are you leaving?" Shane asked.

"This evening. The ship sails at six-thirty."

"Whoa, you weren't kidding when you said you were leaving soon. I'm sure going to miss you, friend. A whole year!"

"We both wish you the best, Mike," Charolette said. "We certainly will miss you." She paused, then said, "I envy you."

"Why's that?"

"You're going to get to see Ashley. I still miss her so much."

"I'll be sure to greet her for you."

"Do that. And tell her she owes me three letters. I haven't heard from her in a long time."

"Will do."

"Greet her for me too, will you?" Shane asked.

"Of course. And I'll tell her that your wedding is planned for Charolette's birthday. She'll be happy to hear that. Well, I guess I'd better head for home. I've still got some packing to do."

Shane and Charolette embraced Mike and told him they would be praying for him and looking forward to his return.

On Sunday evening, March 21, 1858, Mike O'Hanlon boarded the Ireland-bound ship with mixed emotions. He would miss his family and friends…but he was going to see the girl he loved.

The next morning, he pulled his cap low, turned up his coat collar, and walked to the bow of the ship. He stood there with the cold wind biting at his face and squinted against the bright sunlight that reflected off the choppy surface of the Atlantic. The bow of the ship rose and fell in the rough waters, and a light spray struck him in the face.

He lifted his eyes heavenward and prayed, "O Lord Jesus, You know what has been in my heart for so long. I have loved Ashley since she was twelve years old. You've never taken that love out of my heart." The ship's bow went low, then raised high, sending a heavy spray on Mike, but he only tightened his grip on the rail. "Dear Lord, You know that I never let on to Shane nor to Ashley because I never would have come between them. But now...now You've given Charolette to Shane, and here I am — within Your plan — on my way to Ireland. Lord Jesus, I can't look into Your great mind, but could it be possible that my love for Ashley has remained so strong because You have chosen her for me? That You have...or will...put the same kind of love in her heart for me? Lord, I pray that it will be so."

CHAPTER TEN

ike O'Hanlon arrived in Dublin on April 6, 1858. Since there had been no time to send a letter to Donald Kilrain once the decision had been made, Mike himself would be Lewis O'Hanlon's answer to Donald's request.

Mike rode into town on a freight wagon owned by a Dublin merchant named Padriac O'Dwyer, who knew the Jacob O'Hanlon family. He also knew the Kilrains and had seen Donald on several occasions since he and his family had returned to Dublin.

Mike knew the Kilrain's address from the letters that had come from Mavor. O'Dwyer knew the neighborhood well and was kind enough to drive young O'Hanlon right up to the door. Mike thanked him, swung down onto the cobblestone street, and lifted his luggage off the wagon. He carried the four pieces to the door of the large, luxurious house two at a time. The house had a tile roof and was constructed of brick, which only the wealthy could afford. The other homes in the area were also expensive-looking.

Mike rapped the knocker on the door. Light, rapid footsteps preceded the rattle of the latch, then the door swung open. It was Ashley. Her face lit up when she recognized the young man who stood on the porch.

"Mike! Oh, thank the Lord you're here!"

Even as she spoke, she wrapped her arms around him. Mike hugged her too, then held her at arm's length and said, "You're a sight for sore eyes, Ashley! Is everybody in the family all right?"

"Yes, but they'll be even better when they see you! Come in. Daddy just got home. They're all in the library at the back of the house."

Mike set his luggage in the wide entrance hall, then followed Ashley as she led him by the hand to the library. When she led him through the library door, the entire family reacted with surprise, and delight, to see him. Donald and Mavor said he was an answer to prayer. William, who was now sixteen, and Harvey, who was now fourteen, shook his hand warmly.

Mavor and Ashley then hurried to the kitchen and started preparing supper. Donald sat Mike down and told him that somehow he knew Lewis would grant his request. He had already rented Mike an apartment near the factory and had set up his late grandfather's office for him.

The two of them discussed Mike's new job until the meal was ready. At the table, Donald thanked the Lord for bringing Mike safely to them, thanked Him for the food, and they began to eat.

Everyone fired questions at Mike one after the other. When business and family questions had been answered, there were inquiries about different people and what was going on at the church and in town.

It was Donald who asked the inevitable question. After taking a sip of hot tea, he looked at Mike and said, "And how about your friend Shane Donovan? He's in college, I understand. How many girlfriends has he got?"

"Well, sir, you're right. Shane is in college. Doing quite well scholastically. He's become a close friend of Professor Joshua Chamberlain. I guess you knew Mr. Chamberlain was back teaching at Bowdoin."

"Seems someone mentioned that in a letter. Fine man."

"That he is, sir. Shane has only one girlfriend though — that pretty Charolette Thompson. In fact, she's more than a girlfriend. They're now engaged to be married."

Mike noticed a slight bobbing of Ashley's head and a twitch at one corner of her mouth.

"Oh, really?" Mavor said. "That's nice. They're both such fine young people."

"They're getting married on Charolette's birthday…June fourteenth."

He saw Ashley's hands tremble slightly, but she smiled and said, "Oh, that's wonderful. I'm so glad for them. They both deserve to be happy."

"Charolette said to tell you, Ashley, that you owe her three letters. She very much wants to hear from you."

Ashley swung her eyes to her mother. "I know I owe her two. Didn't I answer the one that came last fall?"

"I thought you did," Mavor said. "Maybe it went astray. International mail does that a lot."

"Must be what happened," Ashley said. "I'm just sure I sent that letter. Anyway, I'll write her right away. I've been neglectful in answering the other two letters, and I need to ask her forgiveness."

"She still talks about you a lot, Ashley," Mike said. "I know it'll mean a lot to hear from you."

"I love her dearly and I miss her a lot. It…it's nice that they can be married on her birthday. Too bad you won't be there for the wedding."

"Shane asked me to be his best man. Wish I could've done it, but someone else will have to wear those shoes. I've got a feeling he'll ask Professor Chamberlain."

"How about you, Ashley?" Mike asked, trying to sound as casual as possible. "Any serious boyfriends in your life?" His heart seemed stuck in his throat as he waited for her reply.

She smiled and said, "Nobody special, Mike. I've met and dated several young men, but finding someone who's really dedicated to the Lord is like trying to find a needle in a haystack."

"It's the same with Christian girls. I've dated several who are in First Parish Church. Nice girls and all but not as dedicated as…as you, for instance."

Ashley's features tinted. "I…I just feel that if a person is going to live for the Lord, they should go all the way and give Him their best."

"My sentiments exactly," Mike said. "It's a girl with that kind of dedication that I've been waiting for the Lord to bring into my life."

"And He will," Mavor said. "You're such a fine boy, Mike. I'm sure the Lord has a wonderful girl picked out for you."

Mike couldn't help but look at Ashley. Their eyes met, and she gave him a sweet smile.

Professor Chamberlain dismissed his rhetoric class and was going through papers on his desk in preparation for his next class when he became aware of someone standing over the desk. He looked up to see Shane Donovan smiling down at him.

"What can I do for you, Shane?"

"I was wondering if I could have a few minutes with you sometime today, sir."

"Sure. How long do you need?"

"Not more than five minutes, sir."

"How about right after lunch? Right here?"

"Fine, sir. See you then."

Shane was waiting in the hall after lunch when Chamberlain arrived. The professor commented that Shane was always punctual. He opened the door and gestured for his favorite pupil to sit down in front of the desk, then took his seat behind it.

"All right, Shane, what can I do for you?"

"Well, sir, you're aware that Charolette and I are going to be married on June fourteenth."

"Yes, and I imagine you're starting to get some butterflies."

"Yes, sir. I guess that's to be expected."

"Happens to the best of us. But I don't imagine you came to see me to talk about butterflies."

"No, sir, I came to ask a favor of you. I'd like for you to be my best man in the wedding."

Chamberlain's eyes mirrored the surprise Shane's words brought. It took him a few seconds to reply. "Why, Shane, I would be honored to be your best man. Highly honored."

"The honor will be mine, sir. This will make Charolette happy too. Thank you!"

Shane stood and offered his hand. Chamberlain rose and met his grip.

"Just let me know about wedding practice and all that," Chamberlain said.

"I will, sir. And thank you again."

The next day, Shane was the first to arrive for Greek class. He greeted Chamberlain, who was writing Greek conjugations on the chalkboard. Chamberlain laid the chalk down and walked up to Shane.

"When I got home yesterday afternoon, I told Fannie that you had asked me to be best man in your wedding. She said she wanted to prepare a meal for the wedding party on the day of the rehearsal. It would be at our house afterward. Is that okay?"

"That's awfully kind of her. And yes, that would be great. Thank her for us, will you?"

"I will."

That evening, Shane told Charolette of Fannie's offer, and the bride-to-be was elated. When Sunday came, both Shane and Charolette expressed their appreciation to her, as did Garth and Pearl Donovan.

As the wedding date drew near, Shane and Charolette's love for each other continued to grow. They found a small cottage to rent in Brunswick and began fixing it up like they wanted it.

They talked together about their home and their desire that it would glorify the Lord Jesus Christ. They would teach their children the Word of God and worship together as a family in the church. They agreed to follow the Bible's instructions for disciplining their children.

They decided that since they were doing well financially, Shane would enter graduate school after he received his bachelor's degree. They would not start their family until he had his master's degree and had a steady teaching job. They both hoped the job would be at Bowdoin College.

"I want to follow in the footsteps of Joshua Lawrence Chamberlain," Shane said.

Charolette smiled and said, "You really love that man, don't you?"

"Charly, I would lay down my life for him."

"I hope you don't ever have to do that."

Charolette's birthday — and thus the wedding day — fell on Monday in 1858. On the previous Friday, Shane and Charolette were eating supper in a small Brunswick Café. As they were finishing the meal, Shane noticed a "cat-that-ate-the-canary" look in Charolette's eyes.

"What do you know that I don't?" he asked, cocking his head at her.

"What do you mean?"

"You know what I mean. It's written all over your face. Come on, out with it."

"Well, I've been dying to let you in on it, but I decided to wait till we were through eating."

She dug in her purse and pulled out an envelope. Shane could tell it was addressed to Charolette in feminine handwriting.

"Who from?" he asked.

"Ashley. You remember that I got a letter from her not too long after Mike had gone to Ireland? All she said in that letter was that it was good to see Mike again."

"You told me that."

"Well, wait till you hear this. Do you want me to read it to you or just tell you what's in it?"

Shane eased back on his chair. "Why don't you just tell me what's in it while I sit here and enjoy the view?"

Charolette blushed. "Oh, Shane. You say the sweetest things."

"I just speak the truth, me lady. Go ahead. Tell me what's in the letter."

"All right. Are you ready for this?"

"How can I answer that? I don't know what's in it."

"Well, Ashley says that she and Mike have fallen in love, and they are engaged!"

"No kidding?"

"No kidding. The wedding is set for this coming December tenth."

Shane remembered the special love he and Ashley had promised each other and felt a warm glow spread through his chest. The Lord had guided their lives and provided them with the mates He had planned. Shane loved his Charly with everything that was in him and was superbly happy with God's choice for him...but the little redheaded lass who had been his first love would always have a tender place in his heart.

"Well, I'm mighty happy for them," Shane said, "but I wonder how they fell for each other so quickly. I sure never noticed anything but friendship between them before."

"Well, God works in mysterious ways sometimes."

"Would've been great if we had been able to have a double wedding," Shane said.

"Yes, that would have been nice. But at least we'll get to see Ashley again. Mike will be bringing his bride home to Brunswick with him."

The wedding rehearsal was held on Sunday afternoon, June 13, after which Fannie Chamberlain fed the wedding party, their mates, and their children in the Chamberlain home. During the meal, Shane and Charolette had eyes only for each other.

Dr. George Adams looked on with joy. In his many years of pastoring, he had counseled a great number of couples prior to their wedding. Other than his own daughter and Joshua Chamberlain, he had never seen a couple so in love. In his heart, he thanked God and prayed that their love would grow deeper and stronger all their married lives.

The wedding took place the following evening at the First Parish Congregational Church. The building was packed.

Charolette was a strikingly beautiful bride in her long white-lace-on-white-satin dress with lengthy train. It had a high neck and sleeves that came to a heart-shaped point at her wrists. On her head was a coronet of white lace from which flowed a delicate veil. The crowd looked on with admiration as she walked down the aisle on the arm of Lewis O'Hanlon to meet her groom.

There was pain in Charolette's heart because her father had deserted her and her mother was not alive to see her take her vows. But the pain eased with each step she took toward the man she loved so deeply.

The ceremony was beautifully done, with the Lord Jesus Christ highly honored. Fannie Chamberlain played the organ. In addition to being best man, Joshua Chamberlain sang two solos, one before the bride started her procession and a prayer song while they knelt at the altar just before the pastor pronounced them husband and wife.

The happy bride and groom took a five-day honeymoon in Portland, staying at a hotel and sailing on the Atlantic Ocean. On the last day, they were in a sailboat, drifting with the wind. Charolette was reading Harriet Beecher Stowe's *Uncle Tom's Cabin,* which she had purchased in a Portland bookstore. She had wanted to read it for a long time, but especially so since she had met the author and gotten to know her before the Stowes moved away from Brunswick.

Shane was reading a Portland newspaper and had come across an article telling of trouble in Washington between politicians of northern and southern states over states' rights and slavery.

Charolette noted the concerned look on his face and asked, "What is it, darling?"

"Oh, this slavery issue and states' rights. They're having a heated battle in Congress about it."

"That's what this book's about…slavery. Mrs. Stowe is completely opposed to it. I didn't have to read very far to figure that out."

"Well, so is God," Shane said. "He never intended for one human being to treat another as chattel. If the evolutionists were right, it would be different. They say we're all animals, so humans could be bought and sold like we do cattle and horses and hogs. But God created man in His own image. We didn't evolve from apes. Human beings are not to own one another."

"You're right about that. Slavery is not of the Lord. I hope those politicians get the issue settled before it grows worse. I hate to see Americans at odds with each other."

Shane folded the newspaper and dropped it on the deck of the boat. "Well, if they don't get it settled pretty soon, the battle won't be with words. It'll be with guns. The plantation owners will stir up big trouble if they think they're going to lose the right to own slaves. There's no way they'll just lie down and let their slaves be taken from them. There'll be a bloody war. Can you imagine Americans killing Americans on blood-soaked battlefields?"

"No, I can't."

*****

The next Sunday the newlyweds were back in church, and on Monday they were back at their jobs. As the weeks passed, they found married life sweet and precious with the Lord at the center of their home.

In early September, Shane was given the teenage Sunday school class, and Charolette worked with him as helper. She also did whatever counseling was needed with the girls. The Donovans were full of joy serving the Lord.

College classes began the second week of September, and the weight of study and work was once again on Shane's shoulders. He was glad to have Joshua Chamberlain for three courses.

In Dublin, Ireland, one night in mid-November, Mike and Ashley were alone in the parlor of the Kilrain home, talking of their future. Then the subject turned to family and friends in America.

They were sitting side-by-side on a small couch, facing the blazing fireplace. In the flickering light from the fire, Mike noticed that when they talked of Shane and Charolette, Ashley became visibly nervous. He took hold of her hand and felt it trembling.

"Sweetheart, what's wrong?"

The other hand trembled also as she put it to her mouth.

"Mike, there's something I have to talk to you about."

"Must be serious. You're shaking."

"It is."

"Tell me about it."

She freed her hand from his and stood up.

"Wait here. I'll be right back."

When she returned, she was carrying a small black velvet box. She sat down beside him and opened the lid, displaying a gold necklace adorned with a heart-shaped locket. It was engraved with a male hand and a female hand in a tender grasp of love.

"I recognize that," Mike said. "Shane gave it to you. I remember you wearing it a lot."

"Darling, you know that I love you with all of my heart, don't you?" Ashley said.

"Next to the fact that Jesus loves me, it's the biggest, most wonderful thing in my life. I have to keep shaking myself to make sure I'm not dreaming."

Ashley laid a hand on his cheek and said, "Thank you. Just so you know without a doubt that I love you and I want to become your wife. My greatest desire is to live the rest of my life with you."

"I know that, sweetheart," he said, squeezing her hand. "Now, what about the locket?"

"When Shane gave it to me, we made a promise to each other. We promised we would always have a special love for each other, even if the Lord did not plan for us to marry." Her voice quavered as she proceeded. "Mike, I'm in love with you and you alone. The Lord meant us for each other. That's a settled fact between you and me. But…I still have fond memories of Shane. And I have a special love for him, though not like the love I have for you. Can you understand that?"

He smiled and squeezed her hand again. "Of course I can. I've got a special love for him myself. He and I are best friends. We always will be. What you're asking is, can you keep the locket, right?"

"Yes. As a token of the friendship between Shane and me. But if you want me to get rid of it, I will."

Mike folded Ashley in his arms, kissed her tenderly, and said, "Sweetheart, I'm glad you and my best friend have fond memories of each other. That doesn't bother me at all. And you know why?"

"Why?"

"Because Shane is madly in love with Charolette, but most of all, because I know you love me. It won't bother me at all if you keep it. I want you to."

"Thank you," she said, putting the locket back in the box and closing it. "I'll keep it…but I won't wear it."

Ashley laid the box on a lamp table next to the couch, and they began talking about all the good times they would have with Shane and Charolette when they returned to Brunswick. Ashley said how wonderful it would be to see them and that she hoped she and Charolette could become closer friends yet.

On December 2, a box arrived on a ship from America. Inside were wedding gifts from Shane and Charolette, Uncle Buster Kilrain, and Garth and Pearl Donovan. There was nothing from Mike's family because they were coming for the wedding and bringing their gifts with them.

The wedding took place as scheduled on December 10.

The previous October, Donald Kilrain had hired a new man with experience in the shoe and boot manufacturing business to train for management. Mike understood that the new man would be ready to take over his job by the end of March.

The newlyweds made plans to return to America the first week of April.

CHAPTER ELEVEN

Saturday, April 16, 1859, was a cool, cloudy day. The wind whipped across Casco Bay as the big ship swung off the Atlantic Ocean and headed due west for Portland Harbor.

Mike and Ashley O'Hanlon stood together on the starboard side and, like several hundred of their fellow passengers, squinted against the wind trying to pick out familiar faces in the crowd that waited on the dock. Ashley's long auburn hair kept blowing across her face, blocking her vision. She swept it back and held it there. Only seconds later, she pointed and said, "Mike, there they are! See them?"

It took Mike a moment to find his parents, Buster Kilrain, and Shane and Charolette Donovan, but when he did, he began to wave excitedly.

The ship swung in line with the dock and began to slow. Soon crewmen were tossing ropes to men on the dock, and two massive anchors on heavy chains were lowered into the water. Moments later, the gangplank was lowered, and passengers lined up to rush down to friends and loved ones.

Mike kept an arm around his wife as they descended the gangplank, then released her to hurry into his mother's arms. Shane and Charolette remained slightly aloof to give the O'Hanlons and

Buster Kilrain time to reunite with the newlyweds. Shane, who had been holding Darlene Brainerd, put the six-year-old down and said, "Even though you don't remember Miss Ashley, you can give her a big hug. You remember Mike though, don't you?"

"Yes, sir. He's your goodest friend, isn't he?"

"You've got that right!"

When Buster and the O'Hanlons had been sufficiently greeted, Mike and Ashley looked toward Shane and Charolette. Mike embraced Charolette. Shane and Ashley stood a few feet apart, not quite sure what to do. Their hearts were pounding, and they both seemed frozen on the spot. Then Ashley opened her arms and rushed to Shane, who held her close. She raised up on her tiptoes and kissed his cheek, saying through her tears, "Hello, Shane. It's wonderful to see you again!"

"It's good to see you. You look great. And you've grown up!"

Ashley backed off a step, cuffed him playfully on the upper arm, and said, "What do you mean? I was grown up before I left here!"

Shane laughed, then Mike wrapped him in his arms and hugged him tight.

"Good to see you, old pal!" Mike said. "And I do mean old! Forty-eight days of it."

Shane laughed. "You won't ever let anything die, will you?"

"Not that, my friend. Never! And let me tell you something."

"What's that?"

"I just saw Ashley kiss you on the cheek."

"You did?"

"Yes, I did. And I want you to know that you're the only man outside the Kilrain family I will allow her to kiss!"

"Well, that makes me one privileged bloke, doesn't it?"

"You'd better believe it."

Charolette and Ashley held each other close and mingled their tears of joy.

"Oh, Charolette, I've missed you so much. It's wonderful to see you!"

"It's so good to see you," Charolette said. "I'm never going to let you go away again!"

"I'm so glad for you and Shane. Are you as happy as I suspect you are?"

"Oh, yes, and even more! The Lord has given us such a precious love for each other. You and Mike too, right?"

"Mike's a wonderful husband. We're so much in love."

When the women had finished their embrace, they turned to see Mike hugging little Darlene. Ashley looked at Shane and said, "I wouldn't have known her if Mike hadn't told me who she was. Isn't she a doll?"

"That she is," Shane said. He then took the six-year-old by the hand and led her to Ashley. "Darlene, this is Miss Ashley. She's a very special friend of mine and Aunt Charolette's. How about a big hug for her?"

Darlene gave Ashley a hug, then moved back to Shane and took his hand. "She's pretty, Uncle Shane. I like her."

"Miss Ashley likes you, too. I can tell."

Ashley smiled down at Darlene. "I sure do, honey. You're a very special little girl."

"Shane, has she been told?" Mike asked.

"Yes. A few months ago, Elsa asked if we could come to the house. She felt Darlene was old enough to be told. It was quite a moment."

"I'll say it was," Charolette said. "She put a hug on Shane's neck that night like I've never seen before."

"And Charly cried a bucket of tears," Shane said.

Darlene's bright eyes danced as she looked at Ashley. "Uncle Shane saved me from burning up in the fire when I was a baby, Miss Ashley."

"Yes, I know. I remember when it happened."

"I love him very much. I would have died if he didn't come in the house and get me. I saw you kiss Uncle Shane. You love him too, don't you?"

The child's words tilted Ashley a bit off balance. "Why, of course I do. Your Uncle Shane and I have been friends for a long time."

"Darlene has adopted Shane and me as aunt and uncle," Charolette said. "She comes and stays with us quite often. Sometimes we have her sister and brother with us, too. Darlene stayed with us last night, so we brought her with us to meet you."

Innocent blue eyes looked up at Ashley. "Are you and Mr. Mike going to live with Uncle Shane and Aunt Charolette?"

"No, sweetie. We'll be staying with Mr. Mike's parents until we can get a place of our own."

It took the newlyweds only a few days to find a small cottage, which happened to be in the same block where Shane and Charolette lived. The two couples spent a great deal of time together, including riding to church on Sundays and Wednesday nights. They also attended church social functions together and spent time with other young couples, including Professor and Mrs. Joshua Chamberlain.

During off-work hours for Charolette, she and Ashley sewed together, making themselves dresses. Their friendship deepened, and the love they had for each other grew stronger. Like their husbands, they were the very best of friends.

One day in September, when both husbands were in school, the two young women were sewing at the kitchen table in the O'Hanlon cottage. They chatted about several things as they worked, then the conversation turned to their husbands, their courtships, and how happy they were in their married lives.

Charolette brought up the relationship Ashley and Shane had

had when they were younger and expressed her joy that they could still be such good friends.

"Did you ever have any serious boyfriends before you fell for Shane?" Ashley asked.

"Oh, I had one when I was twelve. His name was Billy Burton." Charolette laughed. "He gave me a cheap little ring to show how much he cared for me. I've still got it, in fact."

"Really? Does Shane know?"

"Oh, yes, but he doesn't care. It's no more than a friendship thing."

There was no conversation for a few minutes, then Charolette said, "My mentioning of the ring Billy gave me just reminded me of that locket Shane gave you — the one with the two hands clasped. Do you still have it?"

"Why, yes I do. Mike took the same attitude toward it that you say Shane took about Billy Burton's ring. I wanted to keep it for the sentimental value it holds." She paused a moment. "Charolette, does it bother you that I still have the locket?"

"Oh, of course not. Not at all. Life in this world gives us enough bad memories. I'm glad you and Shane have some good ones."

"Mike and I are looking forward to being here for dinner tomorrow night. I know you were wanting to have the Chamberlains over before Fannie has her baby. It was awfully nice of you to invite us, too."

"I wouldn't think of inviting them and leaving you two out. Besides, when I invite you, I always get help in the kitchen!"

By March of 1860, the states' rights–slavery issue had heated up. The people of the South were bowing their necks against Northern politicians and newspapers who were speaking out against slavery.

In early April, Joshua Chamberlain addressed the dual issue of states' rights and slavery in his theology class. Though he spoke out against slavery, he expressed his wish that somehow the matter could be settled without violence.

A day later, Chamberlain entered the administration building a few minutes before first hour. Bowdoin's president, Dr. Leonard Woods, was standing in the hall in front of his office, talking to one of the science professors. Woods caught Chamberlain's eye and raised a hand for him to stop. Woods said some final words to the science professor, who then turned and walked away.

The president was a small man with narrow-set eyes that some people said could bore holes through a brick wall. He set those eyes on Joshua Chamberlain.

"Good morning, Professor."

"Good morning, Dr. Woods."

"I have word that you have spoken out on the slavery issue in your theology class."

"Yes, sir."

Woods's normally turned-down mouth curved upward into a wide smile. "I like what I hear. Seems you've got a good handle on this thing."

"Well, thank you, sir. I just felt that since the Bible makes it clear that God is against slavery, the theology class would be a good place to bring it up."

"Excellent, my boy. Tell you what...starting next Monday, I want you to take the next five chapel times and lecture on the subject to the entire student body and faculty."

"I'd be happy to do that, Dr. Woods."

"Good. I'm against slavery from the bottom of my feet to the top of my head, son. I want the students and the faculty of this college to hear what you have to say."

"All right, sir."

"I'll make arrangements for a short song service so you can get right to it. And I want you to speak an hour each time, Monday through Friday. You have enough material, I presume."

"I believe so, sir."

"Good. I want you to close each session with prayer, Professor. I'm sure I don't need to tell you to pray that Abraham Lincoln gets elected in November."

"Fannie and I are already praying that way."

"And well you should. We need to ask the Lord to let the issue be settled peacefully, but we all know that if Mr. Lincoln gets into the White House, slavery will be done away with in this country. By you're public prayer, you'll give an example to everybody on this campus of how to pray between now and November."

"I get the picture."

"And I'll be there on the platform, smiling while you're lecturing and shouting amen when you're praying. About half the people on this campus are old enough to vote, Joshua, and we want them to vote right, don't we?"

"We sure do, sir."

"And all of them are old enough to pray, and we want them to pray right, don't we?"

"Yes, sir."

Woods gave Chamberlain a pat on the back. "Better hurry now, or you'll be late to class. Can't have the professor arriving late to class now, can we?"

"No, sir," Chamberlain said, and darted down the hall.

Bowdoin College's chapel had been built in 1855. It was one of the earliest examples in the United States of German Romanesque architecture. It was a large stone building with twin towers which tapered to sharp spires that pointed boldly to the heavens. In addition to an ample auditorium to provide space for the college's daily chapel assemblies, it housed a huge library, an art gallery, and several meeting rooms.

On the Monday President Woods had designated for Chamberlain's lectures, students and faculty headed for the chapel from the other campus buildings shortly before eleven o'clock. Bibles and notebooks were in their hands. Chamberlain and the president walked together from the administration building, flanked on both sides by students. Other students greeted Woods and Chamberlain as they entered the chapel and headed for the platform.

After one rousing hymn, prayer, and a few announcements, Dr. Woods stood in the pulpit and explained that he had changed the normal program for chapel for that day and the rest of the week because he had asked Professor Chamberlain to bring hour-long lectures on the subject of states' rights and slavery.

There was a warm round of applause for Chamberlain as he stepped to the pulpit. He opened his Bible and directed his hearers to Exodus 1. "This book opens," he said, "with the children of Israel held in slavery by the Egyptians and their Pharaoh. Verse eleven says, 'Therefore they did set over them taskmasters to afflict them with their burdens.' They were *slaves,* my friends. God's earthly people were held in captivity as slaves. Now God allowed them to be taken into slavery as a disciplinary act for their sins, but He did not leave them there. God is against slavery. When the time of discipline was over, He delivered them from slavery. On the night of the Passover, He set them free. And we hear Moses say in chapter thirteen, verse three, 'Remember this day, in which ye came out from Egypt, out of the house of bondage; for by strength of hand the LORD brought you out from this place.' The Lord, I say, is against slavery. He brought them out of the house of bondage.

"And if you know the book of Exodus, you know that the reason Pharaoh continued to resist God and set himself to hang onto his slaves was for the purpose of *free labor*. This is exactly what we've got going on below the Mason–Dixon line today. The wealthy plantation owners and the big businessmen who make money from cotton and other crops planted, cultivated, weeded, and harvested by slaves are determined to keep those slaves and fill their pockets with more and more wealth. This isn't right!"

There was a chorus of amens from the audience.

Chamberlain then closed his Bible and read from newspapers — both Northern and Southern — showing his hearers what was being said about states' rights and slavery. With each pro-slavery article, he quoted additional Scriptures that made it clear God never intended for one human being to own another. When he read the articles that stood for abolition, he lauded the writers, saying they were correct in their thinking.

The hour passed quickly. Professor Chamberlain closed in prayer, asking God to put a man of righteous character in the White House who would abolish slavery.

The next day Chamberlain opened his lecture by reading more Scripture and reminding his hearers of the Scripture they had considered the day before. He read more newspaper articles from both sides of the slavery issue.

"Now, ladies and gentlemen," he proceeded, "our founding fathers laid the foundation of this country on clear biblical principles. We will shoot ourselves in the foot if we stray from those principles.

"Furthermore, the United States was founded as a Union of one people. Our founding fathers did not vote themselves into a people. They recognized and declared that they were *already* a people. Therefore, I think of the people in the singular, as did our fathers. The people living in the states constitute the people of the United States. We all form one indivisible Union. This country and its land belongs to us all...and we to it.

"As you have heard from the articles I've read from Southern newspapers, there is talk in the South of a secession from the Union and a forming of the Confederate States of America. This would be an attack on our foundation as an indivisible people and nothing less than treason! If secession comes, it will be war on the Union and the Constitution. Such unthinkable conflict will bring untold damage, harm, and injury to this people, no matter on which side of the Mason–Dixon line they live."

Chamberlain was filled with emotion and had to stop and gain control of himself. When he resumed, he said, "It is apparent to the Southerners that if Abraham Lincoln is elected president in this coming election, it will be a death knell to their way of life. We must pray for this death knell, for slavery is an abomination to Almighty God. We must earnestly pray for Mr. Lincoln's election, and at the same time, pray that God will somehow keep this conflict from becoming a bloody war with fathers killing sons, sons killing fathers, brothers killing brothers…and worst of all, Christian brothers killing each other across fields of battle!"

Each day, Joshua Chamberlain stirred the emotions of students and faculty alike, giving them more Scripture refuting slavery and laying before them examples of dangerous attitudes being formed in the South. With deep emotion, he closed each session by calling for every one of his hearers to be in earnest prayer for the nation.

With war clouds hanging heavy over the nation, Shane Donovan graduated in May 1860, receiving his bachelor's degree in education. As planned, he soon signed up for the one-year master's program.

The national election was held in November, and Abraham Lincoln was elected president of the United States. Southern political leaders considered Lincoln's election the final affront in a long series of provocations that had pushed their states to the brink of secession. Ironically, it was the Southern political leaders themselves who had split the Democratic ticket, thus insuring Lincoln's election as a Republican.

The United States did not remain united very long.

In December, a secession meeting was held in South Carolina, and that state seceded from the Union. Others were seriously contemplating it. Lincoln hoped to bring the Southerners back, and in the weeks that followed, worked hard to do so. He did not want civil war.

✤ ✤ ✤ ✤ ✤

While the war question festered, Shane labored hard on his studies, while working at the lumber mill and giving Charolette as much of his time as possible. There was also the Sunday school class, which he taught faithfully every Sunday.

By the end of his first semester, Shane was number one on the dean's list in the graduate school. When his name appeared on the president's report, he was summoned to Dr. Woods's office at the close of the school day. The president's secretary ushered Shane into the office, and Dr. Woods rose to his feet behind the desk and gave him one of his rare smiles.

"I was told that you wanted to see me, sir," Shane said.

"That's right, my boy," Woods said, rounding the desk and extending his hand. "I want to be the first to inform you that you are number one on the dean's list in the graduate school. I know the kind of work load you carry, working at the mill for your father. And you're a married man with responsibilities at home. To have achieved these grades, you have to be a master of your time. Congratulations."

"Thank you, sir. I'm determined to be a college professor, as you know, and I want to be as good a professor as Mr. Chamberlain."

"You're well on your way, I'll say that."

Shane cleared his throat nervously. "Sir, since I'm here, may I tell you something that's on my mind?"

"With a mind like yours, you sure can! What is it?"

"Well, sir, I have a big dream. Nothing could make me happier than to teach right here at my alma mater after I receive my master's degree. Would…would you consider my application?"

Woods laid a firm hand on Shane's shoulder and smiled again. "Let's consider the job applied for, son. I happen to know that there will be an opening in the faculty next fall that's right down your line. I'll tell you right now. The job is yours. We'll work on the details next spring."

"Thank you, sir!" Shane said, shaking the president's hand. "Thank you very much! My wife is going to be very happy when I tell her about this!"

CHAPTER TWELVE

By February 1, 1861, six more states had pulled out of the Union: Texas, Florida, Mississippi, Georgia, Alabama, and Louisiana. The seven states were in agreement. Northerners were interfering with the Southern practice of "that particular institution," *slavery*. The seceding states drew up a proclamation, which stated in part: "The people of the North have denounced as sinful the institution of slavery; they have permitted the open establishment among them of abolition societies, and have united in the election of a man to the high office of President of the United States whose opinions and purposes are hostile to slavery."

Even though he had not yet taken office, the president-elect continued to work at trying to bring the Southerners back to the Union; President James Buchanan stood by and did nothing. Lincoln pled with Buchanan to meet with Confederate leaders and do all he could to break down the barriers between the Northern and Southern states. Buchanan turned a deaf ear.

Lincoln then began to contact individual congressmen, attempting to persuade them to negotiate with Southern leaders. Some of them made a few feeble efforts, but they were ineffective.

On February 8, delegates from the seven seceded states met at Montgomery, Alabama, and founded the Confederate States of

America. The next day, the congress of delegates elected Jefferson Davis as their president. Among the plans made to protect the security of their new nation was the seizure of the coastal forts and navy yards in the southern harbors. Jefferson Davis immediately bolstered his military forces to make these seizures a reality.

On March 4, 1861 Lincoln took the oath of office. His inaugural address made his position on secession crystal clear as he spoke to the Southerners: "In your hands and not in mine, is the momentous issue of civil war. No state, upon its own mere action, can lawfully secede from the Union. I shall take care, as the Constitution itself expressly enjoins upon me, that the laws of the Union be faithfully executed in all the states. The power confided to me will be used to hold, occupy, and possess the property and places belonging to the United States government."

Davis's forces had moved swiftly, and by the time Lincoln was inaugurated, only two Southern forts remained under the Federal flag — Fort Sumter at Charleston, South Carolina, and Fort Pickens at Pensacola, Florida. The Union commanders at the forts that were now in Confederate hands had given up and left without a fight, feeling that holding their positions was not worth the risk of civil war. President James Buchanan had concurred, agreeing that they should lay down their arms and peacefully surrender their posts.

At Fort Sumter, however, tension grew between the militant citizens of Charleston and the small Union force stationed there. Major Robert Anderson, Union commander at Sumter, was determined to hold the fort.

Spring came, and along with green grass, budding trees, and flowers came ominous clouds of war.

On Saturday morning, April 13, Shane and Charolette Donovan were sitting at the breakfast table. Shane was in his work clothes, ready to head for the lumber mill. Charolette was still in her robe and slippers, enjoying a second cup of coffee.

Shane had the previous day's edition of the *Brunswick Times* spread before him, and he was shaking his head.

"What is it, darling?" Charolette asked.

Shane raised his eyes to meet hers. "Charly, it's not looking good at all down South. Real trouble is brewing at Fort Sumter."

"The citizens making threats to take the fort?"

"Much worse. Jefferson Davis has General Pierre Beauregard commanding a group of warships at Charleston Harbor. They've got the fort surrounded, and on Thursday, Beauregard demanded that Major Anderson and his men evacuate the fort. Major Anderson has refused to give in. He's willing to stand and fight."

"If Beauregard fires on the fort, we'll be at war, won't we?"

"Yes, we will."

Shane folded the newspaper, laid it on the table, and shoved his chair back. As he stood up, Charolette set down her coffee cup and rose to her feet. She moved to him, and they kissed long and fervently. Shane took his work hat off a peg, dropped it on his head, and the two of them walked to the front door of the small cottage, each with an arm around the other. Shane opened the door, kissed her once more, told her he loved her, and headed across the porch.

The walk to the mill was only about a half-mile. When he was almost to the corner, he turned and looked back. Charolette always watched him from the porch until he passed from view. He waved, and she waved back, throwing him a kiss. He was starting around the corner when he saw a crowd gathered three blocks away near Brunswick's business district. Mike O'Hanlon was running toward him from the same direction.

Shane broke into a run, and as the best friends drew abreast, Mike gasped, "Shane, it happened!"

"What happened?"

"The Confederates bombarded Fort Sumter yesterday, and Major Anderson and his men fought back! We're at war with the

Confederates! The message just came on the telegraph to the *Brunswick Times* from Washington. Their employees are on the streets shouting the news."

Shane's face went white. "I knew it. Charly and I were just talking about it. I told her Major Anderson wouldn't back down."

"Makes me feel sick all over."

"Yeah, me too. The Stars and Stripes are under fire by Southern traitors. Well, guess I better go tell Charly."

Another telegraph message arrived at the Brunswick newspaper late that afternoon, informing them that Fort Sumter had been under heavy fire since dawn that morning, but Major Anderson and his men were still holding firm.

The editor of the *Brunswick Times* ordered his staff to prepare a special edition, putting the story under bold headlines on the front page. The edition was on the streets and in the hands of Brunswick's citizens by 7:00 P.M.

More news came on Sunday, and was spread by word of mouth, since the newspaper offices were closed. The editor had stayed at the office all day to receive any word that might come from his sources in Washington.

By midday Monday, April 15, news had come to the people of Brunswick that in order to save the lives of his men, Major Anderson had surrendered Fort Sumter to General Beauregard on Sunday. The old flag had been hauled down and was in the hands of the traitors.

The first-hour class at Bowdoin College was canceled, and all students, faculty, and college employees gathered solemnly in the chapel. President Leonard Woods stood before the crowd and told them the latest news. With dejection in his voice, he said, "I have asked our Professor Joshua Chamberlain to address us on an impromptu basis in this dark hour. I have the utmost confidence in

Professor Chamberlain and feel that he is best equipped to speak to us at this time."

Woods stepped back from the pulpit and gestured toward Chamberlain. "Professor..."

Chamberlain stepped before the crowd, cleared his throat, and said, "Ladies and gentlemen, I am an American. I love my country, and if some transatlantic force were to attempt to invade these sacred shores, I would be among the very first to take up arms against it."

There was a chorus of amens from the crowd.

"We have all been stunned to learn that the Confederacy has been so bold as to fire on United States property. We do not yet know if there are casualties amongst Major Anderson and his men, but I pray none have been killed or seriously injured. By this deplorable act, the flag of the nation has been insulted, the honor and authority of the Union has been defied, and the integrity and existence of the people of the United States of America have been assailed in open and bitter military attack. If I know our president as I think I do, this kind of aggression will not be taken lightly. Mr. Lincoln will call for retaliation. Civil war is inevitable."

Both men and women were wiping tears. Chamberlain turned to the president, who sat behind him on the platform.

"Dr. Woods, I believe the best thing we can do at this point is to break this crowd up into small groups and have a session of prayer. We must ask God to give wisdom to President Lincoln and our national leaders."

Woods stepped to the pulpit, laid a hand on Chamberlain's shoulder, and said to the crowd, "Let us do as our esteemed professor has suggested."

A cloud of gloom hovered over Brunswick, Maine, as well as over the entire Union. People moved about in every hamlet, town, and city as if they were in a daze.

On Tuesday, April 16, news came that President Lincoln had issued a plea for seventy-five thousand men to enlist in the Northern army. The Confederacy must be put down, and Lincoln felt if he could add that many volunteers to the existing U.S. army, victory could be achieved within three months.

Over three hundred men from Brunswick enlisted, including several single upperclassmen of Bowdoin College. They were lauded by President Woods for their patriotism and were told that upon their return, special classes would be held so they could catch up with their studies.

The volunteers from Brunswick were scheduled to join several hundred other volunteers from the state of Maine at Portland to be transported by ship to an undesignated port in Maryland. They would then march to a military camp set up near Washington, D.C.

All Maine volunteers were to board the ship at Portland Harbor on Saturday afternoon, April 27, at 4:00 P.M. Brunswick's volunteers were set to march out of their town at 9:00 A.M. for the twenty-one-mile hike to Portland. Brunswick's town council put the word out that all the town's citizens and those of the surrounding area should gather on Brunswick's main street to give them a proper send-off.

The crowd gathered, with many waving American flags as the volunteers assembled to begin the march. The street was lined with cheering people of all ages. Every business had closed for the occasion, and all employees were expected to be on hand.

The Bowdoin College band joined with the Brunswick High School band to play a military march. Flags waved and the people cheered as the Maine Volunteers marched southward out of the town, carrying what guns and ammunition they owned.

When they had passed from view, the crowd dispersed, with the people discussing the war and agreeing that it would be over in less than three months.

Joshua Chamberlain, Shane Donovan, and Mike and Lewis

O'Hanlon were talking together. Chamberlain rubbed his heavy mustache and said, "I'd like to be going with them. It would feel good to pay those Rebels back for what they did to Fort Sumter."

"Me too," Shane and Mike said together.

"Time you gentlemen could make it to Washington, it would all be over," Lewis said. "I think Mr. Lincoln is right. Won't take long to put those traitors down on their knees begging for mercy."

"I'm sure you're right, Mr. O'Hanlon," Shane said. "But I'd like to be there to see and hear it."

Graduation day at Bowdoin College came the third week of May. Shane received his master's degree, and the next day he was given a contract as instructor in first-year English, world literature, and American history for the next school year.

Late in May, visions of a quick end to the war began to vanish. There was news every day of Confederate resistance, resulting in skirmishes between Union and Confederate forces in many parts of Virginia. Before the month had ended, President Lincoln called for forty thousand more volunteers.

In June there was a bloody battle at Rich Mountain, Virginia, and the Confederates took a solid whipping. People of the North were again optimistic that the war would be ended inside of three months.

But news of more skirmishes came, not all of them victories for the Union. Northerners once again began to wonder if victory was going to be as simple as had been thought at the outset of the war.

Then came devastation. In mid-July, a fierce, bloody battle took place near Manassas, Virginia, along Bull Run Creek. The Federals were handed an embarrassing rout. The Rebels had come on so strong that hundreds of Yankee soldiers fled in panic from the battlefield.

The Union army returned to Washington like whipped dogs with their tails between their legs. There was no question that the War Between the States was going to last much longer than the Federals had figured.

There were more minor battles and skirmishes from Virginia to Missouri in August and early September, and the Southerners held strong.

When school opened in mid-September, Joshua Chamberlain was first to welcome Shane Donovan to the faculty. Shane was thrilled with his position, but was playfully harassed by Mike O'Hanlon about really being the old man.

As October came, President Lincoln called for more volunteers. Many volunteer regiments were forming in Maine and heading south to get into the war.

One Sunday afternoon in early October, the young Donovans and the young O'Hanlons were at the Chamberlain home, where they had eaten Sunday dinner. While the women were in the kitchen doing dishes and cleaning up, the Chamberlain children took naps. The men were in the parlor, discussing the Civil War.

"I don't know how much longer I'll be able to stand this," Joshua Chamberlain said. "It's hard to sit here in Maine and read about what's going on down south. I feel like it's my duty to join up and do my part."

"That's exactly how I feel, sir," Shane said. "I hate the thought of leaving Charly, but the longer this conflict goes on, the more I want to get into the thick of it."

"I don't want to leave Ashley, either," Mike said. "But there's a job to be done, and I should be in a blue uniform doing my duty."

"I don't have any military experience," Shane said, "but I could learn. I'm pretty good with a musket when it comes to hunting deer."

"Same for me," Mike said. "I've killed many a deer, but I've never carried a gun with the intent of killing human beings. But that's the way it has to be in war."

"I'd have to learn, too," Chamberlain said. "The only military experience I've had is a couple years at military academy in my teens. My brothers went there, too."

"I remember you mentioning your brothers back in the days when you taught our Sunday school class," Shane said. "You have three, if memory serves me. And…one sister?"

"Good memory. I'm the oldest. Horace came next, when I was six. Two years after that, Sarah was born. That was 1836. Then John, and the baby is brother Tom — Thomas Davee. He still lives at home near Brewer with our parents. He's thirteen years younger than I. Just turned twenty."

"They all live in the Brewer area?" Mike asked.

"Actually, Horace and Sarah live in Bangor with their families. John is still single. He lives in a small house between Bangor and Brewer."

The women entered the room, and the men stood up. When the ladies had seated themselves next to their husbands, the men sat down.

"Just when do you gentlemen plan to join the Union army?" Fannie asked.

"Oh, we don't have any plans," Joshua said. "We were just saying we'd like to get into the fight."

"So we heard. We weren't sure if this was just man talk, or if you were making plans we were going to hear about sometime soon."

Ashley laid a hand on her husband's arm and said to the group, "I hate the thought of Mike having to go off to war, but it will be his duty — and the duty of many thousands more — if this war isn't ended soon."

"That's what frightens me," Fannie said. "I know Josh's father has always wanted him to be a soldier. There are many soldiers amongst his ancestors."

"Well, I'm not going to be signing up unless it becomes a necessity," Joshua said.

"Me either," Shane said. "For right now, at least, I'm going to stay here and teach."

When the Donovans arrived home after church on Sunday night, Charolette began to fix them a light snack in the kitchen. Shane was seated at the table, and Charolette was at the cupboard, slicing bread, with her back to him.

"Shane...?"

"Yes, my love."

"The thought of sending you off to war puts ice in my blood. I can't bear to think about it. Oh, I hope it will be over soon."

Her back was still toward him, and tears had surfaced. She felt strong arms slide around her, and he kissed the back of her neck. She laid the knife down, turned, and wrapped her arms around his neck.

"Honey, I have to ask you," Shane said. "If this war does go on and more soldiers are needed...how would you take it if I signed up?"

There was a long silence.

"Darling, thousands of wives have already had to send their husbands off to that awful war. If...if you come to the place where you feel you should put on a uniform, how could I selfishly ask you not to go? I will back you all the way, Shane. Not without a heavy heart, you understand, but I will stand beside you in your decision."

Shane kissed the tip of her nose and said, "Sweetheart, you're the greatest wife a man ever had. I love you so. I would lay down my life to protect you from the Confederates if they invaded our land."

Charolette kissed her husband soundly and said, "Shane, I love you more than I ever realized a woman could love a man."

On Monday, at the Leprechaun Shoe and Boot Manufacturing Company, Lewis O'Hanlon was at his desk when he looked up to see Buster Kilrain standing at the office door, which was open.

"Top o' the mornin' to you, Lewis," Buster said. "Got a minute?"

"Sure. Come on in."

Buster approached the desk and said, "I've got something heavy on me heart, Lewis. I need to talk to you 'boot it."

"Of course. Sit down."

Buster took a seat in front of the desk and said, "Well, me friend, it's 'boot this here Civil War. As you know, ol' Buster Kilrain was a soldier in the Irish Army. I've seen combat and have a couple scars on me body to prove it."

Lewis leaned on the desk, looked Buster in the eye, and said, "Buster, you're in your late forties. Let the younger men do the fighting. Besides, with the new contract from the government to produce thousands of boots and shoes for the army, I need you here worse than McClellan needs you on some battlefield."

"But Lewis, the army needs me fightin' experience. So I'm a little past forty-five. Men are signin' up who are in their seventies. If we don't get this war won, you'll be makin' shoes and boots for Rebel feet…at the point of a gun."

Lewis eased back in his chair, sighed, and said, "How about giving it a little more time? Let's see what happens the next few months, okay? I understand an old soldier wanting to get back into uniform, but let it ride a little longer. Please? I really need you here."

Buster rose from the chair, grinned, and said, "All right, me friend. Since it's you askin', I'll give it a little longer."

"Thank you. Now if things turn for the worse in the war and needing to fight really gets under your hide, come and talk to me again."

"I surely will. You can, ah, bet your boots on it. Pardon the pun."

CHAPTER THIRTEEN

W hile the Civil War proceeded in the South, the name of Dwight Lyman Moody, a Congregational preacher from Northfield, Massachusetts, was on the lips of Christians all over the North.

The twenty-four-year-old evangelist had been converted to Christ out of religious skepticism at seventeen years of age while working as a shoe salesman in Boston. Moody was now making his home in Chicago, and was holding great evangelistic crusades in the larger Northern cities, seeing thousands coming to the Lord Jesus Christ for salvation.

Moody was closing out a series of evangelistic meetings in his hometown of Northfield on Friday, October 25, and Dr. George Adams had him scheduled to preach at First Parish Congregational Church in both morning and evening services on Sunday, October 27.

Placards on the walls of the church and of the main buildings at Bowdoin College announced Moody's coming. There was excitement all over the Brunswick area, and Christians invited lost loved ones and friends to the services to hear the fiery young preacher.

When the big day arrived, the stout-bodied evangelist thrilled the standing-room-only crowds with powerful, straight-forward

Bible preaching both morning and evening. Over a hundred citizens of Brunswick and the surrounding area responded to Moody's impassioned pleas to come to Christ.

After the Sunday evening service, many people stood in line to meet Moody and shake his hand. He was at the front doors of the church vestibule with Dr. and Mrs. Adams, and the line stretched all the way down the center aisle of the large auditorium to the platform. The Chamberlains, the Donovans, and the O'Hanlons were in the middle of the line, which was moving very slowly. They understood why by the time they reached the vestibule. Dwight L. Moody was a warm and personable man. He took time to ask each person if they were saved. If anyone answered no, Moody quickly turned him over to the pastor, who had counselors standing by to take him aside and lead him to Christ.

Ashley leaned close to Fannie and said, "Looks like your father knew that Mr. Moody does evangelistic work at the door, too."

"Yes. Papa hurried him away this morning, but Mr. Moody insisted on meeting the people at the door tonight. I heard Papa telling the counselors before the service this evening to be ready for this."

When the Chamberlains finally reached the evangelist, he greeted the children first, then shook hands with Fannie and Joshua.

"Pastor's daughter, eh?" Moody said, while shaking Fannie's hand. "I love preacher's kids. How long have you been saved?"

"Since I was eleven, Mr. Moody. And what a joy to know Jesus all these years!"

"Amen!" Moody then gripped Joshua's hand and asked, "How about you, preacher's son-in-law? How long have you been saved?"

"Since I was sixteen. I got saved up in Bangor under preaching just like yours."

"Praise the Lord!" Moody said.

Moody also questioned the Donovans and the O'Hanlons as he shook their hands. He was happy to know they could give solid, clear-cut testimonies of their salvation.

"Mr. Moody, I'm one of the instructors at Bowdoin," Shane said. "Are you going to be preaching in chapel tomorrow?"

"Sorry, but I can't. Dr. Woods asked me to, but I have to catch a train in Portland early in the morning. I'm now doing extensive work with the Young Men's Christian Association in Chicago, and I have to be there for a meeting Tuesday morning."

"Well, sir, I'd love to hear you some more. That was great preaching today. The Lord bless you."

"And may He bless you too, Mr. Donovan."

The three couples went to the Chamberlain home, where Shane and Mike played with the children while the women prepared a snack. Grace and Wyllys were fed, then put to bed.

While the couples were eating, the discussion turned to the Civil War. President Lincoln was calling for more volunteers.

"The war is a long way from over unless some miracle takes place," Fannie said. "Our husbands must do their part if it drags on much longer. I'd like for us to ask the Lord to give us wives the grace we'll need if our husbands have to enlist."

"I'll vote for that," Charolette said.

"Me too," Ashley said, taking a tight hold on Mike's hand.

Fall turned to winter, and severe weather set in. Maine winters were notoriously cold and snowy, and January 1862 was worse than normal. While the people of Maine battled the elements, the Civil War went on in the South. President Lincoln called for yet more volunteers, and more regiments formed in Maine and headed for Washington by railroad from Portland.

One day in late March, Ashley stood by as Dr. James Holladay — family physician of both the Donovans and the

O'Hanlons — sat on the bedside of Charolette Donovan, listening to her lungs with a stethoscope. Her face was pale and drawn. Holladay finished listening and dropped the twin prongs of the stethoscope around his neck.

"What do you think, Doctor?" Ashley asked.

Charolette put a hand to her mouth, coughed three times, and set her eyes on the physician.

"Her cold is better. I'd be worried if it wasn't after seven days. Her lungs are not nearly as congested as they were a week ago, and her temperature is almost down to normal. I'm a little concerned that the cough medicine I gave her hasn't done a better job relieving her cough, though." He pulled a dark-colored bottle from his black bag and looked at Charolette. "Let's put you on this. I think it'll work better than the other." Holladay rose to his feet and stuffed his stethoscope in the bag.

"You've been here with her every day, haven't you?" he said, turning to Ashley.

"Yes, sir."

"You're a very good friend, I'll say that."

"I'm her best friend, Doctor. And I'll be here every day until she's on her feet and feeling well again."

"I'll be back to check on you in another week," Holladay said to Charolette. "Of course, if the cough doesn't get better, let me know. I expect, though, that this new medicine will clear it up."

The front door was heard to open and close.

Charolette coughed again and said, "That'll be Shane."

Still in his heavy overcoat and hat, Shane appeared quickly at the bedroom door, smiled at his wife, then at Ashley, and said, "Hello, Dr. Holladay. How's she doing?"

"Her lungs have cleared up a lot, Shane, but her cough is still bad. I'm changing her cough medicine, hoping the new stuff will help her."

"Good. I want her out of that bed real soon." He winked at Charolette. "Ashley's been cooking for us every day since Charolette got sick, and I don't know how Mike makes it eating that horrible stuff all the time."

Ashley laughed and cuffed him playfully on the shoulder. "If I'd left the cooking to you, Charolette would be in her grave by now!"

The doctor chortled, shouldered into his coat, and clapped on his hat. "I'll leave the fighting to you two. I'm a man of peace."

In mid-April, the Chamberlains invited the Donovans and the O'Hanlons to their home for supper. Joshua's brother John had stopped for a couple of days to visit the family before leaving Maine for Washington, D.C.

As they sat at the supper table, Shane looked at the younger Chamberlain and said, "John, the professor tells me you graduated from Bangor Seminary last year."

"That's right."

"So what are you doing now?"

"I've been doing supply preaching in churches all over Maine. Many are those Josh has gotten me into because he knows the pastors. I haven't settled just what part of the ministry the Lord wants me in yet, but with the war on, it's hard to settle on anything. I've been praying about signing up with one of the Maine regiments, and I was about to do that a couple of weeks ago when the Lord opened a door of special service for me."

"Oh, what's that?" Mike said.

"Have you heard of an organization called the Christian Commission?"

"Can't say that I have."

John ran his eyes over the group. "Any of you?"

Every head was shaking no.

"Well, it's fairly new. By the way, Josh, you need to tell Dr. Adams about it. We need the church's support."

"So this Christian Commission you're going to tell us about is funded by support from churches?" Joshua asked.

"Mostly, yes. We do have some wealthy people in Bangor who send us money."

"What does your Christian Commission do, John?" Charolette said.

"We go to the battlefields and tend to the physical and spiritual needs of the soldiers. We distribute Bibles and Christian literature, along with what fruit we can lay our hands on. We write letters home for wounded men who are unable to do so…and just work at cheering up the troops."

"So you're on your way south to the battlefields?" Ashley asked.

"That's right."

"Will you be in danger?" Charolette asked.

"You might say so. Couple of our men have been hit with shrapnel when cannonballs have hit close. We even had one shot by a sniper. Only got a slight wound, though."

Charolette started to speak again, but went into a coughing spell and left the table. As she went to a back room, John looked at Shane. "She have this cough very long?"

"No, just a few weeks. Started with a cold. The cold's gone, but the cough isn't. Nothing the doctor gives her seems to work. He says she'll just have to wear it out."

"I'm afraid it's going to wear her out first," Ashley said. "I can tell she's lost some weight."

"You fellows ought to join the Commission," John said. "Good way to serve your country."

"I think it's fine if that's what the Lord puts on your heart, John," Joshua said. "But if I join anything, it's going to be the Union army. I want to fight those Rebels."

"Me too," Shane said.

"And me," Mike said.

Charolette returned to her place at the table and said, "Forgive me, all of you. I just can't seem to get rid of this miserable cough."

"There's nothing to forgive, Charolette," Fannie said, reaching over and patting her hand. "We've all had coughs. We know you can't help it."

The Civil War continued, and there was no end in sight. The Confederate army had taken a greater toll on the Union troops than any of the military leaders of the North had ever dreamed. General Robert E. Lee was proving to be an able leader, and he had some hardy and intelligent leaders under him, such as Thomas J. "Stonewall" Jackson, James Longstreet, and Pierre G. T. Beauregard.

At the same time, President Lincoln was having problems with his military leadership. There was conflict between Lincoln and his top general, George B. McClellan. In Lincoln's way of thinking, McClellan was not aggressive enough. McClellan insisted that he was simply a careful tactician who moved methodically in order to lose as few men as possible.

On July 1, 1862, Lincoln issued a plea to the governors of the Northern states for 300,000 more men to enlist in the Union army. Governor Israel Washburn of Maine filled the state's newspapers, asking for volunteers to fill the state's quota of eight regiments. Each regiment would be "one thousand strong," according to the governor.

Joshua Chamberlain could stand it no longer. His conscience was bothering him more and more. Other men had left their families to serve their country, and it was time for him to get into the fight.

But first, he must obtain a leave of absence from the college. The board of trustees, willing to part with a few men for the Union's cause, was giving leaves of absence quite readily to instructors. It was different with those of professor status. A man of that stature was more important to the college than to the military.

There was, Chamberlain knew, a legitimate way for him to obtain the leave. After two years of pressure and persuasion from President Leonard Woods and the board of trustees, Chamberlain had agreed to give up his professor of rhetoric position and take the chair of professor of modern languages of Europe. The trustees had offered him a great inducement: a two-year leave of absence to travel Europe whenever he chose, expenses for his family to travel with him, plus regular salary and a $500 bonus.

Chamberlain had planned to take the leave of absence beginning in the fall of 1861. But the war came, and he decided to put off the trip till the war was over. Now, he still had the leave coming, and though there would be no salary or bonus, he could lawfully be gone for the two years. Certainly the war would be over by then. He would talk to Dr. Woods about it.

Chamberlain was sure he could quickly raise the "thousand strong" needed for a regiment. He knew Shane and Mike were on the verge of enlisting, and so was one of his favored students, a single man named Ellis Spear. Ellis had spoken to him on several occasions about enlisting, the last time just two days ago.

And then there was his brother Tom who had come to see him and his family in late June. Tom was also on the verge of enlisting. With Shane, Mike, Ellis, and Tom eager to go to war, they would be good recruiters. With their help, and the help of others who would catch the fever, he was sure he could put a thousand men together in a matter of weeks.

Dr. Woods and the trustees agreed to the leave of absence on July 13. The next day, Chamberlain wrote to Governor Washburn offering his services to the army. Within two days, he had a favorable answer from Washburn and an invitation to come immediately to Augusta and see him. The letter stated that Washburn was pleased at Chamberlain's personal enthusiasm and was encouraged that he felt he could collect enough men for a full regiment.

During the two days it took to hear back from the governor, Chamberlain had told Fannie his plan and received her backing.

He also told Shane, Mike, and Ellis and sent a wire to Tom. Charolette and Ashley gave the same backing to their husbands that Fannie had.

By the afternoon of the second day, Joshua Chamberlain's recruiters had done their work, and over a hundred of his present and former students stated that they were ready to sign up in his regiment.

With the letter in hand, Chamberlain rode a fast horse to Augusta and was warmly welcomed by the governor. Washburn offered Chamberlain a colonel's commission and command of the regiment. Chamberlain was flattered, but told the governor he did not feel qualified since he had no military experience. He would rather start lower under a man who had combat experience and learn soldiering from him.

Washburn told him perhaps he could get Colonel Adelbert Ames to head up the new regiment. Ames, a Regular Army officer and Mainer from Rockland, had been seriously wounded at the Battle of Bull Run in July of 1861. He had now recuperated and was desirous of returning to the war. Washburn would contact him. The governor asked Chamberlain to keep working in the meantime to recruit men for the regiment, which Chamberlain assured him he would do.

Tom Chamberlain arrived in response to his brother's call and went to work with Joshua, Shane, Mike, Ellis, and several other men to sign up more recruits. While other Maine regiments were being put together, those who backed Chamberlain worked the hardest. Each new man contacted several others. Proud and patriotic Maine men, eager to serve their country and their state, signed up — farmers, clerks, lumbermen, storekeepers, lawyers, builders, school teachers, fishermen, merchant sailors, and college and seminary students.

Two days later, Governor Washburn summoned Joshua Chamberlain to his office in Augusta. When Chamberlain entered his office, Washburn shook his hand and said, "Well, Professor, I've got good news. Colonel Ames has signed up. He'll be your commander, and he's elated to be part of a Maine regiment."

"Good! I'm happy to hear it. And you'll be glad to know, sir, that we now have over four hundred men signed up. The recruiting is going well."

"Excellent, Lieutenant Colonel Chamberlain! You're doing a great job."

Joshua's eyes widened. "Lieutenant colonel, sir?"

"That's right. At least you will be officially in another few days."

"Why, thank you, Governor. I figured I might be made a captain, but you surprise me."

"You recall, my friend, that I was willing to make you a colonel, but you disqualified yourself. Since you'll be second in command under Colonel Ames, you should be a lieutenant colonel. I'll be appointing other officers according to how well they do in signing up men for the regiment."

"That's a fair way to do it, sir."

"I've got men working at the moment on a training camp for all the new Maine recruits," Washburn said. "It's on farm land just east of Portland. The farmer is Glenn Mason. He has generously offered to let us use twenty acres for training purposes, so I'm going to call it Camp Mason. Colonel Ames is going to take charge of the camp, as well as being commander of the Twentieth Maine."

"The Twentieth Maine, sir? That's our regiment?"

"Yes. You'll be traveling south with the Sixth, Seventh, Eleventh, Sixteenth, Seventeenth, Eighteenth, and Nineteenth regiments to give those Rebels their due. We're getting boots and shoes from the Leprechaun Company there in your town, and we've got caps and uniforms being hastily made by several clothing manufacturers. The men will have to train in their own clothes and footwear, but we should have sufficient uniforms and footwear by the time all the regiments are ready to head south."

"Sounds like we've got the wheels rolling, sir."

"Have to. We've got to do our part to give President Lincoln the troops he's calling for. We've got to put those Rebels down and end this awful war."

"Yes, sir. I'd like to get it over so all of us can go on with our lives."

"Well put, son. Check back here with me next week…Tuesday, let's say. By then we should have the grounds at Camp Mason ready, and Colonel Ames can begin his training program."

Charolette Donovan sat in Dr. James Holladay's office, with her husband beside her. She had almost gotten over the cough, but now it was coming back.

"So what do you think, Doctor?" Shane asked. "She doesn't have a cold this time."

"The only thing I can figure, Shane, is that about the time she would've gotten over the cough from the cold, we entered pollen and mold season. Her cough is from an allergy, or maybe from several allergies. When we get into fall and the first frost comes, this cough will clear up, I'm sure."

"I hope you're right, Doctor. She's really suffering with this thing."

"I just got some new cough syrup in. Comes highly recommended by the American Medical Association. It's got nothing habit-forming in it, but I believe it'll relieve the cough a great deal and ease the pain in her lungs."

Training for the Maine troops began at Camp Mason on August 14. Colonel Ames was a tall, slender, dark-haired man of twenty-six, and a graduate of West Point. He was all business, and military through and through. He immediately laid down strong disciplinary measures and began whipping the men into shape. Ames's military demeanor made the men all the more eager to fight Rebels. Their enthusiasm gained momentum as new recruits reported for training camp every day.

The married men from Brunswick returned home at night, traveling back and forth in wagons. On a Friday evening in the third week of August, Shane Donovan slid out of the wagon, told the other men he would see them the next morning, and wearily made his way toward the front door of his cottage. It had been a hard day.

Before he reached the porch, the door came open, and Charolette appeared, smiling at him with love in her eyes. It bothered Shane that she was so pale, though the latest cough medicine Dr. Holladay had given her had helped. It also bothered him that she had not gained back any of the weight she had lost.

"How's it been today?" he asked as he took her in his arms.

"How's what been?" she asked, kissing the tip of his grimy chin.

"You know…the cough."

"Oh, maybe a little better." She kissed his dirty chin again.

He laughed. "Honey, you'll get mud in your mouth doing that."

"So?" she said, kissing his grimy cheek this time. "It's your mud, so it's precious mud."

"You're silly," he said, and planted a kiss on her lips. When he released her, he grinned and said, "You ought to see your face. I put a big ol' smudge on it."

"Then I'll never wash it off." She turned her head away and covered her mouth as she coughed.

After Shane had bathed and combed his hair, they ate supper together.

"Does Colonel Ames still have you teaching men how to handle a musket?" Charolette asked.

"Mm-hmm. Tomorrow he's going to begin teaching us how to fight with bayonets."

"Oh, how awful! Shane, I don't like this. I wish this war was over. I can't bear to think of you out there on some battlefield with some Rebel trying to kill you with a bayonet. That's even worse than the idea of bullets flying."

"It's all part of it," he sighed. "War is war. Colonel Chamberlain told me that Mike and Tom and Ellis and I are going to start learning how to fire handguns."

"Really? Why?"

"Because officers wear handguns, and it looks like the four of us are going to be made officers because of how many men we've recruited."

"Well, I'm proud of you. How many men are signed up now?"

"As of yesterday morning, there were nine hundred and four. I know some more came in today, but I didn't hear any final count. We'll have our thousand strong in a few more days, I'm sure."

Charolette suddenly grew quiet. Tears filled her eyes, and her lips began to tremble.

"Aw, sweetheart," Shane said, leaving his chair. He rounded the table and put his arms around her. "Don't cry, Charly." He kissed her cheek. "I'll be home from that ol' war before you can bat an eye. Then we can go on with our lives. I'll be back teaching, and we'll have us a passel of little Shanes and little Charlys running all over this place."

CHAPTER FOURTEEN

The Maine recruits at Camp Mason began to receive heavy shipments of shoes and boots on August 18. Uniforms and caps started arriving in Portland by train on August 22, the same day the Twentieth Maine Regiment attained its "thousand strong." Colonel Ames placed the continuing influx of men into other regiments.

The hot August sun beat down on the camp as men were being drilled at one spot, while at other locations, they were learning hand-to-hand combat and musketry, and young officers were being trained with handguns.

Lieutenant Colonel Joshua Lawrence Chamberlain had caught on to bayonet fighting quickly and was now instructing new recruits in the art. Chamberlain worked with each man about ten minutes at a time. He stopped to rest a few minutes every half hour, then was back with a bayoneted musket in his hands, training another man.

During one half-hour break, he moved within the shade of a tree, took a deep draw on a water jug, and sat down. He was just leaning his head back against the trunk when he saw the stout form of a man with carrot-red hair standing over him.

"Top o' the mornin' to you, Colonel," Buster Kilrain said.

"It's afternoon, Buster." Chamberlain said.

"Aye, so 'tis," Kilrain said, glancing at the sun. "Anyway, nice to see you."

"Just what are *you* doing here?"

"Now, what do ye think a soldier would be a doin' at an army camp, me friend? I'm gettin' ready to go to war."

"You are, huh?"

"Aye."

"And what regiment did they put you in?"

"Well, they haven't yet, y'see. In fact, your commander doesn't even know I'm here. I figured to see you first."

"Buster, are you sure you want to do this?"

"Sure as God in heaven made little green apples."

"And Lewis O'Hanlon turned you loose to join the army?"

"Aye. With a little persuasion, ye understand."

"But you're what — forty-eight years old?"

"Forty-*seven*, I'll have ye know. They're signin' 'em up lots older than me all over the U.S."

"But not in Maine. The oldest man in our outfit is forty-five."

"So? What's two years? An' I bet I c'n whip any one o' them forty-five-year olds. Probably c'n whip 'em all at the same time."

Chamberlain laughed. "Okay, you've convinced me. Go on and tell Colonel Ames you want in."

"But, I don't want in just any regiment. I want in yours."

"We already have our quota, Buster. We were told to sign up a thousand, and we did. A 'thousand strong,' just like the governor said."

Buster leaned down low, looked the lieutenant colonel straight in the eye, and said, "Now, Joshua, you're the second in command in the Twentieth. With that much power, certainly ye c'n make it a thousand-and-*one* strong."

"Well, I could probably swing it."

"And somethin' else."

"Yes?" Chamberlain rose to his feet.

"I've got army experience. Plenty of it."

"Yes, I know."

"Now, I was a sergeant when I mustered out o' the Irish army. Seems to me like I ought to be a sergeant in this army, don't it to you?"

"Well, I'll see what I can do. Come with me." They walked together across the grassy field toward Colonel Ames's tent.

"Son, don't take this wrong," Buster said, "but you look a bit clumsy out there a-teachin' them boys bayonet fightin'."

"Really?"

"No offense, now, but you're goin' at it with your feet too close together…and y'need to hold the musket with your left hand closer to the muzzle."

"So you're experienced at bayonet fighting, are you?"

"Aye. Ye might say that."

Vivian "Buster" Kilrain was inducted into the Maine militia, assigned to the Twentieth Regiment at Joshua Chamberlain's request, and made a sergeant by Colonel Ames on the spot. Twenty minutes later, Chamberlain was sitting in the shade of his favorite tree watching Buster train the young recruits in bayonet fighting.

With sweat pouring off him, the forty-seven-year-old Irishman glanced at the man in the shade and said, "Me and me big mouth!"

The rest of the boots and shoes were there by August 27, and the remaining uniforms and caps arrived the next day. Governor Israel Washburn set departure date for Saturday, August 30. He had notified the railroad several days earlier to be ready on the last weekend of the month. The governor was assured that several trains would be at Portland, ready to haul the troops. One of the trains would have ample flat-bed stock cars to carry the horses the army was providing for the officers.

Among the officers appointed by Governor Washburn were Captain Ellis Spear, Captain Shane Donovan, Lieutenant Mike O'Hanlon, and Lieutenant Tom Chamberlain.

While the officers were at the tent where their uniforms were to be fitted, Mike leaned close to Shane and said, "So you outrank me, eh, captain? I didn't think you came up with that many more recruits than I did."

"Well, tell you what, sonny...Governor Washburn and Colonel Ames took something else into consideration."

"Oh? And what was that?"

"They know that older men are much more mature than younger men, and can handle a higher rank and the tough decisions that go with it."

Mike grabbed his stomach and said, "I think I'm going to be sick!"

The training camp was quiet on Friday, August 29. Those men from farther upstate had already told their families good-bye, and sat around now in the shade, talking in low tones. Those men who lived close enough to spend the day with their families did so. Though they were eager to get into the fight, there was a good deal of sadness.

At the Chamberlain home, Joshua packed his gear, then played with the children for a long time. When they went down for their naps, he sat with Fannie on the parlor couch and held her in his arms. They talked of old times and of their plans for the future. They hoped that this time President Lincoln had enough troops to swarm the enemy and bring surrender. They prayed that Joshua would be home soon and that life would return to normal.

⁎⁎⁎⁎⁎

At the O'Hanlon home, Mike and Ashley spent the day reminiscing about their childhood and marveling at how the Lord had brought them together as husband and wife. Ashley did her best to maintain her composure. She did fine until late in the afternoon. They were standing at the parlor window watching the sun drop below the treetops on the west side of the street. Mike was behind her, with his arms around her. He heard her sniffle and felt her body stiffen.

"Now, I thought we agreed there wouldn't be any tears," he said, turning her around to face him.

"I knew when I agreed to it, I wouldn't be able to keep from it. O Mike, I'm so scared!"

"Now Ashley, we've got to trust the Lord in all of this. He never makes a mistake. If He should let a bullet — "

"No!" she said, placing a trembling finger to his lips. "Don't talk like that! You've got to come home to me, Mike. You've just got to! God knows I need you."

"Then, just leave me in His hands as I go to war, as I must leave you in His hands here at home."

Ashley's entire body shook as she clung to her husband and sobbed as if her heart would shatter.

Shane and Charolette Donovan sat on the back porch of their cottage, holding hands and enjoying the shade from a pair of oak trees that hovered over the yard. For hours, they had talked about the loneliness they would both experience until Shane came home again. Charolette promised to pray for him many times every day, asking the Lord to keep him safe. Soon they grew quiet, each with their own thoughts, and continued to hold hands.

As the sun slowly set, a cool breeze tufted Charolette's long black hair. She smoothed it with her free hand, then coughed suddenly, using the hand to cover her mouth. Concern showed in Shane's eyes as he looked at her.

"I hate to go off and leave you with that cough still bothering you."

"Don't worry about me," she said. "I'll be all right. Soon as the first frost comes, I'll get over it."

"I hope you're right. You still don't have your color back."

"Well, I'll be rosy-cheeked and sassy next time you see me. Just wait and see."

At eleven o'clock on Saturday morning, August 30, 1862, the eight new Maine regiments did a dress parade on the streets of Portland, with spectators there from ten counties.

The people of Brunswick were out in great numbers to observe the Twentieth with a mixture of pride and enthusiasm. Colonel Adelbert Ames had placed the Twentieth Regiment in front of the others when they formed the parade. He and Lieutenant Colonel Joshua Chamberlain rode their horses just ahead of their regiment. Behind the Twentieth and in front of the Nineteenth, which followed next, was the Bowdoin College band.

It was a thrilling sight for all Mainers. The regiments were gloriously arrayed in snappy caps of dark blue with dark-blue uniforms that had shiny gold buttons and brass belt buckles. The officers wore crimson sashes and swords. Their revolvers and gunbelts would be issued, along with new rifles and ammunition for all the troops, when they arrived at the armory in Washington, D.C.

Chamberlain was resplendent astride the beautiful stone-gray stallion the army had provided him. Silver oak leaves denoting his rank gleamed from the gold-edged, light-blue shoulder straps of his dark-blue uniform. A leather belt, with fittings that held his shiny officer's sword and scabbard, wound around his waist and was fastened by a gilt and silver buckle.

The men of the Twentieth Maine admired Colonel Ames, but they admired their lieutenant colonel even more. There was something about Chamberlain's carriage and deportment that instilled confidence in them as they headed for unknown fields of battle.

The parade finally led to a spot in the center of Portland where Governor Washburn waited with the congress of the state of Maine. Fannie Chamberlain, Charolette Donovan, and Ashley O'Hanlon were in the crowd. The three wives held on to each other and wept when the eight thousand men in uniform raised their right hands and followed Governor Washburn as they took their oath of allegiance to the United States of America.

The trains were ready at the Portland depot a block away. The soldiers walked slowly to the depot, many of them accompanied by friends and family. The Chamberlains, the Donovans, and the O'Hanlons found private spots for a few last moments together before the trains pulled out.

Shane held Charolette close and said, "Charly, I love you so much. Please take care of yourself."

"I will, darling," she said. "Don't worry about me. I'll be fine. Just hurry home to me…and don't ever forget that in my heart I'll be right there beside you every minute. I love you, my precious husband, more than mortal words could ever express."

Shane squeezed her tight, then they kissed long and tenderly.

The three wives stood together with tears streaming down their faces as the train that bore their husbands chugged out of the station.

During the next week, Ashley often paced the floor of the cottage, praying and weeping. Lewis and Maureen knew she was having a difficult time and asked her to come and live with them, but she politely turned them down. She felt closer to Mike when she was in their house.

At the Leprechaun Shoe and Boot Company, Charolette had

her moments each day when she had to leave her desk and find a private spot to cry. Along with it, she coughed sometimes until her throat was sore. She returned to Dr. James Holladay, who examined her and assured her that the cough was the result of an allergy. It would clear up when the first frost came and took the pollen and mold out of the air.

By the second week, Charolette and Ashley agreed to trade off staying at each other's homes for the night. In the evenings they read the Bible and prayed together and wrote letters to their husbands…letters they wondered if Shane and Mike would ever receive.

"Where you from?" an idling sailor yelled to the new soldiers marching through Boston from the railroad station to the docks of Boston Harbor. Local residents, who had seen many an inexperienced regiment tramp the city's narrow streets on its way to war, turned to watch.

"We're from the land of spruce gum and buckwheat cakes, friend!" a Maine lumberjack-turned-soldier in the Twentieth Maine shouted back.

Everyone laughed, then an old man in the crowd lifted his cane, swung his hat, and called for three cheers for the men of Maine. "Hip, hip, hooray!" rang pleasantly in the ears of Adelbert Ames and Joshua Chamberlain as they sat astride their horses.

A woman cupped her hands to her mouth and shouted at Chamberlain, "Show ol' Bobby Lee who's boss, will you, handsome?"

Chamberlain smiled at her and lifted a hand.

The Maine regiments reached the wharves of the busy Massachusetts port and were told they would be placed aboard separate ships for their journey to Alexandria, Virginia. The Twentieth was placed aboard the U.S. steamer *Merrimac*. A smaller craft would follow, carrying their horses.

A great crowd of well-wishers had gathered on the docks. As the *Merrimac* began to pull away, the men of the Twentieth saw the arrival of a new regiment of Massachusetts soldiers, dressed in their new uniforms. One of the Massachusetts soldiers stood on the edge of the dock and shouted to the men on the *Merrimac,* "Three cheers for Old Abe and the Red, White, and Blue!"

The men of the Twentieth responded loudly, cheering their president and Old Glory. By the time they were out of the harbor, they were all hoarse from shouting. They were going to the war, and just in time, too. People on the streets had handed them newspapers full of news of a Union defeat at a second battle of Bull Run on August 29 and 30. They were saddened by the news and determined to help turn the tide.

Four days later, as the *Merrimac* carried the men of the Twentieth Maine up the wide Potomac after passing through the southern tip of Chesapeake Bay, the captain showed them George Washington's home at Mount Vernon. The place inspired such awe that many soldiers removed their caps in respect as they floated by.

It was midday when they arrived at Alexandria. Union officers who met them told Colonel Ames that the Twentieth Maine would become part of Third Brigade in the First Division of the Fifth Army Corps, Army of the Potomac under General Daniel Butterfield. They were to make camp on the bank of the Potomac for the night, and would march into Washington the next day, where they would have guns and ammunition issued to them. They would march on to Fort Craig, Virginia, seven miles outside of Washington. The other Maine regiments were attached to different brigades as they landed in Alexandria.

It was hot and humid as the men of the Twentieth did what they could to make themselves comfortable under the trees that lined the river's banks. Mike O'Hanlon was about to sit down under a tree with Shane Donovan and some other men when he noticed a string of boats steaming their way northward toward

Washington. It was what he saw on the boats that captured his attention.

"Shane, look!" he said.

Shane and the dozen or so men close by looked at Mike, who was pointing to the boats. "They've got wounded soldiers and…and *dead* ones on those boats."

Other Maine soldiers had seen them too, by then. All stood gaping as they beheld five boats with wounded men-in-blue lying on the decks. Six boats followed with lifeless forms covered with blankets and sheets.

Buster Kilrain stepped close to Mike, who was now sided by Shane. He sighed and said to both of them, "A hard sight for men who've not yet seen combat."

"Do you ever get used to sights like that, Uncle Buster?" Mike said.

"No, son. Never. It's all a part of this thing called war, but ye never get accustomed to seein' your pals bloodied, maimed, and killed."

Shane put an arm around Mike's neck, locked it snugly in the crook of his arm, and said, "I couldn't stand it if anything happened to you, Mike. You're like a brother to me. We've both got to come through this thing alive."

"I pray we do," Mike said with tears in his eyes. "But…if either of us should be killed, at least we know we'll see the other one in heaven. Thank God we're saved, Shane."

"Yes, praise the Lord for that."

As they prepared to march into Washington the next morning, the men of the Twentieth Maine saw more boats steaming up the Potomac from the south. As with the boats the day before, they were carrying dead and wounded Union soldiers to Washington from the Bull Run battlefield. The sight of them left a solemn feeling with the men from Maine.

They reached the armory in Washington at mid-morning and were issued brand new Enfield rifles and forty rounds of ammunition. The officers were given new Navy Colt .45 revolvers, gunbelts, and as many rounds. Equipped with their weapons, the "thousand-and-one strong" regiment marched through the city toward Fort Craig. The officers rode their horses.

Washington was alive with the military — squads of cavalrymen on their hardy mounts, battery horses pulling big cannons through the streets, wagon trains of supplies, and soldiers any direction one cared to look.

By way of Long Bridge across the Potomac River, the regiment marched seven miles, without a rest break, to join its assigned brigade at Fort Craig, Virginia. For the new recruits, it was a difficult march. Each man was wearing new boots and burdened with his personal possessions, heavy new rifle, and ammunition.

Footsore and weary at the end of the march, the Twentieth joined General Daniel Butterfield and his Third Brigade, First Division, Fifth Army Corps, Army of the Potomac.

There were five veteran regiments camped at the fort from Michigan, New York, and Pennsylvania. They had fought at the second Bull Run battle, and were battle-scarred, worn, and sharply reduced in numbers. They welcomed Colonel Ames and his thousand men warmly.

On September 12, the First Division, Fifth Corps moved out of Fort Craig, and the Twentieth Maine began its first long march. The soldiers of the Twentieth looked down from Arlington Heights to see the blue columns of troops preceding them across the Potomac, followed by artillery, cavalry, and rattling supply wagons. Bands played and sunlight glinted off the burnished rifle barrels.

Chamberlain was at his commander's side, the two of them making a handsome pair sitting erect on their mounts. The men of the regiment marched in a long column, their new uniforms and accouterments contrasting with the worn and sometimes blood-stained uniforms of the veterans. The latter marched with renewed vigor and confidence, their morale bolstered by the thousand men of the Twentieth Maine.

They arrived exhausted at their designated Union camp on the banks of the Monocacy River two miles from Frederick, Maryland, on September 14. While settling in at the Frederick camp, the men of the Twentieth Maine heard their first sounds of war. Distant cannons thundered as elements of the Union army battled the Confederates for possession of three South Mountain passes.

The next morning, orders came for the Twentieth Maine, along with other units, to move out. Robert E. Lee's army was assembling near the small Maryland town of Sharpsburg, and must be met head-on.

Signs of war were all about them as they marched. Wounded soldiers of both armies lay along the roads, and fresh mounds in the fields showed where the dead had been buried. They marched through Turner's Gap, the main pass through South Mountain, and saw more signs of battle. Debris was everywhere, giving evidence that cannonballs had blasted houses, barns, sheds, trees, bushes, animals, and humans.

Deeper in the pass lay unburied bodies of soldiers killed in battle. Some lay with their sightless eyes staring at the sun-filled sky above. All of the bodies were bloody, and some were bloated, turning the stomachs of the men of the Twentieth, who had yet to fire a shot in combat.

At one point, Joshua Chamberlain looked down from his horse and saw a dead Rebel soldier sitting with his back against a tree. There was a New Testament clutched solidly in his stiff fingers. Chamberlain turned to Ames and said, "Just a boy, sir. Probably not more than sixteen or seventeen. I hope he knew the Author of that little Book in his hand. If he did, I'll meet him in heaven someday."

Ames, who made no pretense of being a Christian, mumbled something indistinguishable, and they rode on.

At noon on September 16, 1862, the Twentieth Maine —

along with the other units that had been marching with them —
joined Major General George B. McClellan's massive Union force a
short distance from Sharpsburg.

A bloody battle was about to begin.

CHAPTER FIFTEEN

The Twentieth Maine Regiment camped on the south side of the road that led to Sharpsburg, just outside the small village of Keedysville. Across the way to the north, the sloping grassy meadows were thick with blue-uniformed men, horses, and equipment. Sporadic musket fire could be heard beyond the tree-lined crest of the slopes. Word was that General Joseph Hooker's brigade had crossed Antietam Creek and established itself there under sniper fire, making preparations to attack General Robert E. Lee's left flank the next morning.

A stiff wind whipped up while the reinforced Army of the Potomac made ready to face the Army of Northern Virginia on Union soil. Dark clouds began to form, and soon covered the Maryland sky.

The men of the Twentieth Maine observed as General George B. McClellan met beneath a cluster of oak trees a few yards away with Major General George W. Morell, commander of First Division, and Major General Daniel Butterfield, commander of Third Brigade of First Division. The three generals were in deep discussion.

The men of the Twentieth were amazed to see that General McClellan was of such small stature. They knew he was called Little

Mac, but none had realized he was barely five feet tall.

As they stood looking on, one of the Mainers commented, "It would take two of him to make a good-sized man."

"Tell ye what, soldier," Buster Kilrain said. "Don't judge a man by his size. Sometimes giants come in small bodies. From what I know, these men who have fought under General McClellan see him as just that — a military giant — much as the Frenchmen who fought under Napoleon Bonaparte saw *him*. You're goin' to be fightin' Rebels with the small man as your supreme commander. Learn to respect him for what he is on the inside, not the outside."

The soldier's face flushed and he said nothing more.

Captain Ellis Spear looked around at his fellow officers and said, "I wish we'd had more time for training. Our infantry can barely march in rudimentary formation, let alone quickly load and fire the new Enfields with any precision."

"Maybe that's what they're talking about over there," Mike O'Hanlon said. "Maybe General Butterfield is asking General McClellan to hold us in reserve, since we have no combat experience."

Colonel Adelbert Ames was standing close by and heard his officers talking. "I think not, Captain O'Hanlon," he said, stepping closer. "If Third Brigade is ordered into battle tomorrow, no regiment will be left out. Our men will just have to do the best they can…and while they are, they'll be getting valuable experience."

The wind eased some, but rain began to fall. It rained softly for the rest of the day and into the night. The men of the Twentieth Maine lay in their tents, finding sleep hard to come by. They wondered what part their regiment would have in the coming battle. And each man wondered if he would be among the living when September 17, 1862, was history.

The rain stopped about an hour before dawn, and the sky began to clear. Captain Shane Donovan had slept little. His thoughts had been on the battle at first, but in the last couple of hours, he concentrated on Charly, praying for her and thinking about her health.

Dawn came and with it the sudden sound of musketry and cannon, announcing the advance by General Hooker's brigade on Lee's left flank. Men scrambled about in the Twentieth Maine's camp, making ready under Colonel Ames's orders to be prepared to move out if the command came from General Morell through General Butterfield.

The sounds of battle beyond the crest of the meadows grew louder and more pronounced as the sun put in its appearance, and shortly thereafter, word came to Colonel Ames to push the Twentieth Maine to the top of the tree-lined ridge and wait in reserve.

A quarter-hour later, the Mainers, along with a few other units, were lying low in the wet grass atop the ridge, nerves taut. They watched as General McClellan sent his army to clash with the gray-uniformed invaders along the banks of Antietam Creek.

As the sun rose higher, the deadly spectacle unfolded in bloody panorama. Thousands of soldiers charged and counter-charged each other out of the woods, over cornfields and meadows, amid the deep-throated boom of cannons and the rattle of muskets. Victims were falling like flies beneath the blue-white smoke that formed in shapeless clouds over the field of battle. High-pitched Rebel yells punctuated the deafening roar, along with the shouts of the men in blue.

Shane Donovan lay in the grass between Lieutenant Colonel Joshua Chamberlain and Mike O'Hanlon.

"Colonel, have you ever wondered how you'll do when you're in the middle of a battle like that?" Shane asked.

"You mean if I'll have the desire to turn and run?"

"Something like that. A man can't know what he's made of until he faces the test."

"I think every man wonders just how he'll react when he's facing enemy gunfire."

"I sure do," Mike said. "I hope I don't turn coward and run."

"You aren't going to run, Mike," Chamberlain said. "You'll do just fine."

"I sure hope so, sir." Mike thought of Ashley and told himself he could never look her in the eye again if he showed himself to be a coward in combat.

Chamberlain raised up and ran his gaze over the rest of the Twentieth. Every man except Colonel Ames and Sergeant Kilrain was asking the same question, he told himself.

The battle dragged on, and some of the units held in reserve on top of the ridge were called into the conflict. The men of the Twentieth Maine waited.

The battle raged and the hours passed. Just before 4:00 o'clock, a rider galloped up the slope and found Colonel Ames, who was talking to the leader of a unit from Michigan some thirty yards from where his men sat in the grass under the trees. The rider spoke to Ames, pointing westward, then rode back down the slope. All eyes were on Ames as he hurried to where his officers were clustered.

Ames ran his eyes over the men — who were now on their feet — and said, "We've got orders from General McClellan to move two miles due west. General Franklin's troops are facing heavy opposition near there. General Butterfield says General McClellan wants us on hand for Franklin. We'll probably be called into action to support him."

The Twentieth Maine made a hard run for the designated spot, carrying their guns and ammunition. Only Colonel Ames went on horseback. The word once more was *wait.* They watched the battle rage, and could not believe the carnage taking place before their eyes. The battlefield was littered with dead and wounded soldiers and animals. Ames's regiment was appalled at the sight, but remained ready to charge into the fight when the order came.

Ellis Spear stood next to Joshua Chamberlain and said, "Colonel, I don't know how much more my nerves can stand. I think the rest of our unit is feeling the same way. Look at them."

Chamberlain ran his gaze along the line, observing faces.

There was no question that their nerves were raw.

"I'm feeling the same way," Chamberlain said, "but there's nothing any of us can do about it. General McClellan is on top of this thing. We have to trust him."

Suddenly, the same rider came galloping toward them.

"Look!" one of the men shouted. "That messenger's coming back! We're going into the fight, men! We're going to kill us some Rebels before the sun goes down!"

"We'll have to hurry," cried another. "The sun'll be down in half an hour!"

Every man in the Twentieth was on his feet, ready to go. Colonel Ames stepped up to meet the rider as he skidded to a halt, saluted and said, "Colonel, sir, General Butterfield sent me to tell you he just got orders from General McClellan."

"Yes?"

"You are to return the men to where you were earlier, sir. On the ridge. You are to wait there until you receive further orders."

Ames saw the dejection among his men. He lifted his voice so that all could hear. "Men, this is all part of being soldiers! I know you would rather fight than wait, but we must follow orders. We're to return to the ridge where we were before. Let's move out!"

Darkness had not quite settled over the land when the Twentieth reached the ridge. The sight that lay before them wrenched their stomachs. Thousands of bodies in blue and in gray lay in the fields, on the meadows, and along the creek banks, their silent forms offering a grim portent for the soldiers of the Twentieth Maine.

Orders came shortly for Ames's troops to return to the road where they had set up camp. Their hearts were torn as they marched in the darkness and heard the cries of wounded and dying men all around them.

During the night, General Robert E. Lee picked up his wounded and stealthily marched his army back into Virginia under cover of darkness. Lee's divisions had been severely battered by McClellan's reinforced army.

The next morning, word came to General Butterfield from General Morell to march Third Brigade through Sharpsburg and onto the north bank of the Potomac, where they were to await further orders. Morell warned that they should be alert for any Rebel troops that might have been left behind to safeguard the escape of the battered Confederate army. Colonel Ames passed the warning on to the men of the Twentieth Maine.

Word came down the line as the troops prepared to move out that McClellan's division leaders had tried to persuade him to chase Lee's crippled army down and destroy it. McClellan had refused to discuss it with them further, saying such a pursuit would do no good. It was reported that General Franklin had warned McClellan that President Lincoln would be furious if he bypassed the chance to wipe out Lee's army when it was so vulnerable. McClellan had turned a deaf ear.

As Third Brigade marched out, Ames and Chamberlain were riding side by side. Behind them on horseback were Captains Spear and Donovan and Lieutenants O'Hanlon and Chamberlain.

Ames was heard to sigh and say to Chamberlain, "McClellan's failure to pursue could be his undoing. I agree with Franklin. The president is not going to like it one bit when he hears about this."

With the other units of Third Brigade, the Twentieth Maine marched across yesterday's contested ground. Sprawled, heaped, crumpled bodies in blue and gray lay everywhere, interspersed with dead horses, overturned caissons, ammunition wagons, and cannons.

Just ahead, on the path the Yankee soldiers were taking, lay a wounded Rebel lieutenant who had been overlooked when the Confederates picked up their wounded the night before. Lieutenant

Gregory Downing had been shot twice in the Antietam battle. The first Yankee bullet hit him in the stomach. As he lay there in the meadow, knowing he was slowly bleeding to death, Yankee soldiers came running his way, dodging bullets. Downing pulled his revolver and fired at the closest man in blue. The Yankee went down, and his companions fired several shots at Downing. One of them grazed his head, knocking him unconscious.

Downing had come to sometime during the night, but the darkness was so thick, and he was so weak, he had no choice but to stay where he had fallen. When daylight came, Downing was amazed that he was still alive, though he knew he didn't have long to live. Blood from his abdomen wound was all around him. Not only that, but his pain was almost unbearable. He would rather die than suffer any longer.

The revolver! Where's my revolver? In agony, he twisted his body, searching for the gun. It took only a moment to spot it. It lay no more than the length of his body to his right. All he had to do was crawl a few feet, and he could reach it.

Downing struggled against the pain in his midsection and managed to reach the revolver. He gritted his teeth and rolled onto his back. With trembling thumb, he eared back the hammer. He was about to bring the muzzle to his mouth when he heard a horse blow, followed by the sound of hooves and tramping feet. He strained to raise his head and saw a mass of blue. He blinked and squinted until he brought the marching column of Union soldiers into focus. Out front were some officers on horses.

Why not? They'll put me out of my misery, and this way, I'll take a rotten Yankee officer with me.

Shane Donovan's horse was directly behind the stone-gray stallion that carried Joshua Chamberlain. Shane's mind was on Charly. He knew she would be at work in the factory office right then and wondered if she was thinking of him. His heart ached for her, to see her beautiful face and to hold her in his arms.

Something caught his eye off to the right. Then he saw the

movement again. It was a man in gray, on his side, shakily bringing a revolver to bear on Joshua Chamberlain.

"Colonel Chamberlain! Look out!" Shane shouted, whipping out his revolver. He gouged his horse's sides to put himself between the Rebel officer and Chamberlain.

Shane's horse leaped forward and brushed the rump of Chamberlain's mount, startling the stone-gray and making him do an abrupt side-step. At the same time, Downing's revolver fired. The bullet whizzed past Chamberlain's ear.

Shane steadied his gun on the Rebel officer and shouted, "Don't do it!"

But the officer was dogging back the hammer in a desperate attempt to fire another shot. Shane's gun roared. The slug struck Downing in the temple, killing him instantly.

Colonel Ames raised a hand to halt the column behind him and twisted in the saddle to look at Chamberlain. The lieutenant colonel's face was white as baking powder.

"You all right?" Ames said.

"Yes, sir, I'm fine." Chamberlain looked at Shane, who was off his horse, standing over the man he had just killed.

Mike O'Hanlon was off his mount too, dashing toward his best friend. When he got to him, he put an arm on his shoulder and felt Shane's body shaking.

"You all right?" Mike said.

Shane said nothing. He was looking at the dead Rebel officer, biting his lower lip, on the verge of tears.

Just then Chamberlain and Ames drew up. Ames had commanded the rest of the soldiers to hold their ranks. They looked on wide-eyed, as did the men of the other regiments.

"Shane, you saved my life," Chamberlain said.

"And put himself between you and the Rebel, sir," Mike said. "I saw it, Colonel Chamberlain. That's exactly what he did."

"I saw it, too," Tom Chamberlain said, who was now beside Mike.

Ames moved past Chamberlain and said, "Captain Donovan, you just did a wonderful thing. You put your own life at risk to save that of Colonel Chamberlain. We're all very proud of you."

Shane ran a sleeve across his tear-filled eyes and shook his head. Still staring at the man he had just killed, he said, "I'm glad I was able to keep him from shooting you, Colonel Chamberlain, but…it's the first time I've ever taken the life of another human being."

"These other men will have that first time too, Captain," Ames said. "I had mine at Rich Mountain a year ago in June. But you…you have distinguished yourself by an act of pure heroism."

Shane raised his head, looked at Ames, and said, "I'm no hero, sir. I just did what had to be done to save Colonel Chamberlain's life."

"You are a hero, Shane," Mike said. "Just like when you saved little Darlene Brainerd."

Chamberlain squeezed Shane's shoulder and said, "I'll never forget what you did here, Shane. And Fannie and my children will never forget, either. Words are weak vessels at a moment like this, but thank you. If you hadn't done what you did, I'd be lying dead over there on the road right now."

"It's time to go, gentlemen," Ames said. "We've still got a long way to march today."

As the officers of the Twentieth Maine turned and walked back toward the column of soldiers, a loud cheer went up for Captain Shane Donovan. He grinned shyly, his face tinting.

Before any of the officers mounted up, Ames ran his gaze along the line of men and said, "Captain Donovan is the first man of the Twentieth Maine Regiment to fire a shot in the Civil War. In so doing, he killed an enemy officer at the risk of his own life in order to save the life of his lieutenant colonel."

A louder cheer erupted from the thousand men of the regiment.

✱✱✱✱✱

The Twentieth Maine, along with the other units, marched through Sharpsburg, Maryland, and onto the north bank of the Potomac River, where they set up camp for the night. General Morell's warning for his men to stay alert for Rebel troops was well-spoken. The Rebels were dug in on the south bank of the river, right across from where the Union troops were setting up camp. The river was wide and shallow there and a favorite spot for crossing into Virginia. The Confederates would stay hidden until the Federals showed if they were going to pursue General Lee and his battered troops. If they started across, the Rebel guns would open up.

When morning came, the Confederates watched as all units but one marched away, heading north up the bank. What would the remaining unit do? The Rebels were outnumbered, but they had their orders from General Lee. They must not allow the Yankees to cross the river.

They did have some advantages, however, if the Union troops started across. They were well-hidden in heavy brush and trees. They would have more protection than the Yankees. And they would have the element of surprise.

Colonel Ames had explained to his men before the other troops marched away that General Butterfield had sent orders for the Twentieth to remain and wait for further instructions. He had plans for them, but had to get them approved by General McClellan. It would take a day or two.

Ames sent men to patrol the north bank of the Potomac and to keep a sharp eye for any suspicious activity across the river. He didn't trust the Confederates. They might do just as General Morell had said.

Colonel Ames then had a private conference with his lieutenant colonel, advising Chamberlain that he was going to recommend Shane Donovan for a Presidential Commendation. His act of unselfishness and heroism in saving Chamberlain's life must be recognized. Chamberlain was voicing his agreement when one of the men who had been sent on patrol came toward them, eyes wide.

"Colonel, I saw movement across the river! It was a gray uniform amongst the trees, and I'm sure I saw the mouths of a couple howitzers hidden in the brush!"

"Any of the others on patrol see anything?" Ames asked.

"I don't think so, sir. The instant I saw the Rebel uniform and the cannons, I came here."

"You didn't run, I hope."

"No, sir. I just slowly left the edge of the river and came straight here."

Ames told Chamberlain to send two men downriver till they were out of sight past the bend. They were to cross the Potomac and move up on the Confederate position from its blind side. If they confirmed that the Confederates were there, the Twentieth Maine would cross the shallow spot in the river and attack at dawn.

Chamberlain chose Buster Kilrain and Alex Cowbray for the mission. Before sundown, Buster and Alex returned to report that the man on patrol was indeed correct. They counted four howitzers and a unit of about two hundred men.

Word spread among the Mainers that they were going to make a surprise attack on the Rebel position at dawn. Ames met with the officers, explaining his plan, and the officers took the plans to their units. There was great excitement in the ranks of the Twentieth Maine as they prepared for their first confrontation.

CHAPTER SIXTEEN

It was mid-afternoon on Thursday, September 18, 1862. Charolette Donovan looked up from her desk and saw Fannie Chamberlain and Ashley O'Hanlon come through the office door. Charolette could tell both of them had been crying.

"Fannie...Ashley...what's wrong?" she asked, rising from her chair as they drew up.

Fannie's lips quivered. "I can tell you haven't heard."

"Heard what?"

"News came over the wire at the newspaper about forty-five minutes ago that the Twentieth was involved in a horrible battle yesterday at Sharpsburg, Maryland. There's no actual count yet, but Washington says it's the bloodiest battle the war has seen. Several thousand were killed, and several thousand more were wounded."

Charolette closed her eyes and prayed aloud, "O dear Lord, help us." A cough broke from her lips. She pulled a hanky from her sleeve and coughed into it, putting the other hand to her chest.

Lewis O'Hanlon emerged from his office looking at some papers in his hand. He was about to say something to Charolette when he saw Fannie and Ashley. He stopped, looked at their wan expressions, then looked at Charolette, who was bracing herself against the desk.

"Ladies…what's wrong?" he asked.

"A wire just came in to the *Brunswick Times,*" Fannie said. "Father happened to be there when it came in. Our regiment was involved in the worst battle since the war began. At Sharpsburg, Maryland. All we know is that several thousand were killed, and thousands more were wounded."

Charolette lowered herself onto her chair, her knees feeling watery. Lewis felt his own knees go weak as he laid a hand on Charolette's shoulder and said, "Would you like a cup of water?"

"I'll get it," Ashley said, and went to a nearby cupboard where a jar of water was kept. Several tin cups were lined up, each bearing the name of an office employee. She filled Charolette's cup and hurried back to the desk.

"Father is calling a special prayer meeting at the church tonight at 7:00 o'clock," Fannie said. "I hope you can be there, Mr. O'Hanlon."

"We'll be there. In fact, I'm going to head home right now and tell Maureen. I hate to have to tell her about the battle, but she needs to know."

Charolette was sipping the water when she choked and began to cough again. Ashley patted her back until the coughing subsided, then Lewis said, "Ladies, this war is a terrible thing. We've only one recourse to this kind of news. We must continue to hold our soldiers before the Lord in prayer and trust Him to take care of them."

"If…if we could only know," Charolette said. "If we could only know that they're all right."

Ashley blinked at the tears in her eyes and said, "All we can do is keep praying and wait for an answer to our letters."

"I can think of one good thing that will come out of this horrible war," Fannie said. "It's going to teach us how to lean on the Lord like we never have before."

*****

Just before dawn on Friday, September 19, Colonel Adelbert Ames had his men spread out along the north bank of the Potomac. Five hundred of them were to cross the river, while the other five hundred remained on the bank to provide cover. Half of the five hundred who crossed the river would close in on the west side, and the other half on the east, leaving the center for a barrage of musket fire when Ames launched the surprise attack. Lieutenant Colonel Joshua Chamberlain was on his horse and would lead the unit going in from the west.

Colonel Ames watched as his men waded across the seventy yard span of water. Dawn was breaking, and they looked like specters moving among the mists that hovered thinly over the surface of the Potomac. When the five hundred were ten feet from the shore, Ames gave his signal, and the soldiers on the far bank opened fire. It took the Rebels several minutes to begin firing back, so successful had been Ames's surprise attack.

The barrage went on for nearly half an hour. Suddenly Ames saw Joshua Chamberlain riding into the river, waving his cap and shouting, "Cease fire! Cease fire!"

Ames shouted for the men to stop firing as Chamberlain splashed up on his horse and said, "They took off, Colonel. We'd have had to shoot them in the back to stop them, and I couldn't give that kind of an order."

"You did right, Chamberlain. Anybody get hit?"

"Not on our side, sir. There are some dead Rebels in the brush. Maybe four or five. They took their wounded with them."

"All right. Let's get our men back over here."

For the six weeks that followed the Antietam Battle and the Twentieth Maine's skirmish on the Potomac, the regiment was used to guard some of the Potomac's fords. During that time they were drilled, trained, and toughened by Colonel Ames.

The first day of October brought President Lincoln himself to the banks of the Potomac. He wanted to have a talk with his top general and picked the spot where he could meet with General George B. McClellan and take a look at the troops. Everyone knew the president was perturbed with McClellan for not pursuing the battered and disheartened Confederate army when he had the men, guns, and full opportunity to overpower them.

Though Lincoln's conference with McClellan was held privately in a field tent, the men of the Twentieth Maine were thrilled to see the president when he reviewed their regiment and others camped nearby. When the president had moved from the Twentieth Maine to another regiment, Joshua Chamberlain commented about Lincoln's drawn features and his deep, sad eyes to the officers who stood by him.

On October 15, mail arrived from home. That evening, as men sat beside the campfires, Shane Donovan was sitting alone by a fire, pouring over four letters that had come from Charolette. He looked up to see his best friend standing over him.

"Mind if I sit down?" Mike said.

"Of course not."

"Well, I figure you might want to be alone with Charly…in the letters, I mean."

"I have been for a while. It's okay."

Mike eased down across the fire from Shane, sitting Indian-style. "How many letters did you get?"

"Four from my parents and four from Charly. You?"

"Three from my folks. Four from Ashley."

"Everything all right?"

"Yeah. Sorry about Charly. Ashley filled me in."

"What do you mean?"

"The cough."

Shane looked at the four letters in his hand, then back at his friend. "You'll have to tell me what you mean, Mike. Charly hasn't even mentioned the cough. I figured it had cleared up."

"Why wouldn't she tell you about it?"

"Doesn't want me to worry, I guess. What do you know about it?"

"Well, Ashley says it's getting worse. The last letter said it's already frosted several times in Maine, but the frost didn't help at all. It's not an allergy."

"I had a strong feeling it wasn't an allergy. Any mention by Ashley or your parents about receiving the letters you've sent them?"

"Nope."

"Not in mine either. Guess the mail we've sent home isn't getting through."

"No surprise. Look, Shane, I'm sorry if I've upset you. Guess I should've kept my mouth shut. I…I just figured Charly was letting you know about herself."

"Don't feel bad. You naturally thought Charly would tell me how she was doing. I don't really blame her, either. She just doesn't want her condition weighing heavy on my mind. She knows if she told me it was worse, it would do exactly that."

"And now that I've shot off my big mouth, it *will* weigh heavy on your mind."

"Hey, it's all right. At least knowing that the cough is worse, I can pray more intelligently about it."

Mike walked around the fire and put an arm around Shane's shoulder. "Why don't we pray right now for her?"

Shane smiled, blinked at the tears that had surfaced, and said softly, "Yes. Let's do that."

✳ ✳ ✳ ✳ ✳

Dr. James Holladay stood over Charolette Donovan as she sat on his examining table.

"Do you want me to bring them in and tell them?" he said.

She nodded, biting her lips. A moment later, Garth and Pearl Donovan and Ashley O'Hanlon were seated on straight-backed chairs beside the examining table, deep concern showing in their eyes.

Holladay leaned on the table next to Charolette, looked down at them and said, "There's no question, now. She has consumption. I held out hope that it was something — anything — else, but since she's been coughing up blood these past several days, I can come to no other conclusion. As you know, it was consumption that took her mother in her early thirties."

"What now, Doctor?" Pearl asked.

"Well, she'll have her good days and her bad days. Up to this point, she hasn't missed a day of work, even though she's gone to the factory when she really didn't feel like it. And she's young. The consumption isn't going to go away, but she could get better and have more good days than bad ones."

Garth looked at Charolette and said, "What's Lewis's attitude about this? Will he continue to let you work for him if you should have to ask for a day off now and then?"

"Yes, he told me I could work for him even if I could only come in every other day."

Garth looked at his daughter-in-law with tender eyes. "Charolette, you know that Pearl and I love you as if you were our own daughter."

"Yes. You've shown me that over and over again."

"We've offered to have you come live with us before, and we're offering it again. If it would help, we'd love to have you."

Charolette thought on it for a moment. "Papa Donovan...I love you both so very much, and I appreciate your offer. Maybe the day will come when I'll need to take you up on it. But...our little cottage is where Shane and I started our marriage. I really need to be in the house. I feel so much closer to Shane there. Can you understand that?"

"Yes, of course. Just know that you're welcome at our place at any time should you change your mind."

"Thank you."

Ashley took hold of Charolette's hand. "I don't want to push myself on you, Charolette, but if it would help for me to stay with you on weekends, I'll be glad to do it. We can ride back and forth to church together on Sundays."

"Ashley, you're already doing far more than you should, giving me your nights. I can't ask you to — "

"You didn't ask. I volunteered. And to make it easier for you, I'll come to your house every time rather than you coming to my house every other night during the week. I know that will take some load off you."

"But, Ashley — "

"Ah, ah, ah! There will be no argument. It's a settled matter. Then...if the day comes when you decide to move in with your in-laws, I'll step out of the picture."

Tears filmed Charolette's eyes. She opened her arms, and the two of them embraced.

After a few seconds, Charolette said to Ashley and her in-laws, "I don't want Shane to know that it's consumption. Not now, I mean. He's got enough on his mind as it is."

"But, honey," Pearl said, "he has a right to know. He's your husband."

"Pearl's right," Garth said. "We'll be glad to write him if you say it's okay."

"Well, we don't even know if our letters have reached Shane and Mike," Ashley said. "Even if you wrote to him, you wouldn't know if he got it."

"All we can do is try," Pearl said. "How about it, Charolette?

May Garth and I write and tell him?"

"Maybe I could find him and tell him," came a familiar voice from across the room.

All eyes turned to see John Calhoun Chamberlain standing at the clinic door.

"Hello, John," Garth said. "How long have you been there?"

"We've been here long enough to learn that Charolette's been diagnosed with consumption," Fannie said, stepping around her brother-in-law. "John arrived just this morning on a little furlough. We were across the street at Strother's buying him some new clothes when I saw all of you come into the office."

Fannie moved toward the table and took Charolette in her arms. "O Charolette, I'm so sorry to hear this."

"John, you said maybe you could find Shane and tell him," Garth said. "Are you going where the Twentieth is?"

"Yes, sir. I have to leave tomorrow. I've been up in Brewer visiting my parents and stopped by to see Fannie and the children just for today."

"Do you know about the Twentieth?" Pearl asked. "I mean, how it went for them at Sharpsburg?"

"No, ma'am, I don't. The Christian Commission has had me at Washington up until a week ago working with the wounded soldiers. I tried to see if any of the Twentieth Maine had been wounded at Sharpsburg, but couldn't find out a thing. I do know they're assigned somewhere along the Potomac River, but that's all. I'm going back to Washington two days early so I can find Tom and Joshua. If any of you want to send letters along with me, I'll be glad to take them."

"John," Ashley said, "if you get there and…and find out that Mike and Shane are all right — or if…well, you know. Is there a way you can notify us?"

John shook his head. "Afraid not. The wire service is strictly for military and newspaper use. All I can do is write to you, but things are pretty hectic down there. Looks like it's going to get worse before it gets better. The mail isn't getting through very well."

"We've found that out," Fannie said. "None of us has heard a thing since those men of ours left nearly two months ago."

"Well, you get those letters written," John said, "and I'll do my dead-level best to deliver them."

Charolette looked at Pearl and Garth and said, "I'll write a letter and send it with John. You're right. I hate to worry Shane, but he has a right to know how I am. I certainly would want to know if it was the other way around."

On the afternoon of October 30 (the same day Charolette Donovan learned she had consumption), orders came from General McClellan for the Fifth Corps to march south into Virginia to a spot on the north bank of the Rappahannock River, eight miles south of Warrenton. It would be a full four days' march, and the weather was turning cold. Coats were issued to the entire Fifth Corps.

General McClellan stipulated in his orders that 450 men of Colonel Ames's Twentieth Maine Regiment were to remain in Maryland to continue guarding the fords of the Potomac. Though it was hard to separate from their comrades, the other 550 men of the Twentieth Maine, along with the rest of Fifth Corps, marched south along the east side of the Blue Ridge by the light of the setting sun. Shane Donovan, Ellis Spear, Mike O'Hanlon, Tom Chamberlain, and Buster Kilrain were among those who marched. They marched until midnight, then under a clear, starlit sky and a full moon, they pitched their tents.

As the men of the Fifth Corps lay down for the night, they knew the grounds for war had become even more intense. No longer was the war waged only to preserve the Union and confine slavery to the areas where it existed; now there was a new dimension. Only a few days after the battle of Antietam, President Lincoln had declared his intention to issue on January 1, 1863, his Emancipation Proclamation. This edict would declare the slaves in the Confederate States "thenceforward and forever free." The message had come, along with their marching orders, that Lincoln was going to enforce the edict as planned on New Year's Day. This act would infuriate the Southerners.

The next day found the men of First Division, Fifth Corps, skirting the base of Loudoun Heights and proceeding south through Loudoun Valley. Untouched so far by the war, the valley was one of the most beautiful and fertile in Virginia. As the Union soldiers marched in long blue columns, they kept a sharp eye on the Blue Ridge Range to their right. General Morell had warned that there could be Confederate troops hiding in the shadows of the mountains.

After three more days of marching, First Division arrived without incident at its designated spot on the bank of the Rappahannock River.

The next day, November 4, the men of the Twentieth Maine were busy about their tents. Some shaved, others washed their clothes in the cold waters of the Rappahannock, still others wrote letters, hoping they would somehow arrive at their destination before Christmas.

Shane Donovan and Mike O'Hanlon were hanging their long underwear on a rope stretched between two trees and talking to Joshua Chamberlain. Suddenly Mike's attention was drawn to a familiar face coming toward them.

"Hey, Colonel! Look who's here!"

"John!" Chamberlain exclaimed, dashing to his brother.

The Chamberlain brothers hugged and pounded each other on the back, then John shook hands with Mike and Shane.

"I sure am glad to see you fellows alive! I heard about the Twentieth being in the Sharpsburg battle, but there was no way to find out if you came through it. What about Tom?"

"He's fine too," Joshua told him. "Right now, they have him

leading a guard patrol downriver. He'll sure be glad to see you."

"And me him. Mercy me, I had a hard time catching up with you guys. Good thing I had a horse. I was wondering even then if I'd ever catch up to you."

"Where you coming from?" Mike asked.

"Home." John let a wide smile capture his face. "And I've got some mail, too."

There was elation in the hearts of the three officers as John removed envelopes from his coat pocket and gave two to each of them.

"See you guys later," Shane said, holding his letters close to his heart. "I'm going to find a private spot under a tree somewhere and devour these."

"Me too," Mike said. "See you gentlemen later."

John Chamberlain watched Shane and Mike move away in opposite directions, then said to his brother, "Charolette's letter is going to tear him up, Josh."

"What do you mean?"

"Well…I guess you've known about her cough."

Joshua studied his brother's face. "Don't tell me she's got consumption."

"I'm afraid so."

"Her mother died of consumption while still a young woman. This is going to shake Shane hard. I'll give it a few minutes, then go talk to him."

Shane walked quickly to an old oak tree that stood by itself on the riverbank. He sat down, leaned against the tree, and opened the envelope from his parents. There were two letters inside, one from each. Soon he was wiping tears as he read precious words from his parents. He read both letters twice, then slipped them back in the envelope, anticipating Charolette's letter with a pounding heart.

"Hey, Captain! When did the mail arrive?"

Shane grinned up at a young corporal who was passing by with two others. "This isn't army mail, Corporal Todd. It was delivered personally by Colonel Chamberlain's brother."

Todd snapped his fingers and said, "Oh, to be an officer! They have all the good fortune!" The other corporals agreed in a light-hearted way and moved on.

Shane opened Charolette's envelope. His fingers trembled a little as he unfolded the four handwritten pages and began to read.

Ten minutes later, Joshua Chamberlain and Mike O'Hanlon drew near the tree. They could see Shane sitting at the base of the trunk, his knees pulled up and his arms resting on them. His head lay on his arms. They could hear him weeping and talking softly. They both picked up the word *Lord* and agreed silently to wait.

Soon the talking stopped, but the weeping continued. Chamberlain nodded to Mike, and together they moved up beside him.

CHAPTER SEVENTEEN

S hane…" Joshua Chamberlain said softly.

Shane Donovan raised his head. "Yes, sir?"

"We know about it. John told us."

Shane struggled to bring his voice under control. "I was afraid all along that it was consumption. I just wouldn't let myself believe it."

Mike knelt down and said, "I know you don't need me to tell you this, but God can heal her."

Shane nodded. "He can do anything. I know that. It's just that her mother died of the same disease at a young age, and I…"

"Hey, you're only human. The Lord is aware of that, too. Shane, I can't say that I understand how you feel, because I've never been where you are right now. But I want you to know my heart aches for you, and I'll be praying for both you and Charolette more than I have before."

"So will I, Shane," Joshua said. "And if there's ever anything I can do for either of you — I mean *anything* — don't you hesitate to ask."

Shane met the lieutenant colonel's gaze. "Do you really mean that, sir?"

"I sure do."

"Then, Colonel Chamberlain, Charly needs me right now. And I need to see her. Would you talk to Colonel Ames for me? See if he'll grant me time to go home?"

Chamberlain rubbed his forehead. "That will be quite irregular, but I'll give it a try. You and Mike wait here. I'll be back shortly."

When Chamberlain walked away, Mike said, "Shane, let's pray and ask the Lord to move on the colonel's heart. Charly needs you."

Chamberlain returned ten minutes later. He explained that Colonel Ames had gone into Warrenton with Generals George Morell and Dan Butterfield, who were ordered to a meeting with Abraham Lincoln's general-in-chief, Henry W. Halleck. General Fitz John Porter, commander of Fifth Corps, and General George McClellan himself would also be meeting with them. Morell, Butterfield, and Ames wouldn't be back for several hours. Chamberlain would talk with the colonel as soon as he returned.

Shane said that a meeting with General Halleck had to mean something important was going on. Chamberlain agreed.

With hope that the Lord would do His work in the colonel's heart, Shane went about his daily routine, his heart heavy for Charolette.

The sun went down just before mealtime, and a cold wind swept across the valley. The troops ate supper in their small tents to protect themselves from the biting wind. The nights had been growing colder of late.

Shane and Mike were eating together in Shane's tent when they heard footsteps approach. "Captain Donovan," came a familiar voice.

Shane stuck his head out of the cramped space. "Yes, Colonel Chamberlain?"

"Just wanted to let you know that Colonel Ames is back, and I'll be talking to him as soon as I possibly can."

"Thank you, sir. I'll be right here."

Over an hour later, Chamberlain returned. Shane and Mike saw by the light of a nearby fire that the lieutenant colonel was smiling.

"I explained the situation to the colonel," Chamberlain said, "and he said you can have four days, starting at dawn in the morning. He figures there won't be any fighting within that time. He said to see Sergeant Fillmore tonight. He's the one in charge of the horses. Colonel Ames is right now making arrangements for you to use one."

Shane lifted his eyes heavenward. "Thank You, Lord!"

"You can ride the horse to Washington, leave it at an army camp there, and take the train. That's only going to give you about a day with your Charly."

"That's all right, sir," Shane said. "At least I'll get to see her."

Chamberlain reached into his coat pocket and pulled out two slips of paper. "Here's a map to show you how to find the right camp. And this other paper is to show that Colonel Ames authorized you to leave camp and return home. Has his signature on it. Just show it to the officer in charge of the Washington camp, and any military authority who might question you."

"All right, sir," Shane said as he took the papers.

"You'll note that the dates of your leave are specified in the letter. You must be back here by midnight next Saturday, the eighth. You'll be in deep trouble if you're not."

"I understand, sir. I'll not be late."

"Colonel," Mike said, "did you learn what the meeting in Warrenton was about?"

"Only that General Morell is now meeting with the commanders of all regiments here and that every regiment is going to be addressed by its commander before bedtime. We should be ordered to assemble shortly."

The order came just over a half-hour later.

Several fires burned in the area to give off light. Colonel Ames stood in the cold wind with his cap pulled low and his overcoat collar up and announced to his regiment that President Lincoln had relieved General George Morell of his command of First Division in order to place him at the head of another division stationed further east. Morell was being replaced by General Dan Butterfield, effective immediately.

There was more news. General-in-Chief Henry Halleck had informed the officers that President Lincoln, out of patience with General McClellan's long failure to seek out the enemy and take the fight to him, had relieved him of his command and replaced him with Major General Ambrose Burnside, who had distinguished himself in the battle at Sharpsburg. This change in command would take place the next day, November 5.

By the same directive, Lincoln had ordered McClellan's right-hand-man and commander of the Fifth Corps, Major General Fitz John Porter, removed from his position, with Major General Joseph Hooker placed in his stead.

Colonel Ames then said, "Before we dismiss, men, there's one more thing. Since he is now commander of First Division, General Butterfield is going to introduce to us a bugle tune — one he composed himself — that will be played every night at lights out. It will also be used when we bury men of our division who are killed in battle."[1]

"Colonel Ames..." said a young soldier who stood near the front of the ranks.

"Yes?"

"Did General Butterfield put words to the tune?"

"I don't know, soldier."

"Aye, he did, sir," Buster Kilrain said. "General Butterfield calls it 'Taps.' I heard about it from an Irish lieutenant named O'Leary that I met when we were camped up on the banks o' the Potomac. The words are fittin', Colonel, both for soldiers beddin' down at night and for those laid to rest in their graves."

"And what are those words, Sergeant?"

Kilrain rubbed the back of his neck, pressing his memory for the words. "Let's see...'Day is done, sinks the sun. And the stars all appear one by one. Rest in peace comrades dear, God is near.'"

Ames nodded, then said to the brigade, "All right men, when you hear the bugler tonight, you'll know what he's playing and the words that go with the music. Regiment dismissed!"

✴ ✴ ✴ ✴ ✴

Shane Donovan arrived at Brunswick, Maine, just short of twenty-eight hours after riding out of camp at 4:00 o'clock on Wednesday morning, November 5. He had changed trains in Boston, and upon arriving in Portland, had rented a horse and headed for Brunswick at a full gallop. He wanted to catch Charolette at home before she left for work. It was 7:35 when he slid from the saddle in front of the little cottage and headed for the door.

Not wanting to frighten Charly, he decided to knock rather than walk in. He tapped on the door, his heart pounding wildly, and braced himself. There were light footsteps, followed by the rattle of the doorknob. The door swung open, revealing a thinner Charly with gray circles under her eyes. She was dressed and ready for work. When she saw the face of her husband, her mouth flew open.

"Shane! Oh, you're alive...and all in one piece!"

They embraced, kissed, and embraced again. Charolette clung hard, weeping, and Shane held her tight, shedding his own tears.

"I guess you haven't received any of my letters," he said.

"No."

"I've received five from you. It was the last one that told me about...your sickness. I just had to come and see you."

"Oh, I'm so glad you could come! We heard about the Sharpsburg battle in September, but we couldn't find out anything about your regiment. There's been no way for us to find out if any of you survived. What about Mike? Ashley's been beside herself with worry, just like I have."

"Mike's fine. So is Colonel Chamberlain and Uncle Buster. Tom's okay, too. We didn't actually get into the battle at Sharpsburg, so no one was even scratched. We had a skirmish with some Rebels right after that, but still nobody was hurt. We're camped on the Rappahannock in Virginia now. When your letter came, I asked Colonel Chamberlain if he would try to get me a leave so I could come and see you. He did it in a hurry."

"Well, how long — " she turned her head, covered her mouth, and coughed. "Excuse me. How long can you stay?"

"They gave me a little less than four days. It took me almost twenty-eight hours to get here. I have to report in by midnight Saturday, so I'll have to ride for Portland in the morning at ten."

Charolette looked over his shoulder and said, "Here comes Mr. O'Hanlon."

Lewis O'Hanlon was ecstatic to see Shane and to learn that Mike was alive and well. He gladly gave Charolette the day off, saying she didn't have to come to work on Thursday either. He was going to head home and tell Maureen that their son was fine.

Shane explained that the Twentieth had not yet seen combat, so Lewis could spread the word that everyone in the regiment was all right. He asked Lewis to swing by his parents' house and tell his mother he was home. He wanted to spend a few minutes alone with Charly, then they would come to the house.

There was a sweet reunion with Shane's mother, then Shane told her they were going to see Dr. Holladay. Pearl invited them for supper and said she would invite Ashley, too.

Shane sat with Charolette in the doctor's office and questioned Dr. Holladay thoroughly. The doctor explained that consumption worked differently with different people. Charolette could linger for years with it, or it could end her life in a few months, as it had her mother's.

Shane and Charolette went back home and spent the rest of the day alone. They read the Bible and prayed together, asking God to take the disease from her body. Charolette tried to encourage her husband by staying optimistic.

That evening, a precious time was enjoyed at the Donovan home. When Ashley and Shane saw each other, they embraced, and Shane gave her a letter Mike had hastily written to take to her. She was thrilled to receive it and handed one to Shane to take to Mike. Garth led in special prayer for Charolette and for Shane as he returned to the war. He also prayed for Mike and the others who were known and loved by the O'Hanlon family.

Charolette had a coughing spell right after the prayer. She coughed up pink foam, but hid it from Shane.

Later that evening, Shane and Ashley hugged each other good-bye. She asked him to tell Mike she loved him with all her heart and was looking forward to the day he came home to her. Shane assured her he would convey the message.

The next morning, Garth and Pearl came by to tell Shane good-bye, then left to give him and his wife their final hour together alone.

At ten o'clock, Charolette walked Shane to the front porch of the cottage. The horse was tied to a hitching post, saddled and ready to go. It nickered when it saw them.

Charolette did her best to maintain her composure. As they clung to each other, she said, "Darling, please don't worry about me. I'm in the Lord's hands. We are in His hands. I must trust Him to bring you back safe and sound. You must trust Him to have me waiting here when you come home."

Shane's chest felt as though it were on fire as he battled for composure. He held her at arm's length and said, "The real soldier in this family is you."

They kissed long and lingering, then Shane swung into the saddle. Charolette wiped tears and coughed as she watched him ride away. When he reached the end of the block, he reined in, waved, then rounded the corner and was gone.

Upon reaching the Union camp on the Rappahannock, Shane Donovan learned that the Army of the Potomac's new commander, General Ambrose E. Burnside, had announced that he was planning to move his army south to take Fredericksburg. He would then march to the Confederate capital and take it. When

Richmond was in Union hands, the war would be over.

In order to accomplish his objectives, General Burnside reorganized his army. Changes in command followed as he formed three "Grand Divisions" of two corps each. Burnside appointed General Joseph Hooker to command Center Grand Division, consisting of Second and Fifth Corps. The other four corps formed the Right and Left Grand Divisions. General Dan Butterfield was made commander of Fifth Corps, and Brigadier General Charles Griffin became commander of First Division in his place.

In late November, Burnside deviated from a plan assented to by General-in-Chief Henry W. Halleck and President Lincoln and marched his army southward down the Rappahannock to Falmouth, opposite his first target, Fredericksburg.

Burnside had agreed with his superiors to cross the river above Fredericksburg, occupy the loftiest point behind the town, known as Marye's Heights, and establish a supply base north of the river. Instead, Burnside resolved to cross the Rappahannock on pontoon bridges directly in front of Fredericksburg. When his army was gathered at Falmouth, Burnside decided not to occupy Marye's Heights, believing it was not necessary. He would have the city in hand before the Confederates would know what hit them.

Then things began to go wrong. General Lee was notified that the Federals were making moves to take Fredericksburg. Lee's army had licked its wounds from the whipping at Sharpsburg and had been reinforced. Lee led his army from Richmond with two of his most formidable generals, James Longstreet and Thomas J. "Stonewall" Jackson.

The pontoons failed to arrive as scheduled, and as the days passed, Lee and his Army of Northern Virginia moved in and set up their defensive positions. General Longstreet's division occupied Marye's Heights with artillery and infantry. General Jackson's division set up barriers at ground level.

Panic was building in Burnside. He wired Washington, asking where his pontoons were. There had been a misunderstanding as to when the pontoons would be needed. A rush was put on, and they finally arrived on December 10, more than a week late. By this time, Lee's forces were well-established.

When Lee saw the pontoons from his position on Marye's Heights, he sent a message down to General Jackson to place snipers in buildings along the riverbank to pick off the Federals as they began to connect the floating bridges. Lee then called for Fredericksburg to be evacuated. The Union army had stationed artillery on the heavily forested hills across the river, and he knew bombardment would come. He wanted all civilians out of the city. The command was given late afternoon on December 10, and the evacuation was done on Thursday morning, December 11, under a thick fog.

A four-inch snow had fallen on December 8, followed by freezing cold. None of it had melted off. Fredericksburg's citizens made their way out of the city in a pitiful procession into the foggy forests and fields and set up camps in the snow.

The Twentieth Maine Regiment was sent to the river bank to fire at Stonewall Jackson's snipers, who in spite of the fog were making life miserable for the Union engineers. The Twentieth Maine had excellent cover from which to fire and was able to fend off the Rebel snipers, giving the Union engineers freedom to work.

The pontoon bridges were in place by noon, though the fog had grown thicker. Burnside would now soften up the enemy by bombarding the city. The command was given, and 150 pieces of Union artillery — including several of their largest cannons — opened their iron mouths with a terrific roar, hurling a tempest of destruction upon the city.

Colonel Ames and his Twentieth Maine stood in the icy weather, along with thousands of other men in blue, and listened to the bombardment. The air shook and the ground trembled with the deafening cannonade. Curiously, there was no return fire from Longstreet's guns on Marye's Heights, nor from Jackson's troops on ground level. Rebel soldiers in the city scattered for cover amid the howling of solid shot, the bursting of shells, the crashing of missiles through roofs and walls, and the dull sound of houses and commercial buildings collapsing.

As the bombardment continued, Mike O'Hanlon turned to Joshua Chamberlain and said, "Sir, I don't get it. Why aren't the Rebels shooting back?"

"I don't know. I'm sure Colonel Ames could tell you."

"I'm right here." Ames had been slowly making his way among his men, talking to them in quiet tones. "I couldn't make out the question, but I probably already know what it is. Everybody's asking the same thing. You want to know why Lee isn't firing back."

"Yes, sir," Mike said. "I'd think he'd be retaliating."

"It's quite simple, Lieutenant. General Lee knows we're set up strong enough to take out the city, no matter what he does. So he's waiting to take us on when he can see us and try to make every shot count."

"How soon will we be crossing the bridges, sir?" Chamberlain asked.

"I think General Burnside will put us across under cover of darkness. However, if the fog stays this low and thick, he may start putting us across before dark."

Shane stood next to Mike. "What's the general's purpose in destroying the town, Colonel? Ruining homes and businesses won't shorten the war, will it?"

"No, Captain. If I understand his thinking correctly, it's because the town is full of Rebel soldiers. It's them he's after. He gave the citizens time to evacuate before starting the bombardment. It's too bad, but civilians do suffer in a time of war. And we must remember, the Southerners fired the first shot."

Shane thought of the gospel-preaching churches in Fredericksburg and hated to think of their buildings being destroyed.

The horrible din lasted until after noon. Burnside readied a great number of his troops to cross the bridges even though the fog was breaking up. By one o'clock, the sun was shining through the clouds, revealing the smoking ruins of the city. Many houses, commercial buildings, and churches were on fire.

General Lee stood on Marye's Heights with General Longstreet and watched as the long lines of men in blue crossed the river on the bobbing pontoon bridges. Stonewall Jackson's sharpshooters were firing at them from the west bank of the river, but they were hindered by Union riflemen firing back.

Darkness fell, and the snipers' rifles went silent. A quarter of Burnside's army was on the west bank of the Rappahannock.

December 12 started with heavy fog, making it difficult for the Yankees to cross the bridges. Slowly, however, they made their way across, line after line of them. Burnside's force was massive — 130,000 men. It would take time to get them all across. The fog was one hindrance. The Confederate sharpshooters were another.

Lee's army was much smaller...some 78,000 men. They had an advantage, however. General Burnside's decision to ignore Marye's Heights and the delay of his pontoon bridges gave the Confederates the high ground and time to establish bulwarks at ground level.

The road to Richmond, a sunken road some twenty-five feet wide, ran along the base of Marye's Heights. A long, shoulder-high stone wall ran the length of the hill's base, a perfect entrenchment for 2,500 of Longstreet's riflemen. Furthermore, Longstreet had positioned his artillery atop the heights so that the ground in front of the wall would be vulnerable to a murderous crossfire.

Lee, Longstreet, and Jackson were ready for the big battle that lay ahead of them.

December 13 came with fog once again covering the valley. Burnside now had the bulk of his army on the west side of the Rappahannock. Part of the Union's Fifth Division, including the Twentieth Maine, was kept in reserve in the dense forest on the east side.

Just before ten o'clock, the fog began to lift. From their position on the east bank of the river, Colonel Ames and his lieutenant colonel waited with their 550 men. They agreed that waiting in reserve was harder than being first into battle.

At precisely ten-thirty, the battle erupted. First there was firing in the city, as Union and Confederate soldiers collided, then the artillery units of both sides cut loose. Soon Longstreet's cannons on the heights and his infantry behind the stone wall were firing into brigades of men in blue as they swarmed across the level ground toward the wall and the high hill behind it.

From across the river, the men of the Twentieth Maine waited and watched in horror and fascination. To observe the deadly action and not be able to go to the aid of their comrades was a trial for all of them.

Shane Donovan's mind left the battle from time to time, though his eyes were fixed on it. He thought of Charly and found himself praying for her and wishing he could be with her.

Mike O'Hanlon's line of sight remained steadily on the fierce combat, but like his friend, his mind traveled back to Maine and the auburn-haired woman he had loved for so long. If only he could hold Ashley in his arms and whisper words of love into her ear.

The day ended with the Fifth Corps still in reserve. But before the men of the Fifth laid down for the night, they were told they would all see action the next day. Burnside's forces had been whittled down frightfully by the deadly crossfire that came from Marye's Heights and from behind the stone wall. Tomorrow the Union troops would storm the wall, climb the hill, and overpower Longstreet's artillery with overwhelming numbers.

A common grave was dug on the plain, and "Taps" was played in the light of a clear-edged moon as hundreds of Union soldiers were laid to rest.

There was only light fog on Sunday morning, December 14. The weather had warmed considerably, and what had been frozen ground was now slushy mud.

The battle began just after sunup and raged as violently as it had the day before. The Twentieth Maine watched several regiments that had been in reserve with them cross the river and enter the fight. Their nerves were stretched to the limit knowing that at any time they were going to face enemy guns.

Buster Kilrain found Shane and Mike talking to Joshua Chamberlain.

"Ye blokes ready to get into it?" he asked.

"More than ready," Chamberlain said.

"What's it like to know you're out there charging at men who are bent on killing you, Uncle Buster?" Mike asked.

"Well, son, there really isn't a way to describe it. You'll know soon enough, I'm sure."

Colonel Ames's voice cut the air. "All right, Twentieth Maine! We just got orders to cross the river! Let's go!"

Mike looked at Shane. "Let's stay close to each other, okay?"

"Sure. I can't blame you young boys for wanting a mature man fighting alongside you."

Mike grinned and punched Shane's arm. As they hurried toward the bridges together, he said, "Shane..."

"Yeah?"

"If you should make it and I don't — "

"Stop that kind of talk!"

"We have to be realistic. If I don't make it and you do, tell Ashley I died loving her with all my heart. Okay?"

"I said don't talk that way."

Cannonade thundered and rifle fire rattled as the Twentieth Maine reached the west side of the Rappahannock. Colonel Ames was there to give orders. They were to stay in close ranks and charge across the open plain along with two other regiments — the Sixteenth Michigan and the Eighty-third Pennsylvania — that were collected and ready to go. Their assignment: Charge the wall, kill the riflemen, then climb the hill and wipe out the Confederate soldiers manning the cannons.

Three other regiments — the Twelfth, Seventeenth, and Forty-fourth New York — had gone before them that morning and been repulsed. Hundreds of them lay dead on the field in front of Marye's Heights. The survivors were standing by, ready to join the new reinforcements in a fresh charge as they moved in long blue lines across the open plain.

After the New York Regiments closed ranks with the new ones, the sharp command to charge was given. Thousands of Union soldiers bolted across the open field toward the Confederates who waited at Marye's Heights. As they drew within two hundred yards, the sprawled and crumpled bodies of men who had died in the day's first charge grew thicker, and they had to weave around them or hop over them.

There was no time for fear as they drew near the wall, behind which Longstreet had positioned better than three thousand riflemen. The Confederate artillery opened up, and black muzzles spit fire all along the top of the wall. Cannonballs exploded into the charging swarm of blue, throwing bodies every direction.

The Twentieth Maine was green, but the discipline and hours at drill were paying off. The men who followed Ames and Chamberlain into the storm did not falter.

The gallant Union soldiers came within thirty paces of the stone wall, but encountered such a fire of canister and musketry that they had to fall back. Colonel Ames led his men toward a series of ditches where they could reload in relative safety. He cast a glance at many of his men who had fallen.

"Pure carnage!" he shouted at Chamberlain.

"We should have taken those heights when we had the opportunity!" Chamberlain shouted back.

"General Burnside will have some explaining to do," Ames said as the two of them dropped into a ditch.

Shane and Mike were running side by side toward a section of ditch. Shane could always outrun his best friend. As he began pulling ahead of him, he looked over his shoulder and shouted,

"Come on! Only another thirty yards!"

"You run pretty fast for an old man!" Mike called in return. "But one of these days, I'm going to — "

Shane looked back and saw Mike go down. "Mike!" he cried, whirling and running toward him.

"Don't do it!" a soldier of the Sixteenth Michigan yelled as he came running past. "He's dead!"

"He's my best friend!" Shane shouted.

Shane would not believe Mike was dead. How could that soldier know? While hot lead whizzed all around him and men ran past him, he picked Mike up, cradling him in his arms, and ran to the nearest ditch. He lowered Mike gently into the ditch, then eased down beside him, keeping his head low.

Then he saw it. A bullet had hit Mike in the back of the head. The Michigan soldier was right. Mike was dead.

In solemn quietness, General Burnside's soldiers buried their dead by bright moonlight in a common grave dug hastily in a field a mile from Marye's Heights. Joshua Chamberlain and Buster Kilrain flanked Shane Donovan as he held Mike O'Hanlon's lifeless form in his arms, hesitating to lower it into the deep hole along with the other bodies. A bugler stood near, ready to blow "Taps" when the last body was placed in the ground.

Tears streamed down Shane's cheeks. Chamberlain laid a hand on his shoulder.

"One consolation, Shane."

"Yes, sir. I'll see him again in glory."

"The Christian's hope. Thank God for it."

Shane nodded, then looked into Mike's pale, stone-like face.

"I'll tell her, Mike. I'll tell her."

All of us are acquainted with the haunting refrain known as "Taps." The song is connected in our minds with death and burial, but General Dan Butterfield composed it to *save* lives.

During the Civil War, just about every event in army life was ordered by bugle calls. Military burials, however, were conducted with a volley of rifle shots.

On June 25, 1862, Union and Confederate armies came together on the peninsula at Seven Pines, Virginia, in what was to become known as the Seven Days' Battle. The battle produced forty-three thousand casualties, and bodies were strewn for miles over the rolling, densely-wooded land. General Butterfield and his soldiers were forced by the terrain to camp within firing range of the Confederate forces. When they attempted to bury their dead and fired a volley of shots over the fresh graves, the Confederates thought they were under attack and immediately retaliated. Union soldiers were being killed just for attending the burial of their fallen comrades.

Determined that his dead soldiers would be buried with proper ceremony, General Butterfield composed a short tune for his buglers. He called it "Taps" and ordered it played in the place of the customary rifle volleys. The tune saved the lives of many Union soldiers of the Third Brigade, and it soon was used for "lights out," also. General Butterfield then put words to his tune that in his mind befit either occasion.

When he began to use "Taps" for the entire First Division upon becoming its commander, the tune caught on and spread throughout the Union forces. Before the Civil War was over, the Confederates were using it, too. Our American military has used it ever since.

CHAPTER EIGHTEEN

Major General Ambrose E. Burnside called for a meeting of his officers following the burial ceremony. He wanted to launch another attack on Lee's army at dawn the next morning. Burnside had not perceived that the losses were so heavy that his officers and their troops were ready to back away from Fredericksburg.

Stonewall Jackson's men had fought like tigers, taking losses but killing a higher number of Yankees. The worst onslaught, however, had come from James Longstreet's artillery atop Marye's Heights and the infantry behind the stone wall. Together they produced a deadly crossfire that had killed thousands of Union troops.

The officers protested another attack; their commands had already sustained severe losses and had accomplished nothing. A great part of Fredericksburg had been reduced to rubble, but Lee's army was still intact and in control. General William B. Franklin was brazen enough to remind Burnside that he had deviated from the plan approved by President Lincoln and Henry Halleck, and that his most grievous mistake was not occupying Marye's Heights immediately. Other officers, including Daniel Butterfield, argued that to continue to assault the Confederates in their strong defensive positions would destroy the Union army.

Such strong arguments from his military leaders shook Burnside's resolve, and he ordered the final withdrawal of the Army of the Potomac back across the river. Upon the Union army's return to the camps at Falmouth, the disaster at Fredericksburg weighed heavily on the minds of the soldiers who had left so many of their comrades behind in the common graves.

Though the losses of the Twentieth Maine Regiment were heavy (153 dead and 47 wounded seriously enough to be sent to Washington for medical attention), Colonel Ames was well pleased with his regiment's performance under fire. After the volley of heavy artillery and musketry that had driven them back to the ditches, they had charged the wall again. Though repulsed once more, they had taken a measurable toll on the Rebels.

Ames was convinced his regiment had performed better than any other and had earned that day a reputation for fighting tenacity. The fierce battle had taught his officers and men the value of the hard-learned discipline acquired in seemingly endless hours of drill and instruction. A strong and united fighting unit had emerged from a band of green volunteers.

On the whole, however, the Army of the Potomac was in a low state of mind. Men of every division felt they had been foolishly and needlessly sacrificed by attacking an enemy so well fortified that victory was impossible.

Before January 1863 passed into history, President Lincoln, realizing that Burnside had lost the respect and confidence of his army, replaced him with Major General Joseph Hooker. Dan Butterfield was made Hooker's chief of staff, and George Meade was made commander of Fifth Corps in his place. Hooker did away with the Grand Divisions and reorganized the army, retaining the corps structure. Charles Griffin commanded First Division, and T. W. B. Stockton was made commander of Third Brigade, which still contained the Twentieth Maine Regiment.

Ames went to Meade, requesting that the other segment of his regiment that had been left behind to guard the Potomac fords be brought to Falmouth. He needed them to bolster the numbers of the Twentieth Maine after their heavy losses at Fredericksburg. Meade gladly obliged, and within a week the Twentieth was all together again.

There was relative quiet for the Twentieth Maine in the following weeks. Joshua Chamberlain, concerned that the Twentieth had lost so many men, asked Ames if he could return to Maine to talk to the new governor, Abner Coburn, about recruiting more volunteers.

On February 4, Chamberlain approached a field tent occupied by Shane Donovan. It was a cloudy, cold, blustery day. Buster Kilrain was standing near with his head bent into the wind, in conversation with two young soldiers.

"Good mornin', Colonel," Kilrain said, breaking off his conversation.

"Captain Donovan in his tent?" Chamberlain asked.

"Yes, sir. He's talkin' to Benny Wilson. But I'm sure he won't mind if you interrupt."

Chamberlain was about to call to Shane when the flap came open.

"I heard you ask if I was in here, Colonel," Shane said. "Come on in."

Chamberlain knew Corporal Wilson, who was from Winthrop, Maine. Wilson was eighteen years old and had gone through the Fredericksburg battle. As Chamberlain ducked his head and stepped into the tent, he saw Wilson thumbing tears from his eyes.

"Good morning, Benny."

Wilson smiled through his tears. "It sure is, sir. It's the best morning of my life! I just got saved!"

"Wonderful!" Chamberlain exclaimed. "What brought this about?"

"I've talked to Benny on a few occasions about becoming a Christian," Shane said. "He showed some interest, but that was about it. Well, Fredericksburg put a scare into him. He realizes he could've been killed, and he wouldn't have gone to heaven if he had. It's been eating on him. Or I should say the Holy Spirit has been working on him. He came to me an hour or so ago, wanting to know more about it. Just a few minutes ago he acknowledged to the Lord Jesus that he's a sinner in need of salvation, and called on Him to come into his heart and save him."

Chamberlain shook Wilson's hand. "You just took care of the biggest issue in your life, young man."

"Yes, sir, I know…thanks to Captain Donovan here."

"Well, I hate to interrupt this happy occasion, Wilson, but I need a few private moments with Captain Donovan. So if you'll excuse us…"

"No problem, sir."

When Wilson stepped out of the tent, the first thing he did was tell Buster Kilrain he had received Christ. Buster rejoiced with him.

Shane smiled at Chamberlain and said, "What can I do for you, sir?"

"It's what I can do for you, Shane. How would you like to go home and see Charly?"

The winter sunlight was shining through the bedroom windows, giving ample light, as Charolette Donovan sat in front of the mirror, brushing her long black hair. She was still in her robe, though it was nearly ten o'clock. She heard a knock at her front door. She stood up, laid the brush on the dresser, and wondering who was at the door, took a brief look at her pale features and the dark circles under her eyes.

She crossed the small parlor and could see the shadow of a tall man through the curtains that covered the window in the door. Her heart leaped in her breast. Could it be Shane? She pulled the collar of her robe up around her neck and opened the door.

"Hi, beautiful lady!" said the smiling soldier.

Charolette made a tiny squeal, took his hand, and pulled him inside. Shane shut the door and folded her in his arms.

After several minutes of sweet reunion, he said, "I went to the factory, but Darrell told me you weren't working today."

"Well, I…I haven't been working every day, darling. I just can't do it anymore. I'm…well, I'm just not strong enough. I've been working three days a week."

Shane ushered her to an overstuffed chair, sat her down, then knelt in front of her and took both hands in his.

"O honey, I'm so sorry. Have you seen Dr. Holladay about the loss of strength?"

"He says it just goes with my disease. He says I might take a turn for the better one of these days, and maybe go back to working full time. Ashley's working in my place."

The mention of Ashley sent a cold chill through Shane. He was going to have to tell her about Mike. The government had no system of notifying families of soldiers' deaths. It would fall on him to tell Mike's parents also.

"Honey, listen. Maybe you shouldn't work at all. Maybe it's time you go and live with my folks."

"No. Not yet. I want to work, Shane. It's therapy for me. And…and living in this house keeps me closer to you."

"All right. I just want what's best for you."

"Shane, we all heard about the Fredericksburg battle. It must have been awful. Oh, it's so horrible when I don't know whether you're dead or alive…or maybe alive but wounded. How were you able to come home this time…and how long can you stay?"

Shane told her that Joshua Chamberlain had obtained permission to come to Maine to recruit more volunteers for the Twentieth. Chamberlain had asked Shane if he wanted to come home with him for a couple of days. He had already obtained permission for Shane to take the leave.

"So you'll be here two days?" Charolette asked.

"Colonel Chamberlain and I are scheduled to take the 11:15 train from Portland day after tomorrow."

Shane took a deep breath and said, "Honey — "

A knock at the door cut him off.

"Expecting anybody?" he asked, heading for the door.

"No."

Shane swung the door open, and his heart leaped to his throat at the sight of Ashley O'Hanlon. The way the mid-morning sun struck her hair made it look like burnished copper.

"Hello, Shane," she said. "Darrell told me you were back. I don't mean to interrupt, and I'll only stay a minute, but I just had to hurry over. I knew you could tell me how Mike is."

"Come in," Shane said, praying silently for God's help.

Charolette spoke from her chair, "Hi, Ashley. Colonel Chamberlain was coming to Maine to talk to the governor and invited Shane to travel with him."

"That's wonderful!" Ashley said.

"Take your coat off and come sit down," Charolette said.

"Oh, no. Your time together is too valuable to have an intruder. I just wanted to hear about Mike, and I'll be on my way."

"Go ahead and take the coat off, Ashley," Shane said. "I...have something to explain to you. It'll take some time."

"Something's wrong, Shane," she said, her voice shaky. "What *is* it?" She removed her coat and scarf and laid them on a chair.

"Sit down, Ashley. Here. Next to Charly."

Ashley dropped into the chair, her eyes never leaving Shane's face.

"Shane, what is it? Something's happened to Mike, hasn't it? Is he...is he hurt? Bad?"

Ashley studied Shane's eyes. Her throat was frozen with fear. She waited for him to speak. Charolette rose to her feet and moved to her best friend. She laid a hand on Ashley's shoulder, set her tired eyes on Shane, and waited to hear whatever was coming.

After long seconds of painful silence, Shane knelt in front of

Ashley, drew an uneasy breath, and said, "Ashley...Mike was killed at Fredericksburg."

Charolette sucked in a sharp breath, then leaned over and wrapped her arms around Ashley's shoulders. Ashley's face went the color of gray stone. Charolette could feel her go stiff. Tears welled up in Ashley's eyes. Her lips parted, but she couldn't speak. She sat transfixed, unable to move.

"We...the Twentieth...were attacking a Rebel fortification behind a stone wall. There was heavy artillery unleashing on us from the top of a hill behind the wall. They had us in a crossfire, and our commander signaled for us to retreat. We...we were running across an open field for safety." Shane choked up, bit his lips, and felt tears fill his eyes. "Mike was a few steps behind me. A...a bullet took his life, Ashley. Instantly. He never felt it. He didn't suffer."

Ashley stared at the floor. Her lips quivered. "Where is he...buried?"

"In a field outside of Fredericksburg. Along with hundreds of other Union soldiers."

"I'll never even get to see his grave."

Ashley suddenly burst into tears, wrapping her arms around Charolette. She sobbed as if her very soul would wrench itself from her body. Charolette held her and spoke soft words of understanding and comfort.

Shane and Charolette went with Ashley to inform Mike's family of his death. They left Ashley with her in-laws and went to Shane's family and told them. The next stop was the parsonage of First Parish Congregational Church to tell Dr. and Mrs. George Adams.

The day Shane was to head south with Joshua Chamberlain was a Saturday. Some twenty minutes before Chamberlain was to pick him up, Shane took his wife in his arms and said, "Darling, I can't stand this. It's tearing me up to go off and leave you when you're doing so poorly. I'm going to ask Colonel Chamberlain to get me out of the army. You need me, and I need to be here with you."

Charolette stroked his cheek. "Sweetheart, a lot of people are praying for me. You especially. The Lord doesn't always answer in a hurry. I still have hopes that He will touch me, and I'll take a turn for the better. Besides, Shane, you're a soldier of the United States Army. You must go back. Our country is at war. Thousands of others are making great sacrifices for the Union. Can we do any less?"

Shane bit hard on his lower lip, then said, "No. We can't. It's my duty to help bring this horrid war to an end."

They clung to each other, savoring the precious minutes, then Joshua Chamberlain pulled up in the rented buggy.

As the buggy pulled away, Shane looked back and waved. Charolette waved back, tears streaming down her cheeks. When the buggy reached the corner, the last thing Shane saw was Ashley O'Hanlon hurrying up to Charolette and the two women throwing their arms around each other.

When Joshua Chamberlain and Shane arrived back at the Falmouth camp, they learned that the Army of the Potomac was being ordered back to a camp near Washington.

On March 29, President Lincoln appeared at the camp for a Grand Review. He was pleased to see the rejuvenated fitness and morale of his troops under the leadership of Joseph Hooker. When the Review was over, Lincoln addressed the troops. He spoke words of encouragement and optimism that the Union was going to be victorious. The men in blue cheered, and Lincoln was thrilled with their response.

Before dismissing the army, the president announced that the commanding officers of three regiments had submitted the names of three soldiers who had displayed unusual courage during the battle at Fredericksburg. He was going to present them with

Presidential Commendations for their unselfish and gallant deeds.

The names were called out, and Captain Shane Donovan was surprised to hear his name among the three. The recipients were asked to come to the platform.

Lincoln already had the regiment commanders ready to meet the soldiers on the platform. Colonel Ames smiled broadly at Shane when their eyes met. Shane stood beside his colonel as the commanders of the other regiments told the crowd of soldiers of the brave deeds done by their two men.

After both men had received their written commendations from the president, Colonel Ames was called to speak. Ames explained that he had submitted a written statement of Captain Shane Donovan's act of courage on September 18, 1862, near Sharpsburg, Maryland. Donovan had hazarded his own life to protect Lieutenant Colonel Joshua Chamberlain from a Confederate officer's bullet and had killed the enemy officer in the process.

Eyewitnesses had also told Ames that at Fredericksburg, Captain Donovan had picked up a fallen fellow officer under heavy fire and carried him to safety, not knowing the officer was already dead.

For these two deeds of courage and heroism, Shane Donovan was given the Presidential Commendation by Abraham Lincoln while thousands of his fellow-soldiers cheered and applauded.

April came to Washington, and with it spring warmth. During the first week of April, the Twentieth Maine was given the job of protecting Union telegraph lines in northern Virginia.

Since things were quiet, Shane approached Joshua Chamberlain about getting another leave so he could go home and see Charly. Chamberlain was able to talk Colonel Ames into it, but on the same day, some seventy-five men of the Twentieth Maine fell ill. The entire regiment had been inoculated for smallpox two days earlier, and it was discovered that the seventy-five had been given defective vaccine. The regiment was pulled off telegraph line duty and quarantined until late April. Thirty-eight of the seventy-five died.

When the quarantine was lifted, Shane was making ready for a trip to Maine when things heated up with the Confederates. A battle was about to take place at Chancellorsville, Virginia. Shane's leave was canceled.

The battle started on May 2 and lasted until May 4. After making a promising beginning to his campaign, Joseph Hooker was outmaneuvered by Robert E. Lee and his bold subordinate, Stonewall Jackson. Hooker had started the campaign confident of victory, then was forced to withdraw the army to its Falmouth camps.

The spirits of the Union troops were deflated by the unexpected defeat. They had entertained such high hopes of victory under Hooker's leadership. Though President Lincoln was disappointed with Hooker's performance, he left him in charge of the army.

On May 20, Colonel Ames was promoted to brigadier general and transferred to the Union's Eleventh Corps. Much to the elation of the Twentieth Maine, Joshua Chamberlain was promoted to full colonel and given the Twentieth as his command.

On May 23, 120 new men arrived in response to Chamberlain's request to Governor Coburn for fresh recruits. Among them was Rex Carden, a young man who had worked with Shane at the lumber mill in Brunswick. Though a likable person, Carden had always been a bit "devil-may-care" and unruly.

Shane took Carden aside and warned him that he would have to toe the line in the army, or pay the consequences. Carden assured him that he had changed. Shane had often talked to Carden about the Lord, but the unruly young man had no time for God. When Shane asked him if he had also changed in that way, Carden chuckled nervously and said he had thought about their talks and even recalled some of the Scriptures Shane had quoted him. He would give it some consideration.

On June 1, Colonel Strong Vincent, a native of Pennsylvania, was made commander of the Third Brigade. A robust and handsome man, Vincent was an 1859 graduate of Harvard College and had just passed his twenty-sixth birthday. Vincent was only a year older than Shane, and upon being introduced, they struck an instant friendship.

Shane Donovan rode his horse along the telegraph lines that led through the Virginia hills and valleys to Washington and talked with the men of the Twentieth. None of them had seen any sign of Rebels. So far, Lee hadn't sent any troops to destroy Union communications.

At sundown on June 8, Shane was riding toward the camp, his heart longing for Charly. He hadn't seen her since early February. He had received four letters from her since then, and though she tried to put on that she was doing fine, he knew better. Her handwriting showed signs that she was growing weaker, and she was now living with his parents. Since there was no immediate battle pending as far as he knew, Shane decided to ask Chamberlain for permission to make a quick trip home. When he arrived at the camp, Shane found that Chamberlain had gone to Washington with General Charles Griffin and would not be back for two days.

Strong Vincent looked up as he sat in a canvas-backed chair at the front of his field tent and saw Shane drawing up. Vincent closed the Bible he was reading and stood up.

"Good afternoon, Captain," Vincent said. "What can I do for you?"

Shane eyed the Bible and smiled. "Wonderful Book, isn't it?"

"None like it. A man needs a map to get through this country. Our engineers provide that for us. A man also needs a map to get through this life…and into the next. Our God has provided that for us. This Bible is that map, and Jesus Christ is the Way."

"Amen to that. Man talks like that, makes me think he's a born-again child of God."

"Since October 2, 1860. The young lady who is now my wife led me to Jesus. We were married six months later."

"Thank God for a dedicated Christian young lady."

"That's for sure. She wouldn't date me until I became a Christian. I fought the Lord and His gospel for a while, but finally He broke down my stubborn will. After I received Christ, we had our first date. Things got better, and we finally got married. But let's see...you haven't told me why you came to see me."

"Well, sir, may I take a minute and explain something to you?"

"Certainly. Here's another chair. Sit down."

Shane gave Vincent a brief explanation of Charly's health, without telling him that Charly may be dying, and asked if he could have permission to make a quick trip home to see her. Vincent took it to heart, saying he would go right then to General Hooker and try to persuade him to give leave for Shane to go see his ailing wife.

Shane waited at Vincent's tent. A quarter-hour later the colonel returned, the look on his face conveying that he had bad news.

"I'm sorry, Captain. General Hooker said he wishes he could let you go, but Lee is making moves that spell a big battle in the offing. No leaves are being granted at all."

The denial hit Shane like a club in the chest. "But sir, I can make the trip and be back here in four days. I...I didn't tell you how serious Charly's sickness really is. I'm afraid the Lord is going to take her home. I must see her before that happens. You have a wife that you love with all your heart. Please...put yourself in my place. If you don't feel you can go back and explain this to General Hooker, I'll try to see him myself."

Vincent scrubbed a hand across his clean-shaven face. "Tell you what...I'll take you to him. Maybe my presence will help."

Shane and Vincent were able to see Hooker, but the general

still would not grant the leave. He needed every officer he had on hand. Lee was making a move the Union army was going to have to watch. Small units of gray-uniformed troops were moving northward toward Pennsylvania.

Shane walked away from the general's tent with a heavy heart, but he thanked Colonel Vincent for trying.

By June 14, Robert E. Lee was moving his Army of Northern Virginia toward Pennsylvania in large units. This was enough to press Joseph Hooker into matching Lee in a parallel march. Hooker gathered his Army of the Potomac and began marching northward toward Frederick, Maryland.

Summer had arrived in full, and the hot weather slowed both armies to a snail's pace. They were making only a few miles a day. Many men on both sides were dropping from sunstroke.

On June 25, the heat and humidity were so intense that General Hooker called for a halt in early afternoon. They were at a small creek lined with shade trees, and the entire Union force stopped to take shelter from the sun and to cool off in the creek. Shane Donovan was off his horse and walking beside Buster Kilrain when the news came down the line of General Hooker's order to halt and rest.

"This march to Frederick is going to take a while, Captain," Buster said. "Why don't you talk to Chamberlain and see if he can't get you permission to go see her. Won't hurt to try."

"I'll do it," Shane said. "He's up front of the troops. I'll find him somewhere along the creek and see what he says."

Shane saw a group of soldiers at the head of the Twentieth's lines break rank and make a circle. Suddenly Rex Carden was running toward him, calling, "Captain Donovan!"

Shane handed the reins of his horse to Buster and ran to meet Carden. "What is it, Rex?"

"It's Colonel Chamberlain, Captain! He's passed out!"

Shane hurried toward the spot where Chamberlain's riderless horse stood in the heat of the sun.

Shane Donovan stayed beside Joshua Chamberlain for the rest of the afternoon, dampening his face with water from the creek and using the colonel's cap to fan him. Chamberlain was stretched out on the grass in the shade, and Buster Kilrain sat there, too. From time to time, Chamberlain roused and seemed to be coming to, then he would slip under again.

"Buster, I don't think he's going to come around for a while," Shane said. "I've just got to go to Charly. Looks like I'll have to see if Colonel Vincent will try to help me convince General Hooker to let me go."

"I'll take care of Joshua. You go on and talk to Vincent."

Strong Vincent's heart went out to Shane Donovan, but he shook his head and said, "Captain, I can't get to General Hooker right now. He and President Lincoln are having some problems between them, and the general is in wire contact with the president a couple of miles from here. I think he's going to be tied up there for some time."

"Well, sir, would you give me the leave? I'm about to come apart inside. I've got to get to Charly."

Vincent used a bandanna to mop his brow. "Captain, I wish I could, but General Hooker would have my neck. He absolutely will allow no leaves at this time. You know something's got to explode between us and the Rebels pretty soon. We need every man — especially every officer — we have. I'm really sorry, but you'll have to stay."

Shane reasoned that it would be at least ten days to two weeks before the two armies would go to battle. But another battle was already raging inside him. Shane loved Charly more than he loved life itself. He couldn't let her die without seeing her again. He did not want to disobey his superiors, nor did he want his fellow-soldiers to think he had run away. But he had to see her.

Tom Chamberlain had found his brother and was seated on the grass under the trees with Buster Kilrain as Shane approached.

"How's he doing?" Shane asked, kneeling down next to Buster.

"Still rallies every once in a while," Buster said, "but goes back under again. He'll be all right by mornin', I'm thinkin'."

"Tom, could I talk to you in private?" Shane said.

The two men moved to a relatively private spot in the shade and Tom asked, "What is it, my friend?"

"Tom, you're an officer, and you're my colonel's brother, so I'll tell you."

"Tell me what?"

"You know Charly is very sick."

"Of course. I pray for her often."

"Thank you. Listen, Tom, I know there's a big battle in the cooker. But from what I can put together, it's not going to happen for at least a couple of weeks or so."

"That's probably true."

"I need to go home and see Charly. I think she's dying. Can you understand that?"

"Yes. Have you talked to Josh about it?"

"I was going to when we stopped for the day."

"How about Colonel Vincent?"

"I tried. He says General Hooker's tied up with the president, and he can't give me leave without the general's permission. He says the general wouldn't do it even if he could talk to him."

"Shane, if you just up and go it will appear to the army as desertion."

Shane Donovan's voice was strained as he said, "I've thought of that. But I'm *not* deserting! As I see it, I would be deserting if I ran during battle. Charly's dying, Tom. I feel it in my heart. There's so little time. I've got to see her before she dies!"

"But Shane, why didn't you just take off? Why tell me you're going?"

"Because I'm not deserting, Tom. I'm only going home to see my wife before she dies. Tell your brother I will be back. Within four days. Please don't let anybody stop me. I'll head out when it gets dark."

Tom Chamberlain sleeved sweat from his brow, nodded, and said, "All right, Shane. I won't alert anyone. You go see Charly. I'll tell Josh when he comes around."

CHAPTER NINETEEN

Campfires flickered along the creek, and Union soldiers talked in low tones, discussing the rumored problem between General Hooker and the president. They also expressed their opinions as to when and where the big battle would take place.

Tom Chamberlain was alone with Joshua when he came to. The sunstroke had left him weak and a bit nauseated, and Tom waited till Joshua had taken some water and was sitting up against a tree before telling him about Shane Donovan.

"Tom, please tell me you're joking," Joshua said.

"I wish I was, Josh. But he's gone."

"How long ago?"

"About forty minutes."

"As commander of the Twentieth, I'm duty-bound to report him. But since I'm not feeling well, guess I'll have to give it another couple of hours before I'm strong enough to go to the general's tent and turn in the report."

Tom grinned. "For sure."

✵ ✵ ✵ ✵ ✵

Shane Donovan rode into Brunswick on the afternoon of June 27, 1863, on a horse rented in Portland. As he drew near his parents' house, he saw his youngest brother, Ryan, who was now nineteen, coming up the street from the opposite direction. Lewis O'Hanlon had talked Ryan into working at the shoe and boot factory upon his graduation from high school in May. Patrick had joined the Christian Commission with John Chamberlain and was somewhere down south serving the Federal cause.

Ryan smiled at his oldest brother as Shane swung from the saddle. They embraced. Shane felt relief when Ryan told him Charolette would be plenty happy to see him. He raised his eyes to the window of the bedroom he knew she occupied, but no face appeared.

At that moment, Shane heard a young female voice cry from the front porch, "Uncle Shane!"

Darlene Brainerd was ten years old now, and when school was out, spent a lot of time at his parents' house. He saw his mother standing on the porch as Darlene ran and threw her arms around him. Pearl Donovan was smiling at him and brushing tears from her cheeks.

"Hello, sweetheart," Shane said, giving Darlene a strong hug. "How are you and the rest of your family?"

"We're doing fine, Uncle Shane. Mama will be glad to know you're home and looking good. Do you have to go back to the war?"

"Yes, I'm afraid so."

"I'll be glad when you can come home for good. Aunt Charolette will too. She's going to be real glad to see you!"

Shane walked toward the porch with an arm around Darlene and kissed and embraced his mother. Pearl told him how glad she was to know he was alive and well. She asked how soon he had to head back, and he said he would have to leave at ten the next morning.

Darlene and Ryan followed Pearl and Shane into the house. Shane headed for the staircase, and Pearl said in a hushed voice, "She's not doing well at all, son. She's thinner than when you saw her in February, and she's awfully weak. In bed most of the time. Sits up in her chair in the mornings, but by early afternoon she's down again." She paused, then said, "She may be asleep, but go ahead and wake her. She'll want every minute with you she can have."

"Dear God," Shane said as he mounted the stairs, "thank You that she's still here."

The door was pushed shut, but not latched. Shane quietly pushed it open and saw that Charolette was asleep. Her raven-black hair lay in wavy swirls on the pillow, and her face seemed as white as the pillow case. Indeed, she was thinner, and the circles around her eyes were darker.

As he tiptoed across the room, the floorboards squeaked and Charly stirred. He stopped a few steps from the bed, and when she opened her eyes, she saw him.

"Shane!" she cried in a husky voice, lifting her arms. "O Shane, is it really you, or am I dreaming?"

Shane dropped to his knees beside the bed and took her in his arms. She clung to his neck. They held on to each other for a long time, then he kissed the tip of her nose and said, "You're not dreaming, precious lady. It's really me. General Hooker is moving the army across Maryland into Pennsylvania. There's going to be one whing-ding of a battle somewhere soon. I have to hurry back tomorrow morning, but...I just had to take a little side trip and see my wonderful wife."

They held each other for a long time, then talked about Charolette's health. She was a fighter. Giving up was not in her. She was still trusting God to heal her, and talked of how wonderful it would be when Shane came home for good and they could have their life together.

Shane wanted with all his heart to believe it.

"How's Ashley?" he asked.

"The Lord has given her grace. She still talks a lot about Mike and has her crying spells. Bless her heart, Shane, she comes here every day, even on Sundays between church services, to help take some of the load off your mother. She helps me bathe and washes my hair. I...I can hardly handle the stairs anymore. Ashley carries my meals up to me."

"She's not working at the factory?"

"Lewis hired another woman full-time to take my place. But he still sends a check over here with Ashley every week, same as if I were still working for him."

"You told me about that in a letter. I've got to thank him."

"Ashley does some office work for him as he needs her. She's there probably fifteen hours a week."

"Good she can stay busy."

"She does that, all right. When she's here, she always prays with me and *for* me, and for you...and reads the Bible to me."

"Talk about a real friend. You've got it in her."

"You were that kind of a friend to Mike too, Shane."

"Oh, speaking of Mike...there's something I want to show you."

Shane left the room long enough to go to the head of the stairs and call, "Ryan!"

Ryan came into view quickly. "Yes?"

"On that horse outside there's a blue canvas haversack tied behind the saddle. Has something in it I want to show Charly. Would you bring it up to me, please?"

"I already brought it in and put the horse in the shed out back. I'll bring it right up!"

Shortly thereafter, Shane was sitting on the side of the bed, opening a large brown envelope. He took out an official-looking document and handed it to Charolette. Her eyes focused on the document and she gasped.

"Why, Shane! It's a Presidential Commendation signed by Abraham Lincoln — for courage displayed on the battlefield above and beyond the call of duty! Oh, I'm so proud of you!"

"I hope you don't think I'm showing it to you to boast, or anything like that. I just thought a man's wife ought to know something like this."

"Of course she should. And of course I know you're not boasting. Was this given because of what you did when Mike was shot?"

"That and for an incident when I saved Colonel Chamberlain's life. Did you hear about his promotion to full colonel, and that he's now the commander of the Twentieth?"

"Fannie has made sure the whole state knows about it, I think. I'm so glad for him. He deserves it."

"Sure does. He's a wonderful man. I guess you could say he's my best friend now. On earth, I mean."

"Yes, let's not forget that Mike isn't gone. He's just waiting to see you higher up."

Shane felt his chest grow cold. He feared that soon his beloved Charly would be taken there, too. Suddenly they heard excited voices downstairs, followed by rapid footsteps on the stairs. Then Ashley popped through the door, eyes wide and wearing a warm smile.

"Shane! It's so good to see you!"

The old friends embraced and kissed each other on the cheek. Shane thanked Ashley for the way she was caring for Charly. Ashley said she and Charolette were best friends, just like Mike and Shane had been.

The next morning, Shane tied his haversack on the back of the horse, then went upstairs to tell Charly good-bye. She was in her chair, dressed in a white robe that made her hair look blacker than ever. She seemed to look better. He wondered if it was simply because seeing him had given her a lift, or if it was an indication that her illness might be in remission. With all his heart, he hoped it was the latter.

Shane had spent a little time with his parents and brother the night before. They waited downstairs, knowing he needed the time with Charly. When he had stayed till the last possible minute, he knelt beside the chair, held her in his arms, and told her he loved her with all his heart. They prayed together, then Shane kissed the tip of her nose and rose to his feet.

Charly smiled up at him and said softly, "I'll be lots better next time you come home."

"Promise?"

"Promise."

On June 28, the same day Shane Donovan rode toward Portland with his heart bleeding for Charly, vital changes were taking place in the ranks of the Army of the Potomac, even while it marched toward the Maryland-Pennsylvania line.

By orders from President Lincoln through his general-in-chief, Henry Halleck, Joseph Hooker was relieved as commander of the Union army. His hard-headed insubordination toward Lincoln had run its course. Lincoln replaced him with George G. Meade. By Meade's request, George Sykes became commander of Fifth Corps. The other six corps commanders remained the same. Meade requested that James Barnes be made commander of First Division, Fifth Corps. No other division commanders were changed.

Early on the morning of June 29, the front lines of Meade's army crossed the Pennsylvania border. From what Meade's scouts were telling him, it appeared that the opposing armies would converge at a small Pennsylvania town nine miles north of the border, known as Gettysburg.

At the same time, twenty-five miles south, George Sykes and his Fifth Corps were just arriving at Frederick, Maryland. The citizens of Frederick cheered them, as they had the other Union corps that had passed through before them.

In the heat of the early afternoon on July 1, the Fifth Corps crossed the state line into Pennsylvania. Joshua Chamberlain was riding abreast of Strong Vincent when they crossed into Vincent's home state. Just ahead of them, Old Glory waved in the morning breeze.

Vincent pointed to the flag and lifted his cap. "If I die in this battle, Colonel Chamberlain, what death more glorious could any man desire than to die on the soil of old Pennsylvania fighting for that flag?"

Chamberlain only smiled. He would rather die on Maine soil, but he could not wish that the war would reach the rolling hills and forests of his home state.

Just behind the ranks of the Twentieth Maine was the Eighty-third Pennsylvania Regiment. As the men of that unit crossed the border, their color-bearer unfurled the regiment's battered flag, and the fifes and drums struck up "Yankee Doodle." A tremendous shout went up from hundreds of throats. The enthusiasm spread both ways, and men all along the lines began shouting. Soon every drum was beating and every banner flying, including the battle flag of the Twentieth Maine.

General Robert E. Lee had kept his seventy thousand troops west of Meade's and was leading part of them in close-knit columns down the Chambersburg Pike from Cashtown. Meade's ninety thousand men were still strung out southward over thirty miles.

Neither army was ready to enter into full-scale battle on July 1. Lee insisted that no general engagement be started until the rest of his strung-out army was concentrated between Cashtown and Gettysburg. His plan was to engage the enemy in the fields between the towns, but his scouts reported that Meade already had his engineers laying out a defensive line in the ridges just outside of Gettysburg on the west.

Lee had his Third Corps with him, under the command of Ambrose Powell Hill, who was a fierce fighter. But his other two corps were still miles away. First Corps, under the command of Lee's "Old War Horse," James Longstreet, was almost a day's march to the west. Second Corps, commanded by Richard Ewell, was several miles to the north. Ewell had taken Stonewall Jackson's place as commander of Second Corps when Jackson was killed at Chancellorsville. The death of Jackson had left Lee feeling that he had lost his right arm.

While halted at a small creek for water a mile or so north of the state line, Strong Vincent and Joshua Chamberlain stood in what little shade an old elm tree could give them and drank from their canteens. Vincent cast a long look toward the south, and Chamberlain followed his line of sight.

"Looking for something, Colonel?"

"Some*one.* Your Captain Donovan. I'm beginning to wonder if he's coming back."

Chamberlain was silent for a moment. Did Shane find Charolette dead when he got home? Or if she was still alive, would he really come back as he told Tom he would? Aloud, Chamberlain said, "He'll be back unless providentially hindered."

Colonel Vincent had not taken it well when Chamberlain told him of Shane's departure, though Chamberlain had tried to impress on him that either of them might have done the same thing given similar circumstances. Vincent had said only that it would be wrong, no matter who left the camp without permission.

Chamberlain then told Vincent of Shane Donovan's Presidential Commendation, and why he received it. This caused Vincent to grow quiet for a long time, then having difficulty clearing his voice, he repeated that it was still wrong for a soldier to leave camp without permission.

"Colonel," Vincent said, "if Captain Donovan does come back, you understand I have to put him under arrest and hold him for court-martial."

Chamberlain set steady eyes on him, but did not reply.

Vincent frowned. "I hate to do it, Chamberlain. Especially

because he's my Christian brother. But it's military law. You know that."

"Yes, sir. Military law."

Late afternoon on June 30, Shane Donovan galloped toward Frederick, following the trail of the Union army. By the condition of the animal droppings along the trail, he figured the tail end of the Union lines was not far ahead.

He slowed his horse as he reached the edge of the city and held it to a slow walk. People on the main street waved and smiled at him. He greeted them in return, then spotted an elderly man who was about to cross the dusty street in front of him. Shane rode up to him and leaned from the saddle.

"Good afternoon sir. I'm part of the Twentieth Maine Regiment, which had to have come through here along with the rest of the Army of the Potomac. When did the last bunch go through?"

"Yesterday afternoon. From what I could pick up, they're headed due north. Looks like there's gonna be a big battle somewhere over the line in Pennsylvania."

"Yes, sir. That's what the army officials told me in Washington. Thanks for the information."

"My pleasure. God be with you, son."

"And you, sir."

Shane had ridden two more blocks when a group of young women in front of the general mercantile store took note of him. As he drew near, they began to smile and wave. He touched the bill of his officer's cap and smiled back. His eye fell on a lovely brunette who strongly resembled Charly.

"God bless you, soldier!" one of them cried.

"Send those Rebels home where they belong, Captain!" said another.

When he was past them, Shane breathed a prayer for the one

who was bone of his bones and flesh of his flesh. "O Charly," he whispered, "I love you so much. Please keep your promise. Please be better the next time I come home."

The Fifth Corps pulled off the road some four miles north of the state line shortly before the sun dipped behind the western hills. There were no fires, for General Meade had made it clear they were to leave the Pennsylvania countryside like they found it. They drank water from their canteens and ate beef jerky or salt pork, along with hardtack and dried-out biscuits. As they ate, they heard the sound of artillery and musketry coming from the direction of Gettysburg, some five miles to the north.

Joshua Chamberlain was sitting on the grass in the open field, eating with Tom and Buster Kilrain. Thousands of men in blue surrounded them. The men were quiet, talking little. They were tired, and their minds were fixed on the sounds of the distant guns. Their forward corps were no doubt already in conflict with the enemy. As the sun set, the sounds of battle diminished, then finally went still.

Buster was telling the Chamberlain brothers what he figured Lee had in mind, when Tom looked up and saw two familiar faces coming toward them.

"Josh..."

"Yeah?"

"Shane."

Joshua Chamberlain's head jerked around. Shane Donovan and Rex Carden were walking toward him.

"I knew he'd come back," Buster said almost under his breath.

As Joshua, Tom, and Buster stood up, Rex veered off, saying, "I'll think about it some more, sir."

Other soldiers in the area looked on as Shane halted and said, "Colonel, sir, I caught up to you as fast as I could. They told me at the camp in Washington about the changes in command, and that

General Meade had the army moving toward Pennsylvania."

The Chamberlain brothers and Buster made a small half-circle in front of him.

"What about...Charly?" Joshua asked.

Shane removed his cap and ran a sleeve across his brow. "She's not well, sir."

"Worse than when you saw her last?" Buster asked.

Shane nodded. "She's lost more weight, and she spends most of her time in bed."

"Sorry to hear that, Shane," Tom said.

"I'm not giving up hope, though. The Lord can heal her."

"Aye, He can," Buster said.

Joshua's insides were churning. He took a step closer and said, "Shane, I...I have to take you to Colonel Vincent."

"I'm in trouble, aren't I?"

"Yes. I tried to reason with him, even told him about your Presidential Commendation. But he says it's his duty to put you under arrest and hold you until you can face a court-martial."

Shane took a deep breath. "I'll turn myself in."

"I'll go with you."

"Me and Tom will come too, if ye like," Buster said.

"No need. But thanks anyway."

Dusk was on the land as Shane and Joshua Chamberlain drew near Colonel Vincent's field tent. A rider was just galloping off, heading due north. Vincent's back was to them as he watched the rider thunder away.

"Colonel Vincent, sir..." Shane said.

The colonel turned around slowly, glanced at Chamberlain, then set his gaze on Shane Donovan.

"I've come to turn myself in, sir. I fully realize that I left the camp without your permission. Colonel Chamberlain was sick and unable to talk, and you were not available. I did what I thought was right in view of the circumstances, sir, but I am ready to take my punishment."

"Captain Donovan, may I ask about your wife?"

"She's not well, sir."

Vincent nodded silently. "Do you think this may have been the last time you will see her?"

"On this earth, sir. Unless the Lord intervenes."

Vincent took a deep, tremulous breath and let it out through his nostrils. "I'm sorry."

"Thank you, sir."

Vincent looked at Chamberlain again, then back at Shane. "According to military law, Captain, it is my duty to arrest you and hold you for court martial."

"Yes, sir."

The colonel's face was solemn. "I am a graduate of Harvard Law School, as you may have heard."

"Yes, sir."

"It was my dream to one day become a judge. Judges are given the responsibility of interpreting the law, Captain."

"Yes, sir."

"They must take all circumstances into consideration when doing so."

"Yes, sir."

"Military commanders in the field must often act as judges. I'm sure you understand that because you are my brother in Christ, I would like to just forget your deed. But if Christians do wrong, other Christians cannot condone it."

"I understand that, sir."

"Since discussing your case with Colonel Chamberlain, I have been giving it a lot of thought."

"Yes, sir."

"I decided to take it higher."

"Sir?"

"To Generals Barnes, Sykes, and Meade."

Shane swallowed hard. "Yes, sir."

"After listening to their judgment in your case, Captain

Donovan, I hereby inform you that as far as the generals are concerned, your little trip to Maine never happened." Even as he spoke, Vincent's lips curved into a wide smile.

Astonishment showed in Shane Donovan's face, followed by great relief. "I...I don't know what to say, Colonel."

"Just thank the Lord. It was His doing. I prayed fervently before I went to the generals."

"I do thank Him," Shane said. "And I thank you, sir. And you!" he added, turning to Chamberlain.

After both colonels told Shane he was welcome, Chamberlain asked Vincent, "Was that messenger from General Meade?"

"Yes. He informed me what the fighting was about at Gettysburg that we heard a little while ago. Our First and Seventh Corps fought a desperate battle with part of the Rebel army. A lot of men were killed on both sides. General Meade wants us to march till midnight. We'll stop, sleep three hours, then march again. The rest of Lee's army is marching tonight, too."

When the Fifth Corps started its march at 3:00 A.M., they were but three miles from Gettysburg. As always, moving troops and equipment was slow. When dawn came, the men in blue began to see evidence of a cavalry battle — trampled grain, broken fences, dead horses, and bodies of Yankees and Rebels strewn in the fields.

Fifth Corps, weary and sleepy, arrived at Gettysburg just before 7:00 on Thursday morning, July 2, 1863. They halted at Wolf's Hill, a mile or so southeast of the town's center. The other six corps of the Union army were already there.

Running north and south three-quarters of a mile west of Gettysburg was Seminary Ridge, rising some forty feet above the surrounding fields. The ridge was crowned by the three-story brick building of the Lutheran Theological Seminary.

Due south of town was its cemetery, which was on a gentle

rise that topped out some eighty feet above the town. Cemetery Ridge skirted Cemetery Hill on the south side and curved west, then south. It was about the same height as Seminary Ridge some thousand yards to the west.

Culp's Hill butted up on a portion of the south edge of Cemetery Ridge. The Fifth Corps, having no time for rest nor breakfast, was moved quickly to Culp's Hill. This placed them in the rear of the right of the Union line, which resembled a giant, upside-down fishhook. The hook started with its barb southeast of Culp's Hill, curved north, then ran west to the top of Cemetery Hill. After proceeding around Cemetery Hill, the hook — made up of thousands of Union troops — plunged south along Cemetery Ridge. A half-mile south of Cemetery Ridge stood a granite hill, thick with trees, known as Little Round Top, which stood 170 feet high. Some 500 yards slightly to the southwest of Little Round Top rose the highest prominence in the area, called Big Round Top. It was heavily wooded and cone-shaped and stood 305 feet high.

When the Fifth Corps looked the area over, they were glad to see Union flags atop Cemetery Hill, Cemetery Ridge, both Round Tops, and Culp's Hill. Gaining the high ground was always advantageous. This they remembered from the devastating experience at Fredericksburg. One thing bothered them, however. There was a Confederate flag atop Seminary Ridge. Lee had occupied at least one high spot.

To the west of Little Round Top was a massive jumble of huge granite boulders known as Devil's Den. Beyond Devil's Den toward Seminary Ridge was a large peach orchard. Between Devil's Den and Little Round Top was a marshy, rock-strewn valley. Through it flowed a small stream named Plum Run.

The land that spread out from Cemetery Ridge and the Round Tops south, east, and west contained houses, barns, fields, pastures, and woods of several farms. Fences built from stones cleared from the land ran in several directions across the peaceful terrain, which was about to become a raging, bloody battlefield.

CHAPTER TWENTY

As the sun continued its climb into the Pennsylvania sky, heating up the land as it went, General Robert E. Lee was not yet ready to engage the enemy. He needed to position his troops to assault the Union forces, who had most of the high ground.

At 8:00 A.M., General George Meade met with the officers of Fifth Corps at the field tent atop Cemetery Hill. The way Lee was shifting his army about, Meade knew he had some time before any Confederate assault began. Meade set aside several regiments to be held in reserve. One of those regiments was the Twentieth Maine. Also present for the meeting were Winfield S. Hancock, commander of Second Corps, and Daniel E. Sickles, commander of Third Corps. These men would have some of the reserve regiments at their disposal once the day's battle began. For the time being, the Twentieth Maine was to return to Culp's Hill and wait.

When the meeting was dismissed, Shane Donovan walked a few yards from Meade's tent and in among the tombstones. His heart grew heavy as he read the inscriptions. Was this what he would find when he returned home — Charly's grave with a tombstone coldly declaring the date of her birth and the date of her death?

The tired and hungry men of the Twentieth Maine settled down on Culp's Hill, pulled hardtack, biscuits, salt pork, and beef jerky from their canvas haversacks, and wolfed them down. The temperature was rising, and the air was humid and oppressive. Many took advantage of the wait to doze, while others talked in low tones of the coming battle. Shane and Joshua Chamberlain sat on the sloping hill and read their Bibles together. They were just closing them when Shane saw Rex Carden sitting a few feet away, watching them.

"Hello, Rex," Shane said. "Come join us."

Carden got up and walked to them, then sat down beside Shane.

"So have you been thinking about what we talked about the other day?" Shane asked.

"Yes, sir. But I just don't think I'm ready to get saved."

"We're going into battle, Rex. Are you ready to die?"

The young soldier met Shane's gaze, then looked at the ground. "No."

"Do you remember what the Bible says...that whoever believes in Jesus, God's Son, will not perish but will have everlasting life? All you need to do is call on Jesus, Rex, to put your faith and trust in Him. You can go into battle today knowing that if you should die, you'll spend eternity in heaven. Wouldn't you like to have that assurance?"

"Yes, sir. I'm...just not ready to call on Him, Captain."

"What do you think it will take to make you ready?"

"I don't know, sir. But until I am, I wouldn't mean it if I called on Him."

"Of course I want you to mean it, Rex. But you can put Him off too long and be eternally sorry. He says in this Bible that *now* is the day of salvation. You don't know about tomorrow."

"I know, Captain," said Rex, rising to his feet. "I appreciate your concern...and I'll give what you've said some more thought."

The two armies carefully made plans and positioned their troops and guns as the day grew hotter. Then suddenly at just before 11:00 A.M., a sharp cannonade burst forth from the Confederate guns on Seminary Ridge. The Union artillery answered back, and within minutes, infantrymen were swarming at each other across the open fields. The battle was underway.

By two o'clock, the Twentieth Maine had been moved several times to positions east of Culp's Hill, then near a lumber mill, and finally across a small creek and the Baltimore Pike to a low rise beside the highway. They were expecting to be called into battle at any time. Chamberlain held his men in strict line, ready to go. Colonel Strong Vincent sent a supply wagon, giving twenty rounds of extra ammunition to each man.

Rebel artillery from the north end of Seminary Ridge was concentrating fire on Union artillery and infantry on Cemetery Ridge. From the south end, it was bombarding troops along the west edge of Cemetery Ridge and further south toward Devil's Den, where Meade had placed thousands of men. Meade's artillery pounded them back.

Confederate infantry and cavalry swept through the peach orchard and across a large wheat field to meet the Union infantry and cavalry. Boards of barns, sheds, and houses flew in splinters through the air as cannonballs landed on farm homes. Rock walls shattered, spraying the fields with sharp stone missiles and pelting the fighting men. Exploding shells gouged holes like miniature graves in the earth.

Countless flashes of musket fire began to appear amid the heavy smoke and tongues of flame of the artillery batteries on both sides. Long gray and blue lines came scurrying onto the fields to mix with the battle smoke.

Joshua Chamberlain's regiment sat in the low spot along the Baltimore Pike, waiting, listening. A long, rounded rise just across the Pike blocked their view of the battle that raged less than a mile away. Waiting was harder than fighting. In the quiet of his own mind, a man had time to imagine all kinds of horrible things that could happen to him. In the midst of battle, a man's attention was so riveted he didn't have time for such thoughts. Chamberlain walked among his men and saw the torment written on their sweat-stained faces.

The heat was becoming unbearable. For the most part, the men who waited in reserve along the Baltimore Pike had been born and raised in northern New England. There, summers were comparatively brief and never as hot and humid as what they had found in Virginia, Maryland, and Pennsylvania.

The unseen battle raged on. The Mainers watched the clouds of smoke drift toward the sky on the afternoon breeze — the same breeze that brought them the acrid odor of burnt powder and the unmistakable smell of death.

And death was busy with his grim sickle as the sun slowly ran its course. Men were falling on the ridges, in the peach orchard, on the open fields, and in the small, marshy valley between Little Round Top and Devil's Den. Bodies lay so thick in the valley, men were walking on human flesh to fight each other. Little Plum Run, which ran through the center of the valley, was littered with lifeless forms floating lazily southward in a winding stream of red.

Cannon after cannon along the battery lines of the east and west ridges leaped where they stood as the artillerymen yanked the lanyards, bellowing canister and grape-shot on the enemy.

Still the swarms of fighting men filled the field of battle, advancing under the cries of their leaders. From Gettysburg's south edge all the way to Big Round Top, between the long ridges, stretched an uninterrupted field of conflict. One by one, the reserve regiments on both sides were called into action.

Though the men of the Twentieth Maine waited impatiently, on the battlefield, all sense of time was dulled. The roar of gunfire and the yells of the enemy seemed to fade into the background as impassioned men fought to wipe each other off the face of the earth. Battery men drove deadly charges of canister into a maze of humanity. Cavalrymen charged enemy lines, firing their weapons and thrusting them through with their sabers. Infantrymen fired, reloaded, and fired again, leaving wounded and dying men on the crimsoned grass. Poor, mutilated creatures, some with an arm dangling, some with a leg torn and bleeding, limped and crawled toward the rear.

There was no faltering. Men of blue and gray fought nobly for their cause as the sun, an indistinct ball of fire beyond the smoky mist, began to lower in the western sky.

At the Confederate headquarters atop Seminary Ridge, General Lee and his First Corps commander, James Longstreet, were at odds. Lee had told Lafayette McLaws, a division commander under Longstreet, to pull his division away from First Corps and take up a position at a strategic spot just southwest of Cemetery Hill.

Longstreet, already perturbed at Lee for not capturing the Round Tops before the Union forces arrived at Gettysburg, exploded, telling McLaws to keep his division where it was. Lee lashed back in anger, but his indignation was suddenly interrupted by chest pains. He had to sit down and catch his breath.

In spite of the differences between them, Longstreet loved and admired his commander. He quickly poured Lee a cup of water from a canteen and gave it to him a sip at a time. McLaws stood by, waiting for a final command.

Longstreet was piqued because Lee's arrangements for the complicated battle operations were, in his military mind, incredibly casual. At no time since the Confederate army had converged at Gettysburg had Lee brought together his three corps commanders, upon whose understanding and cooperation the entire campaign depended. During the lull before the battle that morning of July 2,

Lee had acted as his own courier, riding back and forth between Longstreet, Ewell, and Hill at a considerate cost of time.

General Lee had been suffering with severe chest pains since March, and to Longstreet seemed "out of sorts" and not thinking clearly.

Earlier that day, two regiments of John Geary's division of the Union Third Corps occupied Little Round Top. As the battle raged, Major General Daniel Sickles ordered Geary to leave a small signal corps on Little Round Top and remove his regiments to a spot at Culp's Hill.

Geary, a Mexican war veteran, knew that signalmen could never hold Little Round Top. If the Confederates occupied it, they would have a distinct advantage over the Union left wing and turn the tide for the South in the entire battle. To hold Little Round Top was crucial.

Hastily, Geary wrote a note, handed it to the courier who had brought the order, and told him to rush it to Sickles. The note conveyed Geary's opinion that keeping a tight hold on Little Round Top was of critical importance.

Sickles shrugged it off, sending back a message that he would attend to Little Round Top in due time. Geary was to obey the order. Geary returned another message urging the Third Corps commander to reconsider. A third message came, commanding Geary to obey or face the consequences. Geary reluctantly led his regiments off Little Round Top, leaving it virtually undefended.

Captain Samuel R. Johnston rushed up to Robert E. Lee's field tent atop Seminary Ridge and peered through the flap opening. "Pardon me, sirs," he said. "I realize I'm interrupting, but what I have to say to General Lee cannot wait."

"Come in, Captain," Lee said.

As Johnston stepped inside, Lee said to McLaws, "General Longstreet is outranked here. You move your division to the position southwest of Culp's Hill as I told you."

"Yes, sir," McLaws said, giving Longstreet an uneasy glance as he hurried from the tent.

Lee turned his attention to Johnston. "What is it, Captain?"

"Sir, the Yankees have just left Little Round Top."

"What? I can't believe that!"

Longstreet frowned. "You mean they've taken every man off it?"

"They left a signal corps, General. Best we can count are maybe a half-dozen men."

"Why would they do that?" Lee said. "That is the key position on this battlefield. It doesn't make sense."

Lee stood to his feet, swayed a bit, and said to Longstreet, "Who have we got that we can thrust to Little Round Top immediately?"

Longstreet stepped to the table where a crude map of the Gettysburg area was laid out. Lee moved up beside him. Longstreet ran a finger back and forth on the map and said, "Colonel Oates's Fifteenth Alabama, sir. He's had several men killed and wounded, but the last I knew, he still had close to eight hundred men. He's with the Forty-Seventh Alabama right now, trying to take Big Round Top."

"That'll take a while," Lee said, turning to Johnston. "Captain, ride hard and find General Law. Tell him I said to cut William Oates and his Fifteenth Alabama out and send them to take and defend Little Round Top...on the double!"

Major General E. McIver Law responded quickly to Lee's order. In addition to the entire Fifteenth Alabama, he added men from the

Fourth Alabama and the Fourth and Fifth Texas regiments, making a unit of over three thousand men.

Colonel William C. Oates, an officer known for his valor and courage in battle, pulled away from the fighting at Big Round Top and assembled his eager unit amid the heavy trees at its eastern base. They would make a wild run across the five-hundred-yard saddle that lay between the Round Tops.

Oates was convinced that he and his men held the key to victory in the Battle of Gettysburg. By taking Little Round Top with its height and strategic location, they would possess a Gibraltar that they could hold against ten times their number and turn the tide for the Confederacy in the entire war.

It was 3:40 P.M. as they assembled in a dense stand of trees overlooking the space that led to Little Round Top.

At the same time, the Union's chief topographical engineer and a seasoned veteran of the Mexican War, Brigadier General G. K. Warren, was nearing Little Round Top on an errand for General Meade. Warren was on horseback, sided by his staff officer, Ranald Mackenzie. Warren was to observe the situation at Devil's Den and send Mackenzie back with his assessment of how the battle was going. Warren was to then assess the condition of the Union troops at the peach orchard and return to Meade on Cemetery Hill.

Warren's attention was drawn to the crest of Little Round Top, where he saw a signal corpsman waving two flags; a handful of others stood nearby. He wondered why he saw no artillery, nor anyone to man the cannons. Neither did he see one infantryman. He was about to say something about it to Mackenzie when the lieutenant pointed toward Big Round Top and said, "General! Over there in those trees! Looks like the Rebs are getting ready to plunge out of there and head into the open. Where could they be going?"

Warren saw the glistening of gun barrels and bayonets at the edge of the trees and gasped, "Little Round Top, Ranald! Somebody's pulled our fighting men off and left a few signal corpsmen. Those Rebels can see that as well as we can. We've got to man that hill, or they'll have an advantage we can't overcome!"

"What shall we do, sir?"

"You ride to General Sickles. I'll ride to General Sykes. There's enough canister and musket balls flying in that space to make the going slow for those Rebs, but we've got to man Little Round Top before they get there!"

Ranald Mackenzie found his way to General Sickles's position on the battlefield, but Sickles said he could not spare a man. At the same time, General Sykes saw the urgent situation and assured Warren he would take care of it. Sykes sent immediate orders to James Barnes to rush a brigade to the threatened hill. Warren hurried back to Cemetery Hill to tell General Meade what was going on.

Joshua Chamberlain was pacing back and forth with his hands clasped behind his back as the sounds of battle continued to thunder over the hill. Suddenly there was a rider galloping around the south end of the hill, coming as fast as his horse would carry him.

Buster Kilrain moved up beside Chamberlain and said, "Looks like we're finally gonna get into the fight, Colonel."

"It's Colonel Vincent!" Shane Donovan said.

The men of the Twentieth Maine scrambled to their feet as Vincent skidded the lathered animal to a halt.

"Colonel Chamberlain, I need your regiment over at Little Round Top as fast as you can get there!"

He gave a quick explanation of the situation, and rode away as the Twentieth Maine began a hard run in the oppressive heat. The officers rode at a trot ahead of the men, who were eager to get into the fight.

The distance was short, and within minutes, Chamberlain and his troops came near Little Round Top. Three other regiments in Vincent's brigade also had been ordered to the coveted hill — the

Sixteenth Michigan, the Forty-fourth New York, and the Eighty-third Pennsylvania.

As the men of the Twentieth looked out over the land toward Devil's Den and the peach orchard, they saw bayonet fighting in one place, musketry spread wide, and cannonade along the ridges. Across the sloping saddle toward Big Round Top, they saw Colonel Oates attempting to lead his swarm of Rebels toward them, but Union artillery hindered them. At times, they had to hit the ground and hunt for cover.

Oates watched with fiery eyes as the Union troops under the leadership of Colonel Strong Vincent ran toward Little Round Top. General Lee's order had come too late.

Confederate artillery some seven hundred yards west of Little Round Top arched whistling cannonballs down on the troops scurrying toward that hill. Men of the New York, Michigan, and Pennsylvania regiments ahead of the Maine regiment were taking a pounding. Those who escaped the shells ran for the hill as fast as they could. Vincent led them behind Little Round Top on the wooded east side to make the climb. The half-dozen signal corpsmen were at the crest on that side, cheering them on.

The cannonade continued as the men of the Twentieth Maine hastily made their way amid bodies of New York, Michigan, and Pennsylvania soldiers who had preceded them. The officers on horseback were almost around to the safer east side when three...four...five shells struck the line of Mainers. Men were blown every direction.

Those who escaped the shelling kept running. Soon the officers reached the massive boulders at the back side of Little Round Top and left their horses with Vincent's orderlies. More deadly cannonballs fell on the Mainers as the rear lines tried to reach the safety of the hill.

Vincent stayed just below the rocky, forested crest of the hill and gave commands; the regiments formed their positions. The Michigan regiment was on the extreme right, facing west. The New York regiment was placed alongside them and told to man the artillery that General Geary's men had left. The New York had plenty of artillerymen, and there was a modest supply of ammunition. The Pennsylvania regiment was positioned to the New Yorkers' left. Their battle line curved around the southwest turn of the hill. Last was Colonel Chamberlain and his Twentieth Maine, who had taken heavy losses in getting to Little Round Top. The regiment faced south and slightly west on the steep and heavily wooded side.

As they were getting positioned, Rex Carden drew up beside Shane Donovan and said, "That was close, wasn't it? We lost a lot of men!"

"Yes," Shane said sadly. "A lot of men."

"And did you see all those bodies in that low spot where that creek runs...this side of all those huge boulders?"

"I saw them."

"I heard one of the Pennsylvania guys say those boulders are called Devil's Den, and another one said General Meade is calling that low spot the Valley of Death." Rex moved closer. "Isn't there a valley of death in the Bible?"

"Well, there's one implied, but there's no place I know of where a valley is called the valley of death. Jeremiah wrote of a valley of slaughter, and Ezekiel wrote of a valley of dead men's bones. Psalm 23:4 is where the valley of death is implied, but it's called the valley of the *shadow* of death. There's a difference. I — "

"Captain Donovan!" one of the men shouted. "We have a man dying over here!"

Shane excused himself and hurried to where a young soldier lay on the rocky ground. Two of his friends hovered over him. Rex followed and looked on as Shane knelt beside the dying man. He had been hit with shrapnel, and his two friends had picked him up and carried him to the top of the hill.

* * * * *

Several yards away, Colonel Vincent and Colonel Chamberlain were talking together.

"Colonel Chamberlain, I learned that the Rebels headed this way from Big Round Top are led by Colonel Bill Oates. He's a real fighter. He'll get the bulk of his men through all that cannonade of ours soon."

"My men are ready, Colonel."

"Have you had time to make a count?"

"Yes, sir. Best I can come up with, we're down to 386, including me."

"Well, my friend, you're going to find out what your regiment's made of today. Do you understand that you are at the left of the Union line? By that I mean, the Twentieth Maine is at the extreme left of the entire Army of the Potomac."

"I know that, sir."

"Chamberlain, a desperate attack is coming very shortly. You are to hold this ground at all costs. Do you understand? At all costs."

"I understand, sir. We'll do it."

Vincent reached out and grasped Chamberlain's hand. They stood, hands clasped, looking into each other's eyes.

"I know you will," Vincent said. "The victory in this battle, and possibly the ultimate victory in this whole rotten war, depends in large measure on what you and your men do in the next few hours. If you can break Lee's back here and now, maybe you can go home to that family of yours soon."

"I'd like that, sir."

"I must go, Colonel. May the Lord protect you."

With that, Vincent whirled and disappeared around a huge boulder. Joshua Chamberlain had a strange feeling pass over him, a feeling that he had just seen Colonel Strong Vincent for the last time in this world.

The young soldier with the shrapnel wound died before the

eyes of the four men who hovered over him. Rex Carden's face was sheet-white as he walked away beside Shane Donovan.

"Colonel," Rex said, "remember last time you talked to me about repenting of my sin and asking Jesus to come into my heart and save me?"

"Yes."

"And I told you I wasn't ready?"

"Yes."

"Well, I am now."

CHAPTER TWENTY-ONE

R ex, are you sure you mean it?" Shane's heart quickened pace.

"Yes, sir. Ever since you started talking to me about Jesus, God's been working on me. I'm not going to resist Him any more. I want to be saved."

Shane took his Bible from his haversack, opened it, and quickly went over the Scriptures he had shown Rex Carden many times before. After Rex had humbly called on the Lord to save him, Shane prayed with an arm around his shoulder, asking the Lord to help Rex faithfully serve Him.

Tears filled Rex's eyes and he shook his head in wonderment. "Thank you, Captain. Thank you for caring about me and where I spend eternity. How foolish I was to put Jesus off as long as I did."

Both men heard a noise behind them and turned to see Colonel Chamberlain.

"Captain," Chamberlain said, "the Fifteenth Alabama and whoever else they've got with them are about to hit us. We've got maybe ten minutes."

✳ ✳ ✳ ✳ ✳

Colonel Oates found a few moments' lull in the cannonade that hindered his approach to Little Round Top, and when it came, he shouted to his men to charge. They were out in the open, and Oates figured the best thing to do was to take Little Round Top by force. His troops clearly outnumbered Vincent's.

Atop Little Round Top, artillery and infantry were in place. The four regiments of Colonel Strong Vincent's brigade braced themselves for the attack.

At approximately 5:00 P.M., Oates's troops ejected a wild Rebel yell and charged the rocky hill. The wild-eyed Confederates swarmed in on three sides, and the Union regiment commanders shouted for their men to commence fire.

At the bottom of the steep hill, the Fifteenth Alabama and their Texas comrades plunged into the bushes and began crawling over the boulders. Howitzer shells exploded and bullets hissed at them by the hundreds, many of them striking stone and ricocheting away in angry whines.

On the south side of the hill, Joshua Chamberlain stood slightly above his men, sword in one hand and revolver in the other. He saw dozens of Rebels go down in the initial volley unleashed by the Twentieth Maine. But Lee's soldiers meant business. They kept right on coming.

Chamberlain shouted encouragement to his men as he fired his revolver at those Rebels who were climbing closer. He saw Buster Kilrain, below to his left, fire his rifle and drop a charging Rebel, but another took aim at the redheaded Irishman. Just to Kilrain's left, Shane Donovan fired on the Rebel with his revolver. Before the man in gray could squeeze the trigger, Shane's bullet stopped his heart.

Below to Chamberlain's right were his brother, Tom, and Ellis Spear blasting away with their pistols, shouldered on both sides by riflemen. The metallic sound of ramrods punching lead balls into gunpowder rang over the hillside amid the roar of gunfire.

Colonel Vincent's words echoed through Chamberlain's mind: "You are to hold this ground at all costs. Do you understand? At all costs."

The responsibility weighed heavily on Chamberlain's mind and doubled his resolve. If they failed to hold the left flank, the Confederates would gain the rear of the entire Union position where large amounts of supplies and ammunition had been placed. Meade's army would be faced with defeat, resulting in unthinkable disaster to the Union cause. The way to Philadelphia, Baltimore, and Washington would be wide open to a victorious Robert E. Lee.

Chamberlain watched his gallant men carrying the fight to the swarming enemy. These Mainers would do it; they would hold. Most of them were not much more than boys, but they were rugged, disciplined, and tough — veterans of march and battle. They had character, and they knew what they had to do. He remembered their faces as they took their battle positions. There was resolve and courage fixed on each one. And now they were demonstrating it.

Shane Donovan was reloading his revolver when two Confederates pushed through the trees right in front of him, rifles poised to fire. Suddenly there was a staccato of musket fire to his near right. Buster Kilrain and two other men had seen the Confederates and cut them down. Shane grinned and Buster shouted, "Just payin' ye back for an earlier favor!"

Suddenly Buster jerked, hunched, and dropped to the ground, his teeth clenched. Shane punched in the last cartridge with shaky fingers and snapped the cylinder shut. Before he could move, Colonel Chamberlain was beside Buster, calling for a corps medic.

The medic was several yards away, tending to a fallen soldier. He called back that he would be there momentarily, then worked furiously to finish applying a bandage.

The screaming Rebels kept coming through the trees and over the blood-stained boulders and the bodies of their fallen comrades.

Shane fired away keeping Buster in his peripheral vision. Though death was in the air in the form of hot lead, Chamberlain did not leave Buster's side until the medic arrived. As the colonel stood to climb back to his vantage point, Shane called, "How bad is it, Colonel?"

"Got him under the right arm just below the shoulder," Chamberlain called back. "Bullet's lodged somewhere in his chest cavity. He's conscious, but it's not good."

There was no time to go to Buster's side. Colonel Oates's troops were coming too fast and too furious. Rank after rank charged up the slope, taking furious fire from the Twentieth Maine. Bullets buzzed on Little Round Top like hordes of angry hornets, and thick clouds of powder smoke filled the air.

Mainers were dropping here and there, but the real toll was being taken on the brave and determined Rebels. They were falling by the dozens, a mass of torn bodies. Fresh troops appeared from behind the trees and boulders, rushing forward to replace the dead and wounded.

The Mainers tried to find a moment to take a hurried drink from their canteens. Though it was late in the afternoon, the sun's heat was like that of a blast furnace. Chamberlain moved among his men, still bearing his sword and revolver, his entire body soaked with sweat.

"You're doing fine, you bunch of Mainers!" he shouted from time to time. "Keep it up! We're not giving this hill to them! Let them go back to Alabama or Texas and find their own hills!"

Shane was taking a swig from his canteen when a rifleman next to him took a bullet. There was a muffled grunt, and the rifleman fell dead. A swarm of gray uniforms came out of the trees directly in front of him, yelling and firing their muskets on the run.

Mainers unleashed on them, muskets blazing, and Shane fired

his revolver as fast as he could snap back the hammer. Rebels went down two and three at a time.

Shane saw four of them who had just fired their muskets stumble over their fallen comrades. Lying flat, each one started to reload his musket. Shane's revolver had clicked on a spent cartridge in the exchange. It was empty.

The other men of the Twentieth were fully occupied with the seemingly limitless reserve of men in gray. There was no time for Shane to reload his revolver. He had to do something before the four Rebels reloaded or came at him with their bayonets. He picked up the musket of the soldier who had just died next to him and leaped to his feet.

"Drop those muskets!" he yelled, charging at them.

The four Rebels looked at him, eyes wide. One of them said, "He can only get one of us, boys! Let's take him!"

"But which one will it be?" Shane said.

From his high perch, Chamberlain peered through the battle smoke and saw Shane standing alone, holding the musket on four enemy soldiers. The Rebels dropped their guns and placed their hands on top of their heads. Shane waved the muzzle at the Rebels and herded them around to the back side of Little Round Top toward one of the massive boulders.

The sight seemed to Chamberlain to be worthy of some rousing song or sonnet that commemorated the deeds of war heroes. But there was no time for sentiment. The battle was hot, and the enemy was determined.

The Confederates kept coming and the battle roared on. When Shane did not appear after a few minutes, Chamberlain bent low and ran to the boulder. When he rounded it, he almost ran into Shane, who was coming his way. Behind Shane, Chamberlain saw the four Rebels on the ground, trussed up to each other, bound hand and foot with their belts.

"That was good work, Captain," Chamberlain said. "It takes some doing for one man to capture four by himself."

Shane looked over his shoulder at his prisoners and said, "Especially with an empty gun, sir."

"An empty gun!" one of them said.

Shane had the hammer of the musket in cock position. He pulled the trigger, and the hammer made only a dry click as it snapped down.

Though the battle continued to rage on the other sides of Little Round Top, there was a momentary lull for the Twentieth Maine. Joshua and Tom Chamberlain and Shane Donovan rushed to Buster Kilrain. The medic was elsewhere, caring for wounded men, but Buster was conscious. Though he was a bit glassy-eyed, he knew them as they bent down around him.

"Are you in a lot of pain, Sergeant?" the colonel asked.

Buster was gritting his teeth. "Not…for a tough ol' Irishman, laddie. I mean, *Colonel*, sir."

"You can call me anything you want, just so you don't let this wound do you in."

"Colonel!" came a sharp cry. "Here they come again!"

Every man hurried to his station. As Chamberlain was returning to his spot, the sergeant in charge of ammunition ran up to him.

"Colonel, sir, we're running low on powder and bullets!"

"We'll have to make sure we use the ammunition from our dead…and from the enemy dead, Sergeant. Pass the word along."

The sounds of the next assault met the ears of the men in blue. The Rebels came yelling and clawing up through the battle-torn bushes, the shattered trees, over and around the bullet-chipped boulders.

"Stand firm, Mainers!" Chamberlain shouted. "Not once in a century are men permitted to bear such a responsibility! We cannot fold! We must keep fighting!"

And fight they did.

The entire regiment was mantled in fire and smoke, which filled their lungs and stung their eyes. Powder blackened their faces as they tore the paper cartridges with their teeth and stuffed powder into the smoking muzzles. Steel ramrods rattled and clanged in hot barrels. Their valor touched Joshua Chamberlain deeply.

The carnage went on. Within half an hour, the men of the Twentieth Maine were virtually out of ammunition. Sergeant Neil Bulkley ran about, taking powder and lead minié balls off the bodies of Yankees and Rebels alike and distributing them along the lines. Soon there was no more to be found.

Colonel Chamberlain carefully fired the last six rounds in his revolver, making sure every one of them counted. He saw Sergeant Bulkley zigzagging his way among the fighting men, heading toward him. He emptied his revolver before Bulkley reached him.

"Sir, we're out of ammunition," Bulkley gasped. "The men are using up their last rounds now! And…we've lost well over a hundred men, sir. I mean, dead. There are about seventy or eighty wounded scattered about. We haven't got more than two hundred left who can fight."

Even while the sergeant was speaking, the Mainers blasted the Confederates with their last rounds. Chamberlain noticed the Confederates fade back down the hill, as if reforming for a final assault. He was about to give a command when he saw Rex Carden running around the rocky crest from the west. Chamberlain had sent Carden to see how the battle was going with the other three regiments.

"Colonel…the news is not good," Carden said, sucking hard for air. "They're taking a real beating over there. Every one of the regiments has lost nearly half their men."

Chamberlain nodded grimly. Then the commander of the Twentieth Maine shouted, "Fix bayonets! We're going to attack!"

There was no hesitation. The distinct rattle of bayonets being fixed to muskets filled the air.

Chamberlain's empty revolver was in his holster. With his sword in hand, he pointed to the right and said, "I want you spread out in this direction in one long line. We'll charge like a giant swinging door. We've got to stop them this time! We won't get another chance!"

From the bottom of the hill came a high-pitched Rebel yell.

Above the screaming Rebels, Chamberlain shouted, "Charge!" He leaped down from the high spot, yelling over and over. "Charge!"

The whole Twentieth Maine, yelling wildly, followed Chamberlain down through the bushes and trees, over boulders and bodies of dead and wounded, going after the enemy with intent to destroy.

The Rebels, who had reached a point about a fourth of the way up, suddenly froze, eyes wide. The two hundred screaming men surging down the slope with their sharply pointed bayonets was enough to strike terror in the hearts of the most courageous men.

A few raised their rifles and fired, then turned and ran. Some of the Mainers fell.

Shane Donovan was about ten yards behind Rex Carden and saw him take one of the bullets. Rex went down head-over-heels, crashed into a tree, and lay still. Shane wanted to stop, but pressed on.

Colonel Oates was already calling for a retreat, and hundreds of men in gray stampeded from the scene. Hundreds of others, afraid they would be shot if they turned and ran, threw their guns down and raised their hands high in the air.

Eventually all firing stopped on the entire battlefield, and the dust slowly settled. The Confederate army gathered behind Seminary Ridge. General Meade saw it all from his vantage point at Cemetery Hill and did not order his army to pursue them. It would be dark soon. He would fight them again tomorrow.

For Colonel Joshua Chamberlain and his valiant regiment, it was over. The battle for Little Round Top was finished.

It was finished for Rex Carden, who lay dead against the tree as Shane Donovan knelt beside the lifeless form.

It was finished for Buster Kilrain, who had bled to death internally while his fellow-soldiers bounded down the hill and vanquished the enemy.

It was finished for Colonel Strong Vincent, who was killed by a Confederate bullet on the west side of Little Round Top as he bravely rallied his troops.

The men of the Twentieth Maine were bunching up their prisoners when someone shouted that Colonel Chamberlain was down. The colonel was sitting with his cap off at the base of Little Round Top, leaning against a boulder. His brother Tom knelt beside him, and Ellis Spear and Shane Donovan knelt on the other side. The corps medic was hunkered down in front of him.

While some of the men kept the prisoners, the bulk rushed to see what had happened to their colonel.

The medic looked up and said, "He's not seriously hurt. He has a bruised thigh where one of those last Rebel bullets hit his scabbard and ricocheted off. He's also got a slight injury to his right foot. He's not sure when it happened, but his instep was cut through his boot. He wasn't aware of it till he started running down the hill and felt some pain. But he'll be fine."

Chamberlain asked his brother and Shane to help him stand, and he addressed his troops. "Men, we've lost many of our comrades today. They aren't here for me to speak to, but I want to say to every one of you that I am proud to be your commander. I'm sure history will record what happened here today. You did what you were called to do, and you did it with courage and dignity. I must say that our enemies were gallant men in this fight, but they can't hold a candle to you."

"I agree wholeheartedly, Colonel Chamberlain!" came the voice of General George Meade as he threaded his way through the weary men. "And I would like to add one more thing. From what I know about your stand here today, I believe you men gained the victory because of the great man who led you!"

A rousing cheer went up for Joshua Chamberlain.

The four Rebels Shane had captured were brought off the hill and placed with their fellow-prisoners. Then they were taken to the top of Cemetery Hill and held at gunpoint.

To secure Little Round Top, General Meade ordered the Twentieth Maine to spend the night on its crest. Meade felt sure Lee's army would be defeated the next day, and he told Chamberlain that after the tremendous battle his regiment had fought, they needed and deserved a rest. They were to stay on Little Round Top tomorrow and fight only if Lee tried to take it again, which he doubted would happen. Both Round Tops were firmly in Federal hands. The Twentieth Maine was resupplied with ammunition, and their wounded were carried away to be treated by the medics. They would not be able to bury their dead until the full battle was over.

On the morning of July 3, General Lee's attacking forces formed their lines in the cover of the woods near the peach orchard at Seminary Ridge. Lee had assembled Major General George Pickett and his division of six thousand men at the forefront. Picket had yet to fight in the battle. His orders were to converge on Meade's headquarters at Cemetery Hill. It was Lee's last-ditch effort to gain the victory at Gettysburg.

Pickett had argued with his commander in Lee's field tent before sunup. With James Longstreet present, Pickett told Lee the best thing to do was pull what was left of the Confederate army out of Pennsylvania and go back to Virginia. There, on home ground, they could heal their wounds and fight Billy Yank once again. Longstreet voiced his agreement, saying that any more fighting at Gettysburg would lead to disaster.

Lee became angry and told Pickett he must take Cemetery Hill and wipe out Meade's troops. Pickett grew silent, knowing he must obey orders. Lee laid them out. While Pickett was charging Cemetery Hill, Longstreet would lead the other Confederate divisions — battered and diminished as they were — in an attack on Federal forces in the open fields.

As Pickett and Longstreet predicted, July 3 was a disaster for the Confederate army. Longstreet's forces were battered severely, and over three thousand men were killed in Pickett's division, including every one of his officers.[1] Under cover of darkness that night, a dejected Robert E. Lee began moving his devastated army toward Virginia, openly admitting that the defeat was his fault.

---

[1] For the rest of his life, General George Pickett grieved for his men lost in the battle on July 3, 1863, and he blamed Robert E. Lee for the disaster. Five years after the war, when Pickett and the Confederate guerrilla leader John Mosby paid a courtesy call on Lee in Richmond, Virginia, the atmosphere was less than cordial. After leaving the Lee house, Pickett launched into a bitter diatribe, saying, "That old man had my division slaughtered at Gettysburg."

CHAPTER TWENTY-TWO

ll was quiet as the sun rose over the battlefield at Gettysburg on the morning of July 4, 1863. The Confederates were gone.

It was an unforgettable scene for the Union troops as they scanned the vast area between the two ridges. Upon the open fields, bodies were strewn everywhere. There were bodies in crevices of the rocks, in ditches, behind fences, trees, and buildings, and in thickets where bloodied soldiers had crept for safety only to die in agony. By stream or hedge or rock wall — wherever they had fought or crawled or their faltering steps could take them — lay the dead.

All around was the wreckage battling armies leave in their wake — overturned wagons, broken-down caissons, lopsided cannons, muskets bent and twisted. Farmers' implements, barns, sheds, fences, and houses were in shambles. And over all, suffocating the land and poisoning the breath of the living, hung the powerful stench of decaying flesh, both human and animal.

Each regiment found a place to bury its dead. The Twentieth Maine found a small area near the base of Little Round Top where the ground was not filled with rocks. One hundred and eighty-two of them gathered to pay respect to their fallen comrades.

Colonel Joshua Chamberlain used a broken tree limb as a cane to make his way to the forefront to stand in front of the long mound of dirt where the bodies of his dead soldiers had been laid to rest in a common grave. Some of the men attending were bandaged, and many were also leaning on broken tree limbs. Every man stood on his feet, eyes fixed on the colonel as he ran his gaze over their weary, saddened faces.

"Men of the Twentieth Maine, once again I salute you. You are the greatest bunch of fighting men any army has ever produced. This war is not over. General Lee will rebuild his army and fight us again. But I don't think he will ever send his army against the Union flag without remembering Little Round Top and the Twentieth Maine and the losses his thousands sustained fighting our two hundred.

"We have gathered here to honor our dead. It is customary that when soldiers are buried, the highest ranking survivor of the battle conduct the memorial service, usually with the help of a chaplain. We have no chaplain, but I have asked Captain Shane Donovan to take my place and the chaplain's and read some appropriate Scriptures. Captain…"

Shane Donovan took a few minutes to pay tribute to the men of the Twentieth Maine who had given their lives for the Union cause since entering the war. He then paid special tribute to the men they had just buried, bringing many a tear to the eyes of his hearers with his touching words.

Shane then opened his Bible and read the Twenty-third Psalm. When he finished, he explained that salvation comes only through the Shepherd Himself, the Lord Jesus Christ. He urged every man there to open his heart to Jesus. He closed by telling them that Rex Carden had opened his heart to the Shepherd only hours before being killed. Shane invited any man who wanted to be saved to see him, Colonel Chamberlain, or Tom Chamberlain. Then he prayed, asking God to bless and help the families of the dead and to draw men who stood before him to Jesus.

The bugler stepped forward and played "Taps" as the men of the Twentieth stood in silence, shedding tears. When the last sad note died away, Colonel Chamberlain looked up to see General George Meade riding toward them, sided by his aides.

Meade dismounted and stood before the small remnant. With emotion in his voice, he expressed his gratitude to the Twentieth Maine for their courageous stand at Little Round Top. He told them their effort contributed to the Union victory more than any other single unit in the Army of the Potomac. In closing his short speech, Meade said the Twentieth Maine had displayed valor to the ultimate.

Shane's thoughts went to Charly. In his mind, she had shown the greatest valor when she sent him back to the war with death breathing on her heels. Charly…was she yet alive?

When the men were dismissed, several approached Shane and Tom Chamberlain, wanting to receive Christ. By the time General Meade rode away, Shane and Tom had led thirteen men to Christ.

Joshua Chamberlain rejoiced when he was told about it. He then took Shane aside and said, "Captain, I talked to General Meade about you and Charly. He has granted you two weeks' leave to go home. You're to report to Camp Number Seven in Washington on July 18, where we'll be resting up before going back into battle."

Shane blinked at the tears that filled his eyes and embraced his colonel and friend. He thanked him for what he had done, and asked him to thank General Meade for him.

Shane Donovan's heart was in his throat as he rode the rented horse up the street toward his parents' house. There was no sign of life on the entire block, though it was midafternoon, and none at the Donovan house as he reined in and dismounted. He took his blue haversack from behind the saddle and stepped up on the porch. He turned the knob and pushed the door open.

He stepped inside and called in a subdued voice, "Mother!" If Charly was asleep, he didn't want to wake her just yet. He would rather do that while standing over her bed.

He dropped the haversack in the vestibule and proceeded into the parlor and past the staircase toward the kitchen. He called his mother again as he entered the kitchen, keeping his voice low.

The house was perfectly still. All the windows were open, and the curtains fluttered in the warm summer breeze. He smelled the sweet scent of freshly baked oatmeal cookies. His mother always did make great oatmeal cookies. He and his brothers could never get enough of them.

He was moving past the kitchen table to go into the backyard when he spied a note under a salt shaker on the table.

> Ryan
> Ashley and I have gone downtown shopping. We should
> be home shortly. There are oatmeal cookies in the cookie
> jar. Don't eat too many. I want you to eat supper!
>
> > I love you!
> > Mother

Shane walked quickly to the staircase, and his pulse quickened as he mounted the stairs. Charly, are you up there?

The floorboards squeaked as he made his way down the hall toward Charly's room. The door was standing open as he reached it and looked inside. The bed was made up. His mouth went dry, and something cold slid next to his heart.

"Charly!" he whispered.

He entered the room and could see none of her personal things. There was nothing in the room that hinted Charly had ever been there. Suddenly his eyes locked on a white envelope that leaned against the mirror. It had one word written on it: Shane.

Feebly, he moved toward the dresser. He stopped mid-room and took a deep breath. Fear surged through him.

"No!" he gasped, and hurried to the closet. He pulled the door open and saw Charly's dresses and coats hanging in perfect order. Four pairs of her shoes were on the floor, along with some small boxes. He removed the lid of one and found within it the personal items he had expected to see on the dresser.

"No!" he cried again, and dashed to the dresser. He picked up the envelope and found it sealed. With trembling fingers, he opened it. There was a folded note inside. He pulled it out and saw that it was in Charly's handwriting.

My Darling Shane,

I am trusting the Lord to bring you back from that awful war, though I do not know when it might be. This much I know — I'll be gone when you return.

I know I promised to be lots better the next time you came home, and you may think I didn't keep my promise, but I did. I'll be with Jesus when you read this, Shane, so you see, I truly am lots better!

I'm in a better world, darling. There are no battlefields here, not even the personal kind. I'm not coughing anymore, and I have no pain. There is no sickness where I am. I know you will feel pain at my passing, but time and the Lord's hand will heal that. Please don't wish me back in your world, Shane. I've seen the shining face of Jesus now. Your world would be too dark.

One more thing. I know you still carry that special love for Ashley that you knew when both of you were young. She still carries it for you, too. She's so lonely, darling, and I love her so much. And, of course, I love you with all my heart. If you will let Him, I believe the Lord will take that love between you and Ashley and make it what it might have once been.

I want you and Ashley to know that if you find it
in your hearts to marry, you have my blessing.

Yours lovingly,
Charly

Shane Donovan's body shook. The letter trembled in his
hand. He staggered to the bed, fell on it, and wept for several minutes. Then he ran from the room, leaving the tear-stained note on
the wrinkled bedspread. He bounded down the stairs, through the
door, and swung into the saddle.

Brunswick's cemetery was on a hillside just outside the city
limits on the east. Shane guided the horse up the grassy slope on the
small road that led through the cemetery. His eyes roamed among
the grave markers, looking for a fresh mound.

Suddenly, there it was, under a weeping willow tree, the afternoon sun casting a long shadow from the marker. He left the horse
on the road and walked up the slope.

As he drew near, he saw the grave was decorated with flowers.
A strangled moan escaped his lips as his eyes fell on the inscription
carved in stone:

Charolette Donovan
"CHARLY"
Courageous Loved One
June 14, 1839–July 4, 1863
Gone to be with Jesus

Shane fell to his knees beside the grave and wept for a long
time. "Oh, Charly, I love you! I'll miss you. I'm so sorry I didn't
get back in time to say good-bye. I won't wish you back in this
dark world, but how I wish I could see you again. I love you,
Charly! I love you!"

Shane rose to his feet after more than half an hour, wiped his
tears with a bandanna, then stood looking at the grave. Drawing a

deep breath, he turned and walked slowly toward the horse. Suddenly he froze in his tracks. There, standing below him beside the horse, was Ashley. Her auburn hair shone like burnished copper in the late afternoon sun. A smile graced her tear-stained cheeks.

Around her neck was a delicate chain necklace of gold. The necklace was adorned with a gold heart-shaped locket, engraved with a male hand and a female hand in a tender grasp of love.

EPILOGUE

The three-day battle around Gettysburg, Pennsylvania, was the bloodiest of the entire Civil War. Union casualties totaled twenty-three thousand and Confederate casualties twenty-eight thousand.

In his fifty-seventh year as he rode away from the bloody scene, General Robert E. Lee resembled a man thirty years older. His head was bent and his shoulders drooped. The lines in his face seemed to have deepened in the three days he had just endured. Lee knew he had made several poor judgments in the face of resistance by General James Longstreet, and he publicly shouldered the blame for the Confederate loss at Gettysburg.

Within four weeks, Lee asked to be relieved of his command. President Jefferson Davis refused, unwilling to believe that Lee's tactical decisions at Gettysburg were the cause of the defeat. Lee went on to serve the Confederacy until the Civil War ended in April of 1865. He died five years later of heart disease.

On July 4, 1863, a burial detail came upon a dead Union soldier at Gettysburg whose only identification was an ambrotype of three young children held in a death-grip in his stiff fingers.

Though there was no formal system within either government for notifying families of men killed in action, the soldiers themselves wanted to identify every man before they buried him. Word of the ambrotype spread among the Union forces. The two boys and a girl in the picture were dubbed "children of the battlefield," and an all-out campaign blossomed among the Union army.

Thousands of copies of the picture were circulated in the Northern states. A fifty dollar prize was offered for the best poem about the incident, and the winning verse was set to music. Its refrain was a prayer:

> "O Father, guard the soldier's wife,
> And for his orphans care."

In November 1863, a New York woman whose husband was listed as missing recognized the ambrotype. The "children of the battlefield" were hers. She had sent the picture to her husband months before the Gettysburg battle. He was Sergeant Amos Humiston of Company C, 154th New York Infantry.

The story did not end there. Proceeds from sales of the photograph and sheet music were used to establish the Soldiers' Orphans' Home in Gettysburg in 1866. Humiston's widow became its first matron, and his children were educated there.

So many dead were buried at Gettysburg that President Abraham Lincoln declared the hallowed ground a National Cemetery. On November 19, 1863, he traveled to the scene to formally dedicate the cemetery. We have all read his immortal words spoken at the dedication:

> Four score and seven years ago our fathers brought forth on this continent, a new nation, conceived in Liberty, and dedicated to the proposition that all men are created equal.

Now we are engaged in a great civil war, testing whether that nation, or any nation so conceived and so dedicated, can long endure. We are met on a great battle-field of that war. We have come to dedicate a portion of that field, as a final resting place for those who here gave their lives that that nation might live. It is altogether fitting and proper that we should do this.

But, in a larger sense, we cannot dedicate — we cannot consecrate — we cannot hallow — this ground. The brave men, living and dead, who struggled here, have consecrated it, far above our poor power to add or detract. The world will little note, nor long remember what we say here, but it can never forget what they did here. It is for us the living, rather, to be dedicated here to the unfinished work which they who fought here have thus far so nobly advanced. It is rather for us to be here dedicated to the great task remaining before us — that from these honored dead we take increased devotion to that cause for which they gave the last full measure of devotion — that we here highly resolve that these dead shall not have died in vain — that this nation, under God, shall have a new birth of freedom — and that government of the people, by the people, for the people, shall not perish from the earth.

Joshua Lawrence Chamberlain fought in many more battles during the Civil War, and he was promoted twice more — to brigadier general, and later to major general. He was wounded six times and cited for bravery in action four times. For his leadership under fire at Little Round Top, he was thanked by all of his superior officers. Each one stated that the bold and daring stand he took at Little Round Top saved the day for the Union.

Chamberlain recounted soon afterward that the highest praise must go to his regiment. He said not only had the Twentieth Maine immortalized itself, but its conduct was magnificent.

The historian of the Fifth Corps paid this tribute to the regiment's great accomplishment:

> The truth of the history is, that the little brigade of Vincent's with the self-sacrificing valor of the 20th Maine, under the gallant leadership of Joshua L. Chamberlain, fighting amidst the scrub-oak and rocks of Little Round Top on July 2, 1863, saved to the Union arms the historic field of Gettysburg. Had they faltered for one instant — had they not exceeded their actual duty — Gettysburg would have been the mausoleum of departed hopes of the national cause; for the Confederates would have enveloped Little Round Top, captured all on its crest from the rear, and held the key position of the entire battleground.

After the War, Chamberlain was awarded his country's highest veneration, the Congressional Medal of Honor, bestowed on him for his "daring heroism, courage, and great tenacity in holding his position on Little Round Top against repeated enemy assaults."

When General Robert E. Lee surrendered to General Ulysses S. Grant at Appomattox Court House, Virginia, on April 9, 1865, Grant chose Major General Joshua L. Chamberlain to officially command the ceremony of surrender.

In 1866 Chamberlain was elected governor of Maine by the largest majority in the history of the state, and was elected to the office three more times in succession. While still governor of Maine, he was elected president of Bowdoin College in 1871. He remained in that office at Bowdoin until June of 1883, when ill health resulting from his Civil War wounds forced him to resign.

Fannie Chamberlain died from a broken hip on October 18, 1905, at the age of eighty. Joshua died at his Portland, Maine, home on the cold, wintry morning of February 14, 1914, at the age of eighty-five. The cumulative effects of his six war wounds finally took their toll. Two of his children were at his bedside when his soul left the painfully wounded body and made its flight to the arms of the God he served.

A NOTE OF INTEREST

On July 1, 1993, the combined house of representatives and senate of the state of Maine adopted a joint resolution on the 130th anniversary of the Battle of Gettysburg. It is as follows:

STATE OF MAINE

In the Year of Our Lord Nineteen Hundred and Ninety-Three

JOINT RESOLUTION RECOGNIZED
JOSHUA L. CHAMBERLAIN
AND THE TWENTIETH MAINE VOLUNTEER
REGIMENT ON THE OCCASION OF THE
130TH ANNIVERSARY OF
THE BATTLE OF GETTYSBURG

WHEREAS, the State of Maine contributed 73,000 soldiers and sailors to the defense of the Union during the Civil War; and

WHEREAS, July 1st to July 3rd is the 130th anniversary of the pivotal engagement of that horrible conflict, the Battle of Gettysburg; and

WHEREAS, on July 2nd, the second day of that battle, the

20th Maine Volunteer Regiment under the command of Colonel Joshua L. Chamberlain held its position on the extreme left of the Army of the Potomac on a rocky hill called Little Round Top with great heroism, sacrifice and resourcefulness against repeated Confederate assault, thereby preventing an enemy flanking of the Union line and contributing greatly to the eventual Union victory at Gettysburg; and

WHEREAS, the courage and achievement of the 20th Maine Volunteer Regiment is one shining example of the contributions of Maine regiments at Gettysburg and at other battles of the Civil War, citizen soldiers from farms and villages across Maine whose names are now largely forgotten but whose deeds will live forever in the annals of the free nation they fought to preserve; and

WHEREAS, Colonel Joshua L. Chamberlain, born in Brewer, Maine, in 1828; scholar at Bowdoin College; soldier, wounded 6 times, cited 4 times for heroism and awarded the Congressional Medal of Honor for his actions at Little Round Top; promoted to Brigadier General in the field at Petersburg by General Ulysses S. Grant and promoted to Major General after Five Forks; Union officer who received the surrender of the defeated Army of Northern Virginia at Appomattox and led the last Grand Review in Washington, D.C.; Governor of Maine, who was elected four times by unprecedented popular margins and who served with vision, independence and character; who advocated academic innovation as President of Bowdoin College; Major General of the State Militia who defended the public peace without use of force during the 1880 state electoral crisis known as The 12 Days; speaker on *Maine: Her Place in History* at the 1876 Philadelphia Centennial Exposition; representative of Maine and the United States at national and international expositions; commissioner to the 1878 Universal Exposition in Paris; and author of the memoir *The Passing of the Armies,* published after his death in 1914, was during his 85 years a man of courage as he had been on the bloody slopes of Little Round Top; and

WHEREAS, Joshua L. Chamberlain and the 20th Maine Volunteer Regiment contributed significantly to their State and their Nation; now, therefore, be it

RESOLVED: That we, the Members of the One Hundred and Sixteenth Legislature now assembled in the First Regular Session, salute the memory of Joshua L. Chamberlain and the 20th Maine Volunteer Regiment on the 130th anniversary of the Battle of Gettysburg; and be it further

RESOLVED: That suitable copies of this resolution, duly authenticated by the Secretary of State, be transmitted to schools and libraries through the State of Maine.

Joseph W. Mayo, Secretary
HOUSE OF REPRESENTATIVES
Joy J. O'Brien, Secretary
IN SENATE CHAMBER

AL LACY

Books in the Battles of Destiny series:

☛ *A Promise Unbroken*

Two couples battle jealousy and racial hatred amidst a war that would cripple America. From a prosperous Virginia plantation to a grim jail cell outside Lynchburg, follow the dramatic story of a love that could not be destroyed.

☛ *A Heart Divided*

Ryan McGraw—leader of the Confederate Sharpshooters—is nursed back to health by beautiful army nurse Dixie Quade. Their romance would survive the perils of war, but can it withstand the reappearance of a past love?

☛ *Beloved Enemy*

Young Jenny Jordan covers for her father's Confederate spy missions. But as she grows closer to Union soldier Buck Brownell, Jenny finds herself torn between devotion to the South and her feelings for the man she is forbidden to love.

☛ *Shadowed Memories*

Critically wounded on the field of battle and haunted by amnesia, one man struggles to regain his strength and the memories that have slipped away from him.

☛ *Joy from Ashes*

Major Layne Dalton made it through the horrors of the battle of Fredericksburg, but can he rise above his hatred toward the Heglund brothers who brutalized his wife and killed his unborn son?

☛ *Season of Valor*

Shane Donovan fights for the vaunted Twentieth Maine in the historic battle of Gettysburg. His wife, at home in Brunswick, faces a battle of her own — a grave illness that threatens her very life. What awaits Shane when he returns home?

Books in the Journeys of the Stranger series:

☞ *Legacy*

Can John Stranger, a mysterious hero who brings truth, honor, and justice to the Old West, bring Clay Austin back to the right side of the law...and restore the code of honor shared by the woman he loves?

☞ *Silent Abduction*

The mysterious man in black fights to defend a small town targeted by cattle rustlers and to rescue a young woman and child held captive by a local Indian tribe.

☞ *Blizzard*

When three murderers slated for hanging escape from the Colorado Territorial Prison, young U.S. Marshal Ridge Holloway and the mysterious John Stranger join together to track down the infamous convicts.

☞ *Tears of the Sun*

When John Stranger arrives in Apache Junction, Arizona, he finds himself on the edge of a bitter war between sworn enemies: the Tonto Apaches and the Arizona Zunis.

Books in the Angel of Mercy series:

☞ *A Promise for Breanna*

The man who broke Breanna's heart is back. But this time, he's after her life.

☞ *Faithful Heart*

Breanna and her sister Dottie find themselves in a desperate struggle to save a man they love, but can no longer trust.

☞ *Captive Set Free* (coming in March 1996)

Breanna battles a deadly scarlet fever epidemic — and the deceits of a ruthless mine owner.

Printed in the United States
by Baker & Taylor Publisher Services